SHERRI SHACKELFORD

His Substitute Mail-Order Bride

D0037355

 HARLEQUIN® LOVE INSPIRED® HISTORICAL

Special thanks and acknowledgment to Sherri Shackelford
for her contribution to the Return to Cowboy Creek miniseries.

Recycling programs
for this product may
not exist in your area.

LOVE INSPIRED BOOKS

ISBN-13: 978-1-335-36966-6

His Substitute Mail-Order Bride

"Someone is bound to notice if we're seen together." Anna glanced at Russ.

"You're far more likely to attract attention than I am."

"Me?" She backed away, bumping into the table and toppling a bag of seeds to the floor. "No one knows me here."

"Yet." He knelt and reached for the bag. "There's still time to become notorious."

With trembling fingers, she swept the seeds. "I just want a little peace and quiet."

He pressed his hand over her chilled fingers. "I was only trying to lighten the mood. Neither of us is likely to incite comment."

"If you say so."

Russ resumed sifting seeds, his thoughts troubled. The memory of the carefree girl she'd been all those years ago lingered. Surely there was something he could do to bring back that mischievous twinkle in her eyes once more? Perhaps if he knew more about her life, more about her time in Philadelphia, he'd have a better chance at avoiding potential hazards in their friendship. Five years was a long time, and a lot had obviously changed for Anna.

Not all of it for the better.

* * *

Return to Cowboy Creek:
A bride train delivers the promise of new love
and family to a Kansas boomtown

The Rancher Inherits a Family—
Cheryl St.John, April 2018
His Substitute Mail-Order Bride—
Sherri Shackelford, May 2018
Romancing the Runaway Bride—
Karen Kirst, June 2018

Sherri Shackelford is an award-winning author of inspirational books featuring ordinary people discovering extraordinary love. A reformed pessimist, Sherri has a passion for storytelling. Her books are fast-paced and heartfelt with a generous dose of humor. She loves to hear from readers at sherri@sherrishackelford.com. Visit her website at sherrishackelford.com.

Visit the Author Profile page at Harlequin.com for more titles.

The fathers shall not be put to death
for the children, neither shall the children
be put to death for the fathers:
every man shall be put to death for his own sin.
—*Deuteronomy* 24:16

Chapter One

❧

On the road to Cowboy Creek, May 1869

"Something don't feel right," the wagon driver declared, casting an uneasy glance over one shoulder. "I travel this road every Tuesday and Friday delivering eggs to the restaurants in Cowboy Creek. But something don't feel right today."

"How can you tell?" Anna Linford anchored her bonnet with one gloved hand and squinted against the sun. A narrow creek snaked beside the road with scrub brush lining the steep banks. "We haven't seen another soul for miles."

Everything in Kansas was exaggerated and larger than life. The sky was painfully blue, the clouds a preposterous shade of white and the horizon seemingly endless. Even the fluttering prairie grasses were an overblown hue of emerald.

"That's why I'm worried," said the driver, Mr. Ward. "There should be more folks traveling this time of day."

Mr. Ward's skeletal hands trembled on the reins. Anna's reluctant companion was somewhere past sev-

enty and as gnarled and bent as the old oak tree outside
the window of her childhood home. Layers of wrinkles
corrugated his face, rendering his expressions indeci-
pherable. Though he'd politely refrained from smoking
in her presence, the sooty odor lingered on his coat,
and her stomach churned.

As they rounded the corner, the railroad tracks and
what looked to be the site of a previous accident came
into view. Anna sucked in a breath. Two railcars lay
overturned in the ditch, their metal axels twisted. Fresh
weeds growing through the blackened prairie grasses
and long, muddy gashes in the hillside indicated the accident had occurred sometime in the past month. The
loamy scent of freshly turned earth competed with the
stench of machine oil and scorched wood.

A sudden breeze whipped her bonnet ribbons over
her shoulder. "What happened here?"

"Some fool engineer took the curve too fast a month
or so past." The driver grunted. "Those last two cars
have to be separated afore they can drag 'em out of
the ditch. Good thing you didn't arrive with the last
bride train, or you'd have been in the ditch too. Timing is everything in life. Take this morning. Bad timing." He chuckled at his joke. "Too bad the train left
without you."

After founding Cowboy Creek, the council realized
the area needed families to flourish and grow. Since
women were scarce, they sent back east for brides. Some
of the women corresponded with local men before traveling west on a bride train. Others accepted a ticket paid
for by the town, rather than a prospective groom, and
hoped for the best. Anna's unique circumstances had

left her somewhere in the middle—there'd been a correspondence, and she was hoping for the best.

Missing the train in Morgan's Creek had been another stumbling block in a long list of disasters for Anna. Thankfully the distance between towns wasn't far, and the driver from the poultry farm had taken pity on her. She'd learned through the older man's reluctant conversation that Cowboy Creek had grown too quickly for the local suppliers to keep up with demand, encouraging cottage industries in the neighboring communities.

A crack of gunfire sounded, and a bullet struck the ground before the wagon. A plume of dust and a spray of dirt pellets exploded into the air. Anna's heart jerked in her chest. The mule brayed and reared. The cart lurched, and she clutched the seat.

His gun drawn, a man in a long, shapeless duster coat with a hat set back on his head appeared from behind one of the overturned railcars. A second man wearing a similar coat followed close behind. One wore a blue bandanna tied over the lower half of his face, the other wore red.

A chill shivered down Anna's spine.

Beside her, the driver guffawed. "Get along, you two. I'm hauling eggs. We got nothing of value."

"We'll just see about that," the man in the red bandanna said gruffly.

He gestured with his tarnished pistol and approached the wagon. Judging by the way he spoke, Anna marked him as the leader of the pair. He braced his scuffed boot on the wagon wheel, and the bench seat dipped. With careless brutality, he tossed the elderly driver from his seat. The older man yelped.

"Don't hurt him!" Anna gasped. "He's no threat to you."

"You ought to worry about yourself," the outlaw declared ominously. "Tie him up!"

Anna fumed as Mr. Ward was dragged into the ditch and quickly bound and gagged. To her immense relief, the elderly driver put up little fight and appeared no worse for wear considering his rough treatment.

The lead outlaw leaned closer. He flipped back her bonnet with the barrel of his gun, and her pulse jerked.

"You're one of them brides traveling to Cowboy Creek, ain't ya?" he asked. "I heard all about you women at the last train depot." He gestured toward his companion. "The men of Cowboy Creek are hauling in brides by the trainload. It's no wonder the town is growing like stinkweed in a wet spring."

Anna swallowed. "I'm traveling to Cowboy Creek, yes."

She didn't bother correcting the outlaw about being a prospective bride. No man wanted a woman who couldn't bear children. Her late husband had made that fact abundantly clear.

"Must be really desperate to send for a skinny gal like you," the outlaw said, his mocking laughter muffled through his bandanna.

The insult barely registered. The past two years had rendered her immune to even the most vicious slurs. "I suppose."

"How come you ain't on the train with the rest of 'em?"

Her cheeks burned. "I was indisposed when the train departed."

Exhaustion and stress had exacerbated a recent bout

of influenza, and she'd been forced to depart the train at the last minute to visit the washroom. The two brides she'd been traveling with had remained on board since the stop was only long enough to load a freight car with supplies. Though Anna had made the trip as quickly as possible, when she'd rushed outside once more, the caboose was receding into the distance.

"Indisposed, eh? Listen to her talk." The outlaw glanced at his companion. "We got ourselves a real fancy piece."

Not hardly. She couldn't even afford a hotel room for the night. Her late husband's mountain of debts had exhausted every penny of their meager savings and devoured the profits she'd made from selling the house and furnishings. She'd only managed to set aside a few dollars, which had to last indefinitely. Aside from that, she had nothing. No money. No close family. Even her train ticket was a gift from an acquaintance who'd planned on becoming a mail-order bride before falling in love back in Philadelphia.

The bride's change of mind had been Anna's unexpected salvation.

The sound of hoofbeats and a flash of movement in the distance drew her attention.

"Don't move." The outlaw pressed his gun barrel hard against her temple. "We got some unexpected company."

Shimmering through the heat, a rider appeared. The air grew still, and an unnatural silence descended over the outlaws. The rider gradually came into focus, a lone man on a jet-black horse.

As he ambled toward them, a bead of sweat trickled down Anna's spine.

The rider was lean and fit, wearing a dark suit and

boots that gleamed in the sun. His hat brim cast a harsh shadow across his features. He held the reins clasped in one hand, the other loosely fisted on his thigh. The unrelenting black of the sleek horse and the man's crisp suit was broken only by a glimpse of the stark white shirt beneath his vest.

Her breath hitched. "Russ Halloway?"

She'd expected to greet him, but not here. Not now. Not like this. He'd changed in the five years since she'd last seen him in Philadelphia. His face had been rounder and his shoulders narrower. The man seated on the horse before her had none of the softness of youth.

Russ was formidable, exuding an aura of raw power, both mental and physical. He wore his dark brown hair cropped off his collar, and a neatly trimmed goatee highlighted the sharp planes of his strong chin. Despite his careful grooming, there was something uncivilized about him. His features were too rugged for traditional labels. He wasn't handsome so much as compelling.

Confusion flickered in his hazel eyes. "Anna?"

The outlaw gave her a shake. "You know this fellow?"

"She knows me," Russ said, his voice as rough as gravel. "Let her go. I don't want any trouble."

The man in the blue bandanna sauntered around the wagon, his gun drawn.

The lead outlaw cackled. "There's two of us, and one of you. I like my odds."

"Suit yourself."

Her captor grunted. "On your feet, boy, or I shoot the girl."

Russ swung his leg over the side of the horse and casually leaped to the ground.

The lead outlaw kept his gun trained on Russ, while

the second man hopped onto the wagon bed. He tossed crates aside, shattering eggs and spilling hay, then ripped open her carpetbag and dumped the contents over the side. Dozens of small burlap sacks tumbled loose. Several broke open, scattering seeds over the dirt.

The chaotic sight unleashed a sudden rage unlike anything she'd ever felt—not even during the miserable years of her marriage.

"Ain't you got no jewelry or nothing?" The outlaw demanded.

"No." Anna shook her head. "Nothing."

"Maybe you're hiding something."

Her chest seized, and she wrestled back a tide of guilt. The outlaw was searching for valuables. He didn't know about the scandal. She was free. She was innocent. She was haunted by a crime she hadn't committed.

Glancing away, she said, "I'm not hiding anything."

Russ caught her eye and gave an almost imperceptible shake of his head. "Relax, Anna, everything is under control."

"Shut up!" the outlaw ordered.

Anna hung her head. Nothing would ever be fine again. She'd lost everything: her family, her home, her reputation. These men were taking the only thing she had left.

The lead outlaw hopped from the wagon bed and shoved her. "What's all this, anyway?"

"Seeds." Two years of pent-up frustration pulsated through her veins. "Nothing but seeds."

"You're lying. You got jewelry hidden in one of them bags. I heard you talking to the porter in Morgan's Creek. You said your bag was filled with precious cargo and that's why you wasn't letting it out of your sight. Precious cargo, ya said. I heard ya."

"I'm telling the truth." She scooped up the pods and extended her cupped hands. "Look."

"Bucky," the outlaw shouted. "Cut them open. Every one."

"No!" Anna called, throwing her body before the bulk of her hard-earned collection. "These have been carefully collected and cataloged. They're extremely valuable, just not in the way you think."

"Cataloged!" The outlaw chortled. "Well, ain't you something."

The man in the blue bandanna reached for a burlap sack and sliced open the side. Seedpods spilled onto the ground, and something snapped inside her. She was done being a victim.

When the outlaw reached for another bag, she lunged at him. Caught off guard, he flailed in startled surprise. The blade tore through her sleeve, piercing the skin of her forearm. She winced and stumbled backward. The outlaw followed her retreat and caught her around the upper arm.

"That was real stupid, lady."

Russ charged. "Let her go."

The lead outlaw lurched between them, his gun extended. "Hold still or I'll shoot you both!"

The man in the blue bandanna gave her a shake, and his sour breath puffed against her cheek. "What's so valuable that you're willing to throw yourself in front of a knife?"

"You wouldn't understand."

Russ spread his hands in a placating gesture. "Everyone calm down."

"Calm down?" The lead outlaw spat into the dust. "You must be the dumbest feller in the state walking into a holdup all by your lonesome."

"It might look that way," Russ declared, an ominous flicker in his exotic hazel eyes. "But I'm actually the decoy. While you've been flapping your lips, my men have been surrounding you. If you make one threatening move toward the lady, they'll shoot, and they don't miss."

"You're bluffing."

The second outlaw struck Russ in the head with the butt of his gun.

Anna cried out as Russ crumpled to the dirt.

The leader clutched her arm and spun her around. "Leave him be."

She craned her neck, searching for any sign of life. Russ lay sprawled in the middle of the road, his arms akimbo, his black hat crushed beneath his shoulder. Vivid red blood flowed from his forehead.

"Let me tend his wound," she pleaded. "He's bleeding."

"Later."

The outlaw shoved her away from the prone man. "If you don't have anything of value, maybe we can ransom you."

A gunshot echoed through the canyon, and the outlaw's hat flew off. Shocked by the unexpected violence, Anna and the man stumbled apart.

Her captor yanked his blue bandana off his chin and spun around. "What the—"

"That feller wasn't bluffing, Bucky!" his partner shouted. "They're hiding in the creek bed."

"Don't shoot." Bucky dropped the knife and reached for his gun. "Or I'll kill her!"

Another shot sounded, and Bucky jerked. The gun dropped from his slack grip. His knees twitched, but he stayed on his feet. Tearing open his duster coat, he revealed a red stain blooming over his chambray shirt.

The wounded man gaped at something behind her. "I've been hit."

Anna followed the outlaw's gaze, and her jaw dropped. Russ stalked toward them, a smoking pistol dangling from his fingertips. Blood obscured half his face, and a growing scarlet stain darkened his shirt collar.

Unable to reconcile the sudden change of events, she stared in stunned silence. Russ had been unconscious a moment before, and now he was swooping toward them like an avenging savior.

A shot whizzed past her ear. Stifling a shriek, Anna pressed her hands against her mouth. Without slowing his stride, Russ shoved the stunned outlaw, dropping the wounded man instantly. Shock rendered her immobile, and she remained rooted to the spot.

The remaining outlaw took one look at the gun in Russ's hand and stumbled toward the ditch, then disappeared behind the derailed cattle cars.

"C'mon, Anna." Russ grasped her around the waist. "Stay down."

The urgent note in his voice cut through her torpor, and she willed her legs to move.

Russ urged her toward the wagon. He crouched behind the spoked wheel, shielding her with his body, his gun at the ready. With the back of his hand, he swiped at the blood streaming down his face.

"I've got two men hiding near the creek," he said. "Stay out of the crossfire."

A thunderous volley echoed over them. Russ fired several shots at the overturned cattle cars. Her ears rang, and the pungent scent of gunpowder filled the air. The frightened mule lunged, jerking the wagon. Anna dove forward and grasped the trailing reins. Bracing her heels in the dirt, she leaned back, tugging with all her might. As the mule brayed and bucked, the leather dug painfully into her palms.

Russ reached to help, and she shook him off. "I've got this. You keep shooting."

"Don't worry," he said. "It's over."

The chaotic scene went eerily quiet. The mule stilled. Anna dropped the reins, collapsing against the buckboard. For a long moment, the ominous silence was broken only by the steady tick-tick-tick of the watch in Russ's pocket and the harsh sound of her labored breathing.

He turned and cupped her cheek. "Are you all right?"

"I'm f-fine. What about the driver?"

"He's safe, don't worry."

For the past five years, hatred for this man had been her constant companion. He'd broken her sister's heart, he'd torn apart their family, and he'd set in motion a chain of events that had ended in disaster. Yet his striking hazel eyes held nothing but concern.

Where was the villain she'd clung to all these years?

An earsplitting whistle sounded, startling her.

Russ heaved a sigh. "You're safe, Miss Darby."

"It's Mrs. Linford now," she corrected automatically.

"Is your husband traveling separately?"

"I'm widowed."

That one innocuous word did little to encompass her current situation. Her late husband had been murdered in broad daylight by an unknown assailant. Shot dead on the walkway outside his office building. The police had assumed the brazen killing was a crime of passion. Rather than having too few suspects, they had too many. Her late husband's philandering was well known around the city. The extensive list of scorned women had produced plenty of enticing leads, but no conclusive evidence.

Following an unflattering story on the front page of the morning post, she'd been outright shunned by the people she'd once considered close friends. The newspaper had gone into great detail about her husband's numerous infidelities. Though she'd been cleared of any wrongdoing by the lead detective, vicious rumors had forced her from town.

Everyone who mattered was convinced she'd murdered her husband.

His head throbbing, Russ stood. "We obviously have a lot to catch up on, but now isn't the time. Can you stand?"

"Yes. I'm fine. Just a bit shaken." Anna pulled an embroidered handkerchief from her sleeve and dabbed at his forehead. "But you're bleeding."

Russ touched the spot. Their fingers brushed, and she quickly pulled away.

He raked a hand through his hair. She was as skittish as a newborn foal, and his appearance probably wasn't calming her nerves any. He retrieved his plain handkerchief and wiped away the rest of the blood as best he could, his fingers brushing the growing lump.

Satisfied he was somewhat respectable once more, he held out his hand, and Anna clasped his fingers.

She leaned heavily on his aid with a mumbled apology. Once she'd steadied herself, he placed a firm hand on the small of her back.

She eyed him warily, and something shifted in his chest. Perhaps it was their previous acquaintance, or perhaps it was her slight frame, but he felt unaccountably protective toward her.

When he'd last seen Anna, she'd been a round-faced cherub on the edge of womanhood. There'd been a sparkle of mischief in her green eyes and a ready smile hovering on her impish lips. The woman before him was a shadow of that memory. Anna was thin, painfully so. Her cheeks were sunken, and the bones of her wrist pronounced.

Despite her gaunt frame, there was a beauty and elegance about her that hadn't been there before. She'd lost her bonnet in the melee, and her hair was a shimmering waterfall of golden brown. Her emerald traveling suit highlighted the lustrous strands and brought out the green patina of her eyes. She was delicate and composed, though he sensed a sadness that hadn't been there before.

Hoofbeats sounded in the distance, and Russ turned toward the sound. The approaching rider sat tall in the saddle, an air of authority about him, as though he was accustomed to giving orders.

Anna started.

"Don't worry, he's with me," Russ said, halting her retreat. "That's Will Canfield, the current mayor of Cowboy Creek. Tell me, Mrs. Linford, did you happen to board the train in Philadelphia?"

Her gaze skittered away. "I did."

"Then perhaps you met Susannah Lowe." He was a cad interrogating Anna following her ordeal, but he'd been filled with worry since the arrival of the bride train. No one seemed to know anything about his intended. "Susannah should have boarded the train in Philadelphia, as well. I spoke with the other brides, but no one recognized the name. I know you've had a shock, but I was hoping you could help. Did you see her at the train station?"

Without meeting his eyes, Anna fished an envelope from her pocket and extended her hand. His name was scrawled over the front in Susannah's now-familiar handwriting.

"She isn't coming," Anna said.

"Is she all right?" Shock and confusion burned through him. "Did something happen?"

"She's met someone."

Russ staggered back a step. He and Susannah had only corresponded, but they'd both agreed they'd suit. Nothing in her letters had given him any indication that she'd had second thoughts about becoming his mail-order bride.

"I don't think she meant to fall in love," Anna continued, her hands clasped. "She was quite remorseful about misleading you."

"Misleading me?" he repeated.

Everything fell into place. Susannah's letters had been long and rambling, and he'd taken to skimming the contents. They'd come to an agreement, after all, and they'd said all they needed to say to each other until they met in person. He'd made excuses instead of reading between the lines.

Anna gazed at him with pity in her emerald eyes. "You're not angry, are you?"

"Odd, isn't it?" The past came rushing back, and a

strange sense of inevitability overcame him. "We've already played this scene before, haven't we?"

"I'm so sorry." A greenish pallor swept over Anna's face, and she pressed her fingers against her lips. "I don't feel well."

Russ immediately recognized the urgent nature of the problem. He stuffed the envelope into his pocket and scooped her into his arms.

She gasped and wrapped her arms around his neck. "What are you doing?"

"I'll take you to the stream." His questions about Susannah could wait given Anna's current condition. "You'll feel better after splashing some cool water on your face."

Her cheeks flamed, and she pressed her face against his shoulder. She was slight and delicate in his arms, and his pulse quickened. Recalling the outlaw's gun pressed against her temple, his gut clenched. He maneuvered down the embankment in three long strides and gently set her on the soft grass near the stream.

She waved him away. "Please go."

He hesitated, his hand hovering near her shoulder.

"Please," she whispered.

She was visibly embarrassed, though she needn't be. He'd seen far worse. "Call if you need assistance. I'll be near."

He moved a distance away, lingering on the edge of the steep embankment. This was not at all how he'd expected to spend his day. He thought he'd be introducing Susannah to his mother and brother soon. Instead, he'd be explaining her absence. Having gone through this once before when he was jilted by Anna's sister, Charlotte, he dreaded the coming days. The compassion of friends and family only seemed to worsen the humiliation.

Russ stifled a groan. He'd missed the signs both times. Was there something fundamentally wrong with his character? An inherent insensitivity to the feelings of others?

He discreetly checked on Anna, then looked away before she caught him. Susannah's betrayal wasn't her responsibility any more than Charlotte's had been, yet her presence exacerbated his shame and frustration.

Given his past acquaintance with Anna's family, however, he couldn't avoid her during her time of need.

He raised his voice over the gurgling stream. "Can I get you anything, Mrs. Linford?"

"Perhaps a drink of water," she replied, her voice strained.

He glanced toward the creek bed, and his chest grew heavy. Why was she traveling alone with Susannah's letter? Did she need more than a drink of water? And what had become of the carefree girl he recalled from all those years ago?

He didn't know Anna's plans, but he doubted Cowboy Creek was her ultimate destination. Her family was well-to-do, and though the town was rapidly adding all the amenities of an Eastern city, they were still a long way from the civilized Philadelphia society teas she and her sister had attended.

Given her current difficulties, there'd be time enough to sort out the details later. She'd been attacked by outlaws—rendering his own problem pale in comparison. She deserved his sympathy—not the irritation of his self-pity.

"Back in a moment," he said. "I'll signal my return, Mrs. Linford."

With a last look over his shoulder, he reluctantly strode toward his friend.

Will Canfield was a lanky man with an engaging charm and a wry wit. Since Russ's arrival in Cowboy Creek, Will had been an ally and a mentor. He'd guided Russ through the rough and corrupt world of land grabbing and false deeds. The mayor had even encouraged him to send for a bride.

Will reined his horse near the wagon and surveyed the damage. "The driver, Mr. Ward, is bruised, but he'll be all right. No bones were broken. What about the woman?"

"Her name is Mrs. Linford," Russ interjected quickly—lest Will think they'd discovered Susannah. "She's a widow. She needed a moment to collect herself."

"What about you? That was quite a hit you took."

"It's nothing." Russ lied, his head pounding. "Looks worse than it is."

"Shouldn't have happened. We took too long getting in place."

When the three men discovered one of the brides had missed the train, they assumed the woman was Russ's intended, and decided to escort her personally. Upon hearing the gunshots, they'd immediately realized the overturned railcars were the ideal place for an ambush. Russ had volunteered to distract the outlaws while Daniel and Will took cover near the creek and surrounded the men.

"I knew what I was agreeing to," Russ said.

"Go back to town," Will ordered. "Perhaps there's been some news about your bride."

"Miss Lowe isn't coming." Russ balked at leaving Anna this soon after her ordeal. She was a stranger in town, to everyone but him. She wasn't feeling well, and she needed a friend. "Susannah met someone else. She sent a letter forward with Mrs. Linford."

Shock flickered over Will's face before he quickly masked the emotion. "I'm sorry. That wasn't the news I was expecting."

"It's not your fault."

"I talked you into sending for a bride," Will said, his voice heavy. "I bear some of the responsibility."

There it was: the compassion, the sympathy. It should have made Russ feel better. It didn't. "What's done is done."

Will scratched his temple. "How does Mrs. Linford fit into all this? I thought perhaps they'd mistaken the name of the bride who missed the train. Linford and Lowe are close enough."

"That's the thing. There's more."

"More?" Will guffawed. "Save something for dinner, will you? A missing bride and a shoot-out before lunch is plenty."

"I know Anna Linford," Russ said.

A familiar pang squeezed his chest. He'd been jilted twice. Once by Susannah, and once by Anna's sister, Charlotte.

And Anna had delivered both letters.

Chapter Two

Reluctant to abandon the peaceful scene for the chaos on the road, Anna lingered by the stream as long as she could before struggling to her feet. The sparkling water gurgled over polished rocks, and a butterfly skipped along the fluttering prairie grasses. Crickets chirped, and birds called from the shrub trees. A spring-scented breeze caught a strand of her hair, and she tucked the lock behind one ear. With the sheltering limbs providing much-needed shade from the sun, she might have been picnicking. Only her torn and bloodied dress belied the peaceful scene.

She climbed a few steps before another wave of nausea overcame her. Pausing, she took a few deep, fortifying breaths.

Though she hadn't meant to eavesdrop, voices sounded near her.

"How fortunate that you know Mrs. Linford," said the man Russ had introduced as Mayor Canfield. "I'll leave her in your care. She'll want to be near someone who's familiar after what's happened."

Blinking rapidly, Anna pressed a hand against her

roiling stomach. As the messenger, she'd been prepared for Russ's annoyance—even his recriminations. His kindness had thrown her off balance. Her eyes burned, and she pressed the heels of her hands against the telling weakness until she saw stars. She wasn't usually given to bouts of tears, but lately she couldn't seem to control her emotions.

"What about the outlaws?" she heard Russ ask.

"Dead. Both of 'em. Daniel and the driver are on their way back to town to fetch the undertaker." Mayor Canfield made a sound of frustration. "How is it that Sheriff Getman is never around when he's needed?"

"He's new. Give him a chance."

"He's wearing on my nerves," the mayor grumbled. "No need to rush Mrs. Linford. I'll clean up the worst of the mess."

"Appreciate that," Russ replied. "Start with the outlaws. The lady's stomach isn't strong at the moment."

A flush of heat swept over her face. What an awful time for a relapse of her influenza. She'd been feeling much stronger earlier in the week, and the timing of Susannah's ticket had been too fortuitous to ignore.

"Understood," the mayor said. "You might want to clean up yourself. You don't look so good."

"You wanted a distraction, and I gave you one."

Anna touched her cheek. Russ had put himself in danger for her. *No*, that wasn't exactly the truth. He'd been looking for Susannah. He hadn't known that someone else would be delivering a letter in his intended's place.

Anna wasn't special. He'd have done the same thing for anyone else.

The mayor grumbled. "I don't want to lose my replacement."

Replacement? What did he mean by that? Not that Russ's future was any of her concern.

How odd that circumstances had conspired to bring them together once more after all this time. The other brides on the train had been so optimistic, so eager to meet the men of Cowboy Creek—their prospective bridegrooms—that Anna had kept her opinions to herself. Following the war, men were scarce back east, and the choices limited. Unlike Susannah, none of the other prospective brides had corresponded with the bachelors of Cowboy Creek beyond arranging their travels.

Anna had been out of place amongst their cheerful ranks. Not only because she was traveling under false pretenses, but because she couldn't share their enthusiasm for marriage. Her brief time as someone's wife had left her soured on the institution. She didn't begrudge them their optimism; she only worried their dreams might not match reality.

The mayor muttered something she couldn't quite discern before saying, "That wallop saved the day. Gave Daniel and me time to get in place."

Anna pivoted toward the creek. Russ's suggestion of a little refreshing water splashed on her face was the perfect excuse for a delay. If she appeared now, they'd know she'd been listening, albeit unintentionally.

She located a large, flat rock and knelt on the hard surface. After tugging off her gloves, she dipped her hands in the cool water.

Footsteps sounded, and she glanced up. Canteen in hand, Russ made his way down the embankment once more. Her stomach dipped, and she whipped around.

Everything had seemed so simple back in Philadelphia. Given the unexpected turn of events, her justifications for taking Susannah's ticket were rapidly evaporating. She'd painted Russ a villain, but he wasn't living down to her expectations.

"Here." Russ extended the canteen. "Water will help."

Though her life might have turned out drastically different had Russ married her sister, she couldn't use the past as an excuse to defend her current questionable behavior.

Anna offered a weak smile. "Thank you."

He dipped his handkerchief in the clear water and knelt beside her. "You've got some, um, dirt on your face."

Her hands trembling, she accepted the cloth and wiped her cheek.

"Your arm." His eyes widened. "You've been cut. You're bleeding."

"It's nothing."

He took her hand and gently turned her arm until her palm was facing up. The scratch was several inches long, though not deep, and the bleeding had slowed. With everything else happening, the sting barely rose above the rest of her aches and pains.

"We'd best wrap this," he said.

Confused by his actions, Anna remained passive as he carefully wound the handkerchief around the gash. Why was he being kind?

Her carefully practiced speech hinged on diffusing his anger. First, she'd planned on appealing to their past connection. If that didn't work, she'd appeal to his conscience and hope the man her sister had initially fallen in love with was still present in the man who'd eventually jilted her.

What Anna hadn't expected was Russ's immediate compassion, and she didn't know what to make of him. Trust did not come effortlessly these days.

She caught his eyes, and her breath hitched. "You don't have to do that."

"I insist." He knotted the length of material and leaned back. "Can you stand?"

Perhaps he was merely acting this way because the mayor was near. Her late husband had been adept at playing different roles based on the company he kept. Only when they were alone did he show his true character.

"Yes," she said. "I'm fine now."

She pushed off and stood, then wobbled.

"Let me help you, Anna."

She instinctively backed away, and he followed.

"I can manage."

"Please. I can't have you tumbling into the creek." He softened his words with an engaging smile. "I'll ruin my new shoes wading in after you."

"All right," she reluctantly conceded.

Let him put on a show for the mayor. She needed his help, and distancing herself served no purpose. She'd made it as far as Kansas alone, but her meager funds were swiftly depleting. Finding work wasn't easy for a woman, and she desperately needed a job.

She allowed Russ to take her elbow as they ascended the hill but stepped away immediately once they reached the top. A tarp covered a body on the side of the road, and the scene bustled with people and activity. A man wearing a tin star pinned to his barrel chest glanced at her and quickly looked away, a blush staining his ruddy cheeks. Anna frowned and glanced behind her. She wasn't the sort of person who turned heads. Another man tipped his hat her way.

Russ placed his hand on the small of her back in a proprietary gesture. "I'm afraid you'll have to get used to the attention. The arrival of the bride train is always cause for hope."

"They're interested in courting me?" She scoffed. Times must be truly desperate in Cowboy Creek if the men were casting glances her way. "How should I correct the assumption?"

Russ frowned. "If you didn't want to become a bride, why take Susannah's ticket? Cowboy Creek isn't the usual place for widows to relocate."

"It's a long story."

"Give it time, then. Will and I will do our best to staunch any speculation."

His authority and importance were evident in the deference the men paid to him. She'd known Russ held a notable position in Cowboy Creek, but she'd thought Susanna had exaggerated his reputation.

In the center of the street, Mr. Ward's mule stood placidly, still hitched to the wagon. To Anna's amazement, the animal was unharmed despite the volley of bullets.

She crossed the distance and shook her head. "Poor Mr. Ward. They've broken all his eggs."

"Don't worry, Mrs. Linford," the mayor said from where he knelt beside the wagon. "I'll see that he's reimbursed. If any of your clothing has suffered, the town will reimburse you for the expense, as well. You were traveling under our care, after all."

"That's very kind of you," she said, knowing she'd never take him up on the offer.

She wasn't traveling under anyone's care—not really. Though she fully intended to repay Russ for the cost of the ticket, she mustn't accrue any more debt in the process. Her clothing would survive. She'd sold most of her best dresses anyway. The frills and fripperies required for Philadelphia society weren't appropriate for her new life.

She bypassed the hastily arranged pile of clothing from her carpetbag in favor of the scattered burlap sacks. The damage was even worse than she recalled, and a wave of exhaustion crashed over her.

Unwanted emotion forced its way past her defenses, and she pressed a fist over her mouth, stifling a sob. Of all the things the outlaws could have vandalized, why had they destroyed her collection?

"What's all this?" Russ asked.

He and Will exchanged a glance. They must think her odd, crying over a bunch of sacks.

"Seeds," she said, her voice hoarse with unshed tears. "I know it seems stupid, but I've been collecting them for years. Some of these varieties don't exist anymore except in those bags."

She'd always enjoyed gardening, and she'd become obsessive with her hobby during the years of her marriage. There was something infinitely satisfying about nurturing a flourishing plant from a tiny seedling. In nature, there was no prevarication. Water and sunlight created a thriving sprout. Neglect led to death.

When her world was falling apart around her, there was order in the beauty of her garden. Flowers bloomed, and the plants bore fruit. Even after a harsh winter, delicate hyacinth, beautiful harbingers of spring, pushed through the soil and snow. There was always new life in nature. There was always a fresh start.

Will rubbed his chin. "Can you sift the dirt and sort the seeds?"

"I suppose." She stifled a sigh. The process would take ages. Time she didn't have.

In order to survive, she must find work immediately. A tide of despair threatened to overwhelm her, and she wrestled with her emotions. What was wrong with her? She'd always considered herself a sturdy, practical person. Lately, everything seemed overwhelming and impossible. Perhaps if she shook off this lingering illness and managed a little rest, she'd be more resilient.

Russ knelt and grasped her torn carpetbag. "Why don't we gather everything together, and I'll help you sort them later? The task won't seem as daunting when you're rested."

"Thank you." She gazed at him, perplexed by the suggestion. "But why would you do that?"

"Why wouldn't I?"

"You must be quite busy."

"I'm never too busy for an old friend," he said. "Although Philadelphia must seem a lifetime away."

They weren't friends. Not really. He was offering now, but he'd make some excuse later, out of the mayor's earshot. Especially when he realized that she couldn't immediately pay him back for the cost of Susannah's train ticket.

An odd set of circumstances had conspired to throw them together. It was logical that Russ had sent for a bride through people he knew and trusted, but Anna had been shocked when Susannah had come to call. Their connection was tenuous at best. The social community in Philadelphia had many overlaps, and Susannah's family had known Anna's through mutual acquaintances. Not the sort of relationship that inspired confidences.

The prospective bride had initially written to Russ after an argument with her current beau. Moving halfway across the country to escape her woes had seemed the perfect solution. As time passed, Susannah had come to regret her impetuous decision. Cowboy Creek was too isolated, and the conditions too remote from her society friends. Then her beau had come calling with flowers and profuse apologies.

All of Susannah's reasons for abandoning a move to Cowboy Creek had struck a chord with Anna. The town was halfway across the country from Philadelphia and the incessant gossip thwarting any chance of living a quiet, peaceful life.

She'd known the moment she appeared that Russ would be disappointed at best, angry at worst. Brides were not cogs in a wheel to be interchanged at will, and she had no desire to marry again. But at least she'd be a thousand miles from the scandal.

Desperate times required desperate measures.

The mayor doffed his hat and dusted the brim against his trousers. "I don't believe we've been properly introduced. I'm Will Canfield, ma'am. I hope you won't let this experience sour your first impression of Cowboy Creek." He gave a shallow bow, then he turned to his friend. "You don't have to stay, Russ. Have the doc take a look at both of you. I'll make certain every one of those seeds is collected and have them delivered to The Cattleman. Your hotel room has already been arranged. Mrs. Linford."

"But I can't—"

Will held up one hand. "I insist."

The ground rumbled, and Will replaced his hat. "That will be the cavalry, so to speak. You two take the wagon back to town. I'll see to Mr. Ward. Rest as long as you need, Mrs. Linford. When you're fully recovered, you and Russ will join my wife and me for dinner."

As though accustomed to having his orders followed without question, Will didn't wait for her answer. He strode toward the new arrivals.

Anna shivered despite the warm afternoon. "He's very sure of himself."

She wasn't quite certain if she liked him or not. She'd had her fill of men who insisted on giving orders rather than issuing requests.

"Yes." Russ appeared resigned to the mayor's high-handed behavior. "He has to be, given his job."

"I can't possibly accept his generosity."

"You heard the man. He insisted. There's no harm in accepting."

"But the room was arranged for Susannah."

"He knows about Miss Lowe. He's also aware that you and I knew each other in Philadelphia."

"Surely our previous relationship is too tenuous for such a generous offer?" Anna lifted her chin. She'd stretched her morality to the breaking point by asking for Russ's help given their flimsy connection, and she refused to impose on his friends. "I simply cannot accept his hospitality."

"This solution is best." Russ motioned toward the wagon. "If you stay at the boardinghouse, people will assume you're a prospective bride, and you'll be under even more scrutiny. That's why we arranged for Susannah to stay at the hotel. Don't be surprised if you're still inundated with offers, though."

"But…but…I'm a widow." A childless widow.

"Single women are a much-sought-after commodity in Cowboy Creek."

"I won't marry again." Anna set her jaw. She'd been married once, and that experience had been enough. "I'm not ever getting married again. Never."

Why must everything be so complicated? She didn't want to be noticed or courted. She wanted to live a quiet life in solitude. She didn't need much. A patch of land for gardening and enough money to see her through the winter.

She hadn't considered all the ramifications of a single woman in a town full of unattached men.

"You never know," Russ said. "You might change your mind."

Her stomach twisted. She'd gone from the frying pan straight into the fire. Coming to Cowboy Creek had been an awful mistake, and now she was trapped by her impulsive decision.

"I won't change my mind."

Fifteen minutes later, they were on the road. As Russ carefully formulated his next question, Anna sat stiff and silent beside him. Mindful of her earlier bout of sickness, Russ kept the pace of the wagon unhurried. He sneaked a glance at his taciturn traveling companion. She didn't appear comfortable being alone with him, and he wasn't certain how to put her at ease.

He'd never considered himself an excessively curious man. As a lawyer, he dealt in facts. Extraneous details only muddied the waters. Yet even he had to admit that why a person wound up in a particular place was at least as noteworthy as how.

Anna, a recent widow judging by the faint shadow around her ring finger, had boarded the train in Susannah's place. The facts were simple. The motivation was not.

She'd traveled halfway across the country. Alone. But *why*? She'd hitched a ride with a poultry farmer rather than stay an extra day and catch the next train. If she was destitute and isolated, why not ask her sister for assistance?

"Are you all right?" he asked. "Do we need to stop?"

"I'm fine." She flashed a weary smile. "That's the fourth time you've asked me that question in so many minutes. Do I look as bad as all that?"

"You look lovely."

She snorted softly. "You needn't charm me. The mayor isn't here."

"What does the mayor have to do with anything?"

"Nothing." She ducked her head. "I'm out of sorts."

"You have every right, considering what you've been through."

She blinked him at him with eyes that reminded him of a lost foundling, and his heart did an unexpected zigzag in his chest. She was being incredibly brave, but she was nearing the end of her endurance. The sooner they returned to town, the better. He had plenty of questions, but they'd all have to wait.

"There was an influenza epidemic in Philadelphia," she said softly. "Hundreds of people died. Don't worry. The doctor assured me that I was no longer contagious."

"Is that what happened to your husband?"

"No. Um. His death was sudden. Unexpected."

"I'm sorry. This must be a very difficult time for you."

She muttered something noncommittal, further stirring his curiosity. She didn't appear interested in discussing her late husband. He respected her mourning. Her reticence must mean she loved her husband very much. Not that he had personal experience with the sentiment. For Russ, love was an elusive emotion.

Four years before, he'd been engaged to Anna's older sister, Charlotte. The war between the states had left the country in tatters, and he was finishing up his law degree. The time was ripe to settle down and plan for a future. Charlotte was the daughter of a business associate in Philadelphia, and the match had been celebrated by both families. He'd thought he'd loved her. He'd certainly been infatuated.

His chest constricted. He hadn't known that his fiancée was in love with another man until she'd broken off the engagement. She'd begged him to accept the blame, and Russ had gone along with the ruse. Her father, Mr. Darby, had a reputation as a harsh man, and Russ had been swayed by Charlotte's pleading.

He kept his eyes fixed on the road ahead. "How is your sister? Well, I hope."

"I don't know. I haven't heard from her in years. Not since she, um, not since she married."

Not since she'd thrown him over and eloped. "Surely you write letters."

"No."

Russ raised an eyebrow. The clipped answer effectively slammed the door on any further questions. He searched his memory but couldn't recall any animosity between the sisters. Then again, he'd been distracted.

Though he'd worked as a lawyer in the army, his title had been more honorary than official. He'd had to apply for his law license upon his discharge. He'd been finishing up the studies he'd abandoned upon his conscription while working long hours as an apprentice at a law firm.

He didn't remember the Darby family with any warmth. The episode with Charlotte had been publicly humiliating. Her father's tirade had been blistering. Though Russ had taken the blame for breaking off the engagement, Charlotte's speedy elopement had spoken volumes. Only the most gullible of the gossips had been fooled. His fiancée had been in love with someone else the whole time he'd been courting her. Russ was only human, after all, and the betrayal had smarted.

Anna had been one of the few pleasant memories he recalled from that time. She'd had a ready smile and a sharp humor, even at her young age. While Charlotte had been demure and shy, Anna was an energetic hoyden with a taste for adventure.

She'd also been given to pranks. "Do you recall the time you climbed the oak tree in the backyard and dropped acorns on us?"

"Yes." A ghost of a smile danced around the edges of her mouth. "Charlotte was livid. It wasn't the first time I'd ruined a romantic moment between her and one of her suitors." Two dots of color appeared on Anna's cheeks. "I'm sorry. I shouldn't have said that."

"It's all right." Russ shrugged. "Everything worked out for the best. Both Charlotte and I arrived where we needed to be. We just took the long way around."

He hadn't known Charlotte any more than he'd known Susannah. Given his current circumstances, Charlotte's elopement had been a blessing in disguise.

If he'd stayed in Philadelphia, he'd still be toiling in the basement of a crowded law firm as an underling. Out west, he'd thrived in his practice. As the years passed, he recognized that his pride had pained him more than his heart, but back then, he'd been too young to tell the difference.

Anna met his sidelong gaze. "Then you're content living in Cowboy Creek?"

"I am." Russ cleared his throat. "What are your plans? You've come all this way, after all."

She caught her lower lip between her teeth. "If you want to read Susannah's letter, I can drive the mule."

The change of subject piqued his curiosity. Each time he asked a personal question, she turned the tables on him.

"Reading the letter won't change anything," Russ said. "Your explanation seemed clear enough."

Two months before, Will had convinced him to send for a mail-order bride. The mayor had decided to run for the Senate and had convinced Russ to campaign for the local office in his place. Voters preferred the stability of a married man over a bachelor, and Russ was ready to settle down and start a family. After corresponding with Susannah Lowe, he'd finally sent for her. Their letters had been cordial. They'd both agreed to a marriage of mutual convenience. Russ had needed a wife to legitimize his political career, and Susannah had been looking for a husband.

For the second time, his fiancée had left him for another man. At least with Susannah, they'd never actually met in person. Charlotte's betrayal had been more difficult to bear. Especially since he suspected that Charlotte had only been encouraging him to make another man jealous. A colleague had hinted at the rumors, but Russ had ignored the warning. His frustration at Charlotte's behavior had been directed as much at Charlotte as at himself. He'd seen what he wanted to see. A fault that ran in his family.

Nine years before, a drought had struck his hometown of Big Bend, Missouri, and the ranchers had fallen upon hard times. A ruthless entrepreneur, Zane Ogden, had appeared with a charming smile and a friendly offer of assistance. With a seemingly endless supply of money, he made loans to various ranchers. The initial deals had seemed too good to be true. They were. The fine print required ruinous interest payments and stiff penalties, including the loss of the ranches put up as collateral.

Russ's father, Gilbert, had been the unofficial leader of the local ranching community, and he'd warned people to stay away from Ogden. When several friends became entangled in Ogden's web, his father had agreed to speak with the man and see if anything could be done. Those were the facts that Russ knew for certain. The subsequent events were filled with conjecture and guesswork, a mystery that had torn a rift between his two brothers, Seth and Adam.

As far as anyone knew, their father had gone to Ogden's home late one evening and had never returned. To everyone's shock, despite his advice to others, their father had taken out a loan. When he couldn't repay the balance, he'd fled from his debts and his responsibilities. Russ had initially been skeptical, but Zane had produced paperwork containing a signature from their father, with the sheriff as the witness, showing that he'd taken out a substantial loan. Russ figured his father must have lied to his friends about borrowing the money because he was ashamed. Unable to pay back the loan, he'd abandoned his family.

Initially, Russ had struggled with the truth. The man he knew as his father was forthright and honorable. He'd never abandon his family. Over the years, Russ's opinion had shifted. There were people in this world who could sell sand in the desert. There were people who could steal the pension from a widowed grandmother without blinking. There were people who made their living off the misfortunes of others. His father, like so many others before and after, had merely fallen prey to a charming swindler.

By working around the clock to squeeze out every cent of profit, his older brother, Seth, was able to pay off the loan in full, saving the family ranch from foreclosure.

Seth was convinced their father had never signed the paperwork and was killed, though the body had never been found. Russ believed their father had signed the paperwork and abandoned the family. The difference of opinion had driven a wedge between the brothers.

His father's shame had compelled Russ in his law career to assist those being swindled or left out in the cold due to flaws in bureaucracy. He'd made a name for himself fighting for veterans' rights after the Civil War, which put him in correspondence with various former soldiers, including the leaders of Cowboy Creek.

Eventually, Will Canfield invited him to come out and open a law practice in their booming town. Russ had accepted, and when he saw the endless opportunities in the area, he'd encouraged his mother and Seth to sell the ranch and buy land in Kansas. Though Russ had his own house and business in town, at least they'd all be closer. Last autumn, they'd taken him up on the offer.

He'd put the incident with Charlotte in the past, or so he'd thought. Apparently, the past had just caught up to him. Anna's unexpected arrival along with Susannah's defection had stirred up all the old feelings. He was as much embarrassed for the man he'd been as for what had happened. There was too much of his father in him. He'd run from Charlotte's betrayal rather than face the humiliation.

There'd be no running this time.

"Did Susannah confide in you?" he asked.

Susannah's letters tended to be unfocused and rambling. He might as well get to the heart of the matter rather than wade through a sea of frivolous words.

"Just what you already know," Anna said. "Susannah wanted me to send her sincerest apologies. She didn't mean to fall in love with someone else. It just, well, it just happened."

"Just happened, huh?" Russ didn't bother to disguise the bitterness in his voice. "I've heard that before."

How could he fault his father for running from his mistakes when there were times when Russ wanted nothing more than to do the same himself? Cowboy Creek was a fresh start, but now he felt like the boy he'd been all those years ago, his pride wounded.

No matter his own feelings, Susannah's change of mind didn't explain Anna's unexpected appearance. While Susannah's letter might shed light on the matter, Russ wanted to hear what Anna had to say first.

This time, he wasn't falling for a change of subject. "How do you know Susannah?"

"She's a friend." Anna twisted her hands in the material of her skirt. "More of an acquaintance, really."

"And you hand-delivered a letter, traveling hundreds of miles across patches of hostile territory, from an acquaintance?"

"The social groups in Philadelphia overlap. Surely you remember how things were? When Susannah fell in love, she came to me for advice. Since you were once engaged to Charlotte, she thought I might be of help."

"I see."

He didn't understand anything. Why compound the betrayal by introducing someone from his past?

"I borrowed Susannah's ticket," Anna said. "I hope you'll excuse the imposition, but I'm unable to reimburse you for the fare right away. I promise I'll pay you back as soon as I can."

"A train ticket is the least of my worries."

He wasn't a struggling law clerk pinching every penny anymore. While his heart wasn't involved, there were practical decisions to consider. How was he going to explain to his mother and brother that he'd been jilted yet again? Seth might have laughed at him before, but now that he had a family of his own, he was eager for his brother to follow suit. Adam, if he were here, would probably call him foolish for sending for someone he'd never met in the first place.

There was also his political career to consider. Married men were considered more attractive candidates to hold public office. He'd set his plan in motion to run for mayor, and single men didn't win political races.

Anna glanced at him from beneath her eyelashes. "Susannah mentioned that you were quite successful in Cowboy Creek."

A prickly sensation raised the hairs on the back of his neck. "Business is going well."

"Considering our past connection, I was hoping to ask a small favor of you?"

His heart beat a strange, uneven rhythm. "Other than using my fiancée's train ticket?"

Anna's already pale complexion turned ashen. "It was nothing."

"I'm sorry, Anna." Russ scrubbed a hand down his face. All the tattered feelings had come rushing back. He'd been looking forward to starting a new life and raising a family and hadn't yet adjusted to the disappointment. Having the sister of his former fiancée staring at him like a lost waif wasn't helping matters. "For Charlotte's sake, I'll do whatever I can to help you."

"You have every right to be angry with me."

"I'm not angry, Anna. I'm frustrated. Have you ever been traveling along a path, only to find that nothing is turning out the way you expected?"

"I've had that sensation. Yes."

A jolt spiked through him. That's all he felt. Frustration. Not sadness or disappointment. Not heartbreak. If anything, he was annoyed. He and Susannah had struck a deal, and now she was changing the deal. He'd approached their relationship as though he was approaching a contract negotiation. They both wanted something the other had: Susannah had craved the security a husband could provide, and he'd wanted a family and children. While emotions were best left out of contract negotiations, they seeped into personal matters.

"I'm sorry," he said. The weary note in Anna's voice sent a pang of regret through him. "I shouldn't have asked. You're not in the middle of this any more than you were in the middle of what happened between Charlotte and me."

"You don't have to apologize."

He'd been so young and naive with Charlotte. Anna had been even younger. They were a thousand days and a thousand miles from who'd they'd been all those years ago. He'd approached his relationship with Charlotte as an eager schoolboy, and he'd kept a level head with Susannah. Neither approach had saved him from disappointment.

Rehashing the past wasn't doing either of them any good. "You said you needed a favor. How can I help?"

There was an exhausted slope to Anna's shoulders that reminded him of the battle-hardened soldiers he'd met during the war. Her eyes spoke of a soul-deep sorrow, and his heart softened.

"I need a job." She rushed ahead. "I'm a hard worker. I can cook and clean. I even assisted my late husband in his law office. I heard there's a new hotel in town. Perhaps they need a maid? You must know people."

He barely managed to hide his shock at her request. What catastrophe had forced her on this path? Her family had been quite well off. Had she fallen on hard times before or after her marriage? Why did that even matter? She was here now. Here and in need. Plenty of men had gained and lost fortunes while the country rebuilt. Following the war, more than one man had made imprudent investments.

"You're exhausted," he said. She was in no shape to clean hotel rooms. "We'll settle everything after you've had a chance to rest."

"Never mind. I shouldn't have imposed."

Russ flipped back the edge of his coat and planted

one hand on his hip. The throbbing in his head intensified. He wasn't putting her off. He was truly concerned about her current state. Why did she insist on reading the worst into his innocent words?

The deep creases around Anna's eyes spoke of too little sleep and too much worry. She was fatigued beyond a lengthy train journey.

Russ looked at her for the first time. *Really* looked at her. A thousand tiny clues added together. Anna was widowed. She was riding the train on a borrowed ticket. She was too thin. She was desperate for a job but hadn't gone to her sister for help.

Something had gone terribly wrong in her young life.

She was evading the real question, and though it pained him to push her, he craved answers. "I could better help you if you told me the truth."

Chapter Three

Why did Russ have to be so perceptive?

Pursing her lips, Anna pointed at the distant horizon. "Is that Cowboy Creek?"

"Yes."

"It's larger than I expected."

"The train route helps. We have a thriving depot."

"That's nice."

"I promise I only have your best interests in mind," Russ said. "If you reconsider, and you'd like a friend, I'm here for you."

She was desperately trying to evade his questions. Most men enjoyed talking about themselves. Why must he keep turning the conversation back to her?

"You know the truth." She twisted a bonnet ribbon around her finger. "I'm a widow. I borrowed Susannah's ticket. I need work. You know everything there is to know about me."

Her pulse thrummed in her ears. Though she longed to confide in someone, she caught the words before they escaped. If he knew what they were saying about her in Philadelphia, he'd never agree to help. At best, he'd treat her with pity, at worst, derision. This was her one chance to start over. She didn't have any other choice but to remain silent.

"Anna," he began, "I don't feel I know you at all. Not anymore."

"All I need is a job reference," she said. "Finding work benefits both of us. I'll be able to repay the cost of the ticket sooner. Unless you're uncomfortable. We haven't seen each other in years, after all."

"I'm happy to give you a reference. I'll do whatever I can. You have to know that you can count on me for help."

Anna narrowed her gaze. What if she was making a terrible mistake? Trusting the wrong man had led her down the path of destruction once before. What if he wanted something in repayment for helping her? She didn't have much to give. Perhaps he was being charitable, or perhaps not. These past few years had her questioning everyone's motives. Though he must know she had nothing to offer, she'd best be on her guard.

"Thank you," she said. "I didn't mean to sound surly."

She'd take him at his word that he'd help her find a job. Nothing more. Cowboy Creek was her best chance at living free of the scandal, and she most certainly wasn't confiding in anyone about her recent troubles. Especially Russ. With his past connections in Philadelphia, he could rip open the story before she had a chance to escape again.

"I understand pride, Anna." He glanced at her askance. "Just remember that pride often comes before a fall."

"Pride is not the problem."

She had more important things to consider. Things like surviving to the next week, the next month, the next year. Pride was the least of her worries. The news in Philadelphia had shredded whatever vanity she might have possessed.

"Then I won't press you," Russ said.

Her heartbeat slowed to a normal rhythm once again. "Thank you."

"We're almost there. I'm sure you'll want to rest after we've visited the doctor."

For now, she'd be grateful for the things that had turned out well. At least she wasn't stranded in the next town over. At least she'd made it this far. At least he didn't know about the scandal. *Yet.*

He was suspicious of her. Sooner or later that skepticism was going to get the better of him, and he was going to make inquiries. He'd sent to Philadelphia for a bride, after all, which meant he kept in touch with people he knew there. How long could she hide? Once he mentioned their renewed acquaintance to his friends back east, someone was bound to share the salacious gossip. After all, it had only been three months since Edward's death had made her a widow.

At least letters traveled slowly in this part of the country. Perhaps by the time he discovered her secret, she'd have enough money to relocate to another town.

"I don't need a doctor," she grumbled. "I just need a little rest." She stifled a yawn. Lately, it felt as though no matter how much she slept, she still needed another hour or two.

Russ touched the gash on his forehead. "The doctor is for me."

"I'm sorry. I didn't mean…"

"Relax, Anna. I'm teasing you. I'm trying to put you at ease. You used to enjoy my jokes."

She tugged at a loose button on the wrist of her glove. "That was a long time ago. A lot has happened since then."

He rested his hand over hers, dwarfing her fingers in a brief embrace before pulling away. "You have my condolences on your father."

His touch stirred up long-dormant feelings. The statement was a diplomatic concession considering the treatment he'd received from her father following the jilting.

"His death was painless." Her stomach dropped. Russ knew her father had passed away, therefore he must keep in touch with people back home. People who might share the circumstances of her husband's untimely death. "He didn't suffer."

"Losing a loved one is never easy."

Her heart pounded against her ribs once more. He was going to discover the truth, and then what? Would he keep her secret?

"He always seemed invincible." She tugged on the loose thread. If she lost the button on her glove, she'd never find a match. She'd have to replace them all. "He was always such a powerful presence, I somehow thought he'd live forever."

"I suppose we all think our parents are invincible when we're young."

A memory tugged at the edges of her recollections. There was a hint of scandal surrounding Russ's father, though she couldn't recall the exact circumstances. She'd been too young at the time, and whispered conversations had come to a halt when she entered the room.

She yanked the button free. What did buttons matter? What did any of this matter anyway? There was no use delving into either of their pasts. After today, she doubted she'd see Russ again. He probably wanted to be rid of her just as quickly as she wanted to escape his company.

Disappointment warred with relief. The less he saw of her, the less likely he was to consider her past.

If only he was the ogre she'd invented over the past five years instead of this handsome, solicitous savior. Then again, nothing else had gone as planned; why should her experience with Russ be any different? She'd missed the train, she'd been accosted by outlaws, and Russ wasn't the cruel villain she'd invented after he'd jilted her sister. The more she knew about him, the more he challenged the assumptions she'd brought forward from all those years ago.

She was tired. She was out of sorts. Perhaps she simply wasn't reading beneath the surface of his actions. The facts were firmly embedded in her memory: Charlotte had eloped weeks after the jilting to avoid the scandal, and their father had disowned her. Anna hadn't spoken to her sister since.

If Charlotte and Russ had married, then Anna would still be in touch with her sister. If she'd had Charlotte to lean on after their father's death, she might not have entered such a hasty and unfortunate marriage. If Russ had greeted her announcement about Susannah with anger and recriminations instead of pushing his feelings aside, then she'd feel better about deceiving him.

If. If. If.

The disparity in the villain she'd created and the man before her made her all the more determined to repay her debt quickly. Yet more questions balanced on the tip of her tongue. Considering the outsize role Russ had played in her life, she didn't know much about him. He'd been in the war. His father was gone. He had siblings. That's all Anna could recall.

Against her better judgment, she was hungry for information about the life Russ led outside of his law practice. Perhaps the information might even be useful as she settled, albeit temporarily, in the town.

"You lost your father, too, didn't you?" she asked.

"He's not part of our family any longer."

Shock rippled through her. She'd always assumed the hint of scandal was linked to his father's death, but the evasive answer pointed to something else. "What was he like?"

She didn't know why she'd asked such a personal question beyond a nagging sense of puzzlement about his father. Even if Charlotte had known the truth, she was hardly likely to confide in her younger sister.

"He was a good man," Russ said, his voice flat. "Proud. Honorable. Loyal to his family. Too proud, sometimes."

The hairs on the back of her neck stirred. Though his words were glowing with praise, the tone didn't match his sentiment. There was a slight edge in Russ's voice, a pursing of his lips when he spoke. As someone familiar with keeping secrets, she recognized the signs. There was more to Russ's father than what he was saying.

"You have a brother, as well, don't you?" she prodded.

"Two of them, to be precise. Seth lives just outside of Cowboy Creek with his new wife. They recently adopted three boys and his wife's niece."

"Oh my, that's quite a household."

"I haven't seen my younger brother, Adam, in years." This time the sorrow in Russ's voice was obvious. "I used to receive letters, but I haven't gotten one in months. I don't even know if he's alive. I have to believe he's still out there somewhere. I don't know why, but I feel as though I'd know if he was gone." Russ scoffed. "That probably sounds stupid."

"Not at all."

Anna's eyes burned. Charlotte had always been a distant, ethereal creature. The years between them had been a chasm. Charlotte had been older and elegant, with little patience for a younger sister with dirt beneath her fingernails and muddy circles over her knees from digging in the garden.

Even during the war, Charlotte had been sought after by the young bachelors in the community. She'd had pale blond hair, soft blue eyes and a delicate figure. She spoke in a voice that was barely more than a whisper. Everything about her seemed to attract men like honeybees to nectar.

How many times had Anna knelt on the balcony above the parlor, peeking through the railings, when Charlotte was holding court? Charlotte had been a fragile porcelain figurine. She was to be looked upon and admired but never touched or bothered. Most of her beaus had ignored Anna. Not Russ. He'd always brought her a sweet or an extra flower. He'd wink at her, as though they shared a special secret.

For someone who was largely ignored in the household, she'd found his attention heady. Anna had adored his visits. Then he'd betrayed Charlotte. He'd betrayed their family. He'd betrayed *her*.

Yet despite her better judgment, Anna was still

drawn to the man before her. Did she trust her feelings or the facts? Did she trust the man who'd been kind to a lonely young girl, or did she accept that he'd callously thrown aside her sister and tossed their family into disarray? How did those two men exist in the same person?

A wagon passed them, and the driver tipped his hat.

"We're almost home," Russ said. "The traffic will be heavy soon."

Home. For now. The future remained uncertain.

A skyline of boxy structures appeared above the horizon. The town was larger than she'd expected. Buildings sprawled into the distance, undulating over the rolling hills. Additional frame structures in various stages of completion surrounded the outskirts. A few of the buildings rose three stories into the sky. A train whistle blew, and she caught sight of a steam engine leaving a trail of smoke.

Another rider passed them at a gallop, the horse's tail whipping in the wind.

The nearer they moved toward the town, the more wagons and riders appeared. Everyone seemed to know Russ. He made introductions and soon all the faces blurred together. After meeting countless new people, she gave up even trying to remember their names.

As though sensing she was overwhelmed, Russ caught her gaze. "New visitors are always a curiosity. Especially when a bride train comes in."

She touched the side of her bonnet. "Will there be any awkwardness for you, because of Susannah?"

"No." He bent his head. "I kept the news to a select few. I'll tell them all soon enough. After I've read Susannah's letter."

Anna recalled the letter with a jolt. Had Susannah

mentioned the scandal? The thought hadn't even occurred to her before now. Pressing a hand against her pounding heart, Anna took a deep breath. There was no reason for Susannah to reveal anything about her. Anna was merely the messenger. Her role hardly warranted a mention.

Russ pointed toward a shopfront. "Marlys Mason is the town doctor. She's got some newfangled ideas about how to treat illness, but she has an excellent rate of success, so people mostly take her advice. It's too bad that some of the old timers won't see a woman no matter what the circumstances."

"A lady doctor?" Anna had never considered such a thing but immediately liked the idea. "Why shouldn't a woman be a doctor?"

"Folks get stuck in their ways, but times change. Sometimes it just takes a little longer than we'd like."

"Women should get to be whatever they want to be."

Anna had wanted to write articles about gardening for the local newspaper, but her husband had disapproved. He didn't want his colleagues to think his wife had to work for a living. Especially at something as coarse and common as the women's pages.

Russ made a sound of frustration. "Looks like the doc is out. She often assists the town midwife, Leah Gardner, when there's a challenging case. It's difficult to keep regular hours."

A large chalkboard had been set up beside the etched glass window of the doctor's office. Russ climbed from the wagon, retrieved the whittled piece of chalk dangling from a length of twine, then wrote Anna's name along with The Cattleman as her place of residence.

Anna made a note of the street. She'd return later

and erase her name. A doctor's visit was an added expense she could ill afford.

"Put down your name, too," Anna insisted. "You should have that cut stitched."

"I'm fine. It's too late for stitching anyway."

"If I must see the doctor, then so must you."

Russ dutifully wrote his name and her gaze narrowed. She had a suspicion he'd come back and erase it too as soon as he ensured she was settled. She stifled a giggle. They'd run into each other if she wasn't careful.

"I'm going to ask Dr. Mason tomorrow if you've come for a visit," she said.

Chagrin flickered over his features, and she grinned.

"All right," he said. "But this works both ways. I'll know if you've skipped your appointment, too."

Heat crept up her neck. "Except I wasn't hit over the head." She couldn't very well ask the doctor if he'd visited if she wasn't planning on doing the same. "I'm fine."

"You've been ill, and someone should look at that cut on your arm." He climbed into the wagon once more. "Don't worry, the visit will be charged to the town."

Her cheeks burned. The only thing more humiliating than being destitute was having everyone else know her circumstances. One needn't be a Pinkerton detective to ascertain the situation. She hadn't exactly concealed the fact. She'd begged Russ for a job before, and she was traveling on a borrowed train ticket she couldn't repay. As demeaning as her circumstances may be, she didn't suppose there was any harm if Russ knew the truth of her finances. He'd be more likely to assist her if he knew the dire nature of her situation.

"I'm not one of the brides," she said. "And I can't

accept any preferential treatment on false pretenses."
She might as well set her circumstances straight from
the beginning.

"The mayor is responsible for the reputation of the
town. Having a lady accosted on the road outside of
Cowboy Creek is most definitely bad press. Indulge
him, if only for the sake of community pride."

"If a visit to the doctor will set the mayor's mind at
ease, I suppose I can concede the point."

"That's the spirit."

Perhaps Dr. Mason had some suggestions for regain-
ing her energy. The next few months were going to be
difficult, and she needed her stamina. She had to stash
as much money as possible before Russ—or someone
else—discovered her secret.

"This may be my only opportunity to meet a real live
lady doctor. How can I pass that up?" she said.

"You never know, we may have as many female as
male doctors in the future."

"The mills of the gods grind slow," she quoted.

"But they grind fine," Russ completed Plutarch's
line.

Perhaps finding a job here wouldn't be as difficult
as in Philadelphia. A little anonymity didn't hurt. Having one's name slandered in the newspapers impeded
gainful employment.

The town vibrated with activity. Men on horseback
and people driving wagons laden with supplies jockeyed
for position along the wide, well-kept streets. Shoulders
brushed, and a sea of hats bobbed along the boardwalk.
Townspeople passed each other in opposite directions,
many calling greetings to one another. Russ was forced

to wait several minutes before he eased the wagon onto the street once more.

A low whistle sounded, and she glanced around. A man tipped his hat at her with a leering grin.

Russ glared at the man, and the whistler rapidly disappeared into the crowd.

"I'm sorry for that," Russ apologized. "Let me know if you have any trouble. In some respects, Cowboy Creek is little more than a glorified cow town. Women are still somewhat of a novelty around here."

Another wave of nausea that had nothing to do with her previous illness rippled through her stomach. She didn't want attention. She didn't want to be courted.

"How do I make them stop?"

"Get married, I suppose."

"Not likely."

His expression shifted. "I'm sorry, Anna. That was a thoughtless comment given your circumstances. Please accept my apologies."

He thought her a grieving widow. He couldn't be further from the truth. One thing was certain, for someone who'd had her fill of men, she'd picked a terrible place to start over.

"It's not your fault." She didn't want him to be kind. She'd forgotten kindness even existed. "If anyone should be apologizing, it's me. None of this would have happened if I hadn't missed the train."

"Why did you miss the train?"

"Bad timing. That's what Mr. Ward said this morning. He said life is all about timing."

Even if she'd been older when Russ had come to call on her sister, he'd have never glanced her way. There were few women who didn't pale in comparison to Charlotte. There was no use pining over the past.

Life was all about timing, and she'd been handicapped by a faulty watch.

Chapter Four

The sun had reached its zenith by the time Russ was able to break for the noon meal. After delivering Anna safely to the hotel, he'd visited the office before returning home at midday. There'd been some confusion over Anna's name at the hotel—the porter had been expecting Susannah—but Russ had smoothed over the awkward moment as best he could. He tipped his chair against the side of the house and rested his crossed ankles on the porch rail. A cool breeze stirred the warm air, and he'd slung his coat over the back of the chair.

Susannah's letter rested on the table beside him. She'd apologized profusely in tiny script for several pages. The explanation was better delivered succinctly, but brevity had never been Susannah's strong suit. His attention had drifted after her third apology, which only seemed to exacerbate the sting, and he'd skimmed the last page before the postscript had piqued his curiosity.

Look out for Anna. The past three months haven't been easy, and she deserves better.

For all Susannah's lengthy elocution, that line had been sparse. He figured she referred to Anna's husband's death. A pang of regret reverberated through his chest. Great sorrow only came with great love. Anna had said her husband's death was "sudden" without revealing more. What must it be like, loving someone so much that you couldn't let them go, even in death? What kind of man had Anna loved? Given her family connections and her father's ambitions, her husband must have held some prominence in the community.

If he'd been a community leader, Mr. Linford's death would be noted in the newspapers. A fellow law school graduate had recently sent Russ a copy of the *Philadelphia Morning Post* after winning an influential case. If Russ recalled correctly, the paper had been dated about three months before. He hadn't cleaned off the dining room table in ages, and the newspaper was probably buried beneath a stack of legal documents.

He half stood and then sat back down again. Digging into the past felt intrusive. Anna Linford's life was none of his business. He was protective of her, that was all. A natural inclination given their previous acquaintance. He had no romantic aspirations toward her or anyone else. Having lost out in love twice already, competing with the memory of a dead man held no appeal.

He'd seen that sort of soul-deep love before in his parents' marriage before his father's fall from grace. As though she were summoned by his thoughts, he recognized his mother's silhouette near the end of the block, her steps long and purposeful. Dread filled his stomach. He'd have to tell her about Susannah, but perhaps news of the attack on the road had failed to circulate.

Moments later, she climbed the shallow porch stairs and leaned against the banister. "Lovely afternoon we're having."

Sunlight glinted off the dark hair beneath the brim of her ribboned hat. Though she'd never admitted as much, she was still mourning the disappearance of her husband nearly a decade before. Once or twice, Russ had broached the subject, and she'd gently but firmly rebuked his questions. Whatever she thought of her husband's defection, she kept the feelings to herself. Instead, she clung to his memory with love.

"Isn't today your meeting with the committee?" Russ righted his chair. "I didn't expect to see you."

On Mondays, she met with the opera house committee and often stayed well into the afternoon. They invariably dined at one of the restaurants in town.

She hoisted a perfectly winged eyebrow. "I heard there were outlaws in the area."

Russ heaved a sigh. "Not anymore." Keeping the encounter a secret had been too much to ask. Gossip spread faster than a plague of locusts.

His mother gestured toward the house. "Did you find your lunch?"

"Yes, but you don't have to cook for me. I can eat at The Cattleman on the days you have meetings."

"I like to take care of you once in a while."

"Then I won't argue. Too much. Having home-cooked meals has been a rare treat."

While his mother spent the bulk of her time living with Seth on his ranch outside of town, she was staying with Russ for a few weeks while Seth and Marigold adjusted to married life with an instant family.

Just last month, Seth had become the guardian of three boys following the death of a childhood friend. Though a confirmed bachelor, Seth had taken on the added responsibility of raising three precocious children. The pretty, new schoolteacher had assisted with the transition. His brother had fallen head over heels for Marigold, and the two had recently married and adopted the three boys, as well as Marigold's young niece, Violet, who had come to town. Seth's bachelor home had gone from a hollow shell to a house brimming with love practically overnight. The transformation in his brother was both astonishing and heartwarming.

Russ pulled out a chair. "Did you visit Seth today?"

"I watched the boys for a few hours. Violet is still adjusting. She's only seven and the last few months have been difficult. Before she lived for that brief time with her father, she was accustomed to having Marigold's attention all to herself. Now she has three brothers to contend with. Marigold and Seth wanted a little time alone with her."

Russ nodded. "She's gone through a lot, losing her mother and being taken from her aunt. She appears resilient, though."

"She's an absolute delight. I took the boys to the opera house. I think Harper has a natural talent for the theater. He did cartwheels across the stage while Pippa was attempting to rehearse. And now James Johnson is taking them fishing for the afternoon."

James was married to the local dressmaker in town, and they had a daughter, Ava. He did odd jobs around town when he wasn't working at the stockyards. The boys had been fascinated by his beaded jacket with the leather fringe, and they'd struck up a friendship. When work at the stockyards was slow, James occasionally took them fishing.

"I didn't realize Pippa was in town."

"Her husband is visiting on railroad business. She's

using the opportunity to stage a performance of *Lord Dundreary Abroad.* The committee has approved the funding for a new set and costumes. Should be our best show yet."

Pippa and her husband, Gideon Kendrick, had met and married in Cowboy Creek. Though Gideon's work with the railroad took him all over the country, they returned to Cowboy Creek whenever possible. A talented actress, Pippa was also masterful with costumes and makeup. Everyone looked forward to attending the theater when she performed.

"If Pippa is involved," Russ said, "I'm already looking forward to the performance. I'll escort you on debut night."

"I'd like that. Perhaps Seth and Marigold can join us."

"Seth isn't much for the theater," Russ said, "but he'll go anywhere Marigold leads him. She's good for him. I'm happy for Seth."

"I am, too. I spent too many years leaning on him after…after what happened with your father. It wasn't fair to him, having all that responsibility."

"Adam and I were just as guilty of depending on Seth too much."

Seth had always been the responsible son. He'd become the patriarch of the family after their father disappeared, rebuilding the family legacy while Adam and Russ had pursued other interests. All three of them had taken Seth's hard work and dedication for granted.

Seth had repaid the loan to Ogden by selling off some of the land, only to lose the herd when he left for war. Thankfully, they'd sent their mother to live in Philadelphia before armies from both sides had burned and looted their way through Missouri. A dutiful son, Seth had regained his fortunes in the cattle markets of Colorado.

Without uttering a single word of complaint, Seth had put his wants and needs aside and sent for their mother. He'd come to Cowboy Creek to start over yet again, and his hard work was finally paying off.

None of them had realized how much of a burden he'd shouldered until he took on the added responsibility of the three Radner boys after the death of their parents. Seeing the change in his brother following his marriage to Marigold, Russ was ashamed he hadn't taken notice sooner. He hadn't realized how unhappy his brother had been until he'd seen him happy.

His mother took a seat on the proffered chair. "Marigold has been a darling, and she takes excellent care of the boys." His mother adored the Radner children and enjoyed living on the ranch, helping Marigold and caring for her four new grandchildren. "We all owe Seth a debt of gratitude." His mother scuffed the ground with her toe. "Have you heard from Adam recently?"

"Not in months. You know how it is with him. His work takes him to places we can't follow."

Following the war, Adam had joined the Pinkerton Detective Agency. He'd sent a few letters over the years, but he didn't correspond regularly. Russ didn't know the details of his brother's work, but he knew Adam was often in dangerous situations.

His mother dabbed at her eye. "I pray for him every day."

"I'm sure he's fine, mother. The agency would contact us if something happened."

"You boys mean the world to me." Unshed tears

thickened her voice. "I'd be devastated if anything happened to you."

His anger flared. The next time he saw Adam, they were going to have a long talk. Their mother deserved better. Adam could at least write a letter now and again, letting her know he was alive.

"Nothing is going to happen to any of us," Russ said. "Especially me. I'm just a pencil pusher. Nothing dangerous in my line of work."

"Oh really?" She dropped the handkerchief from her eye and pursed her lips. "Then what about this afternoon?"

A guilty flush crept up his neck. The tone of her voice yanked him back to being scolded as a child. No matter his age, she was still his mother. "I'm sure whatever you heard has been exaggerated."

"I would have preferred to hear about the incident from you," she declared. "I can't believe I had to learn about your outlaw encounter in a conversation with Tomasina. Imagine my surprise when I bumped into her at the opera house, and she regaled everyone with your brave rescue. She assumed I knew."

Tomasina was the mayor's wife, a spitfire redhead who'd ridden into town on a cattle drive last year. Though she and Will were as different as chalk and cheese, they somehow managed to be perfect for each other at the same time.

"There was nothing brave about it," Russ said. "Tomasina is exaggerating."

"What exactly happened then? And what's this I hear about Susannah missing the train? How does one miss a train? They run on a schedule, after all."

A part of him had been dreading this encounter with

his mother since the arrival of the bride train, but now that she was here, he figured he might as well get it over with.

"Susannah isn't coming," he said, cutting right to the point.

"Is she all right?" His mother's annoyance instantly transformed into concern. "Has something happened?"

"She's fine. She merely had a change of heart."

"A change of heart?" His mother snorted. "Did she at least have the decency to send a letter?"

"Yes."

"A letter? That's all? A letter!" The concern returned to annoyance just as quickly. "I don't know what's wrong with women these days. If all she can do is send a letter, then it's her loss. You deserve someone better. I don't know why you had to send to Philadelphia for a wife anyway. I mean, certainly I understand why some of the men of Cowboy Creek feel that a mail-order bride is their only choice, but you're not just anyone. You're handsome and successful."

"You have to say those things." Russ lifted his eyes heavenward. "You're my mother."

"You're going to be the mayor someday!"

"My political career is uncertain."

Especially now. He'd been so sure about what he wanted and where he was going. This morning had changed everything. The hitch in his plans had left him unbalanced for the first time since Charlotte had thrown him over. He was growing heartily tired of having his life derailed by fickle women who just *happened* to fall in love with other people.

"You're going to be the mayor, and we both know it," his mother declared. "There's no need for false modesty. You're absolutely the most qualified man for the position. Anyone would be a fool not to vote for you."

"Now you're exaggerating."

"I'd say that even if I wasn't your mother."

Russ chuckled. "I'm certain you would."

"You deserve someone like Marigold. Someone who is mad about you. You deserve love, not some…some… ramshackle agreement with a stranger."

Susannah's words rattled around in his head: *Anna deserves better.* There was nothing like contemplating the misfortunes of others to put one's priorities back in place. While he was wallowing in humiliation, Anna was dreadfully alone in the world. At least he had his mother and Seth. He had Will and his friends in Cowboy Creek. Near as he could tell, Anna had no one.

"Do you recall Anna Darby?" he asked.

"Charlotte's younger sister?"

"That's the one."

"Hmm." A wrinkle appeared between his mother's brows. "She enjoyed playing in the dirt all the time, as I recall."

"I believe the term you're searching for is gardening."

His mother shuddered delicately. "Same difference. While I enjoy a beautiful garden as much as the next person, I far prefer the finished product more than the process. Just like I can adore a beautiful bonnet without seeing how it's made."

"Anna is here. In Cowboy Creek."

"Are you quite certain? I cannot, for the life of me, imagine one of the Darby sisters in Kansas. I thought their father was strategically marrying them off to build his dynasty?"

"Mr. Darby passed away."

"I'm sorry to hear that, of course." His mother patted the side of her bonnet. "But he was a difficult man. While I shouldn't speak ill of the dead, I was never very fond of him. He treated those poor girls as though they were bargaining chips for his personal advancement."

"She's a widow now. Mrs. Anna Linford." He heaved a great sigh. "And you can't paint the sisters with the same brush. Anna wasn't anything like Charlotte."

"Thank the stars for that."

"Charlotte was fragile," Russ said, not for the first time. His mother had taken Charlotte's elopement and the subsequent gossip personally. "She did the best she could given the circumstances."

"Hmph. I know her father was a difficult man, but making you take the blame for her actions showed a distinctive lack of character." His mother swept her skirts aside and stood. "Not that you didn't try and do the honorable thing by assuming responsibility, but I never believed a word of it. Now that we've exhausted our conversation about the Darby sisters, what happened on that road today? How were you injured? What were you doing out there to begin with?"

She leaned forward and touched the gash and purpling bruise on his temple.

He winced. "It's nothing."

"It doesn't look like nothing."

"After we discovered one of the brides had missed the train at the last stop before Cowboy Creek, Will decided to escort her personally. The next train wasn't until the following day. It occurred to me that someone might have mistaken the woman's name, Lowe for Linford. Either way, I volunteered to accompany Will, and we met Daniel on the road. He was traveling to Morgan's Creek for business. And have you met Mr. Ward? The poultry farmer?"

"As old as Methuselah and just as friendly?"

"That's the one," he said.

"On with your story," his mother prodded. "You still haven't told me about the outlaws."

"As it happened, Anna was the absent bride. Well, not a bride exactly, that's another story. Mr. Ward had offered to take Anna the rest of way after she missed the train." Russ considered his next words carefully. His mother needn't know every detail. She'd worry if she knew how close they'd all come to death. "We heard gunshots and stumbled onto a holdup. Anna and Mr. Ward didn't stand a chance against two men with guns."

"Why didn't you at least wait for help? You might have been killed."

"There wasn't time. Besides, there were three of us against two of them. The odds were on our side. We feared they'd ransom Anna if they didn't find anything of value. I created a distraction, and we were able to defuse the situation."

"You created a distraction with your head, or so I hear."

"What else did Tomasina say?"

"She said that you saved Mrs. Linford's life." His mother leaned over and touched his forehead again. "What does Dr. Mason think of that gash on your hard head?"

"Nothing. She wasn't in her office."

"Promise you'll visit her first thing tomorrow," his mother ordered. "She arrives early. I see her light on during my morning walk."

"Yes. I promise." He hesitated over his next request.

"Mrs. Linford is moving to Cowboy Creek indefinitely. Since she doesn't know anyone, I thought you might introduce her around. She's staying at The Cattleman."

His mother quirked an eyebrow. "I'd be delighted. I'm sure she's charming."

He didn't want his mother reading any more into the situation than necessary. He considered Anna a friend, and she'd had a quite an ordeal this afternoon.

"I'm worried about her," he admitted.

"Was she injured this afternoon?" His mother rested a hand against her chest. "Tomasina didn't say."

"Slightly. She was more shaken than hurt. There's more, though. She was ill at the last stop, and that's why she missed the train. She was ill again after the holdup."

"Outlaws, gunfire and witnessing a bludgeoning would be hard on anyone's constitution." His mother paused. "How long has she been a widow? Grief can be exhausting."

"I didn't ask, but I suspect three months or so."

"I'll introduce her around. It's difficult, losing one's husband. Any children?"

Russ started. He hadn't considered that she might have children. "She wasn't traveling with any."

"She couldn't have been married very long. Sounds as if she could use a friend."

Russ exhaled. "Thank you."

His mother patted his knee. "You work too hard. You need a rest."

"I enjoy my work."

"You're as bad as Seth. At least he spends time with his family these days. You should let Simon do more work. He's ready for the responsibility."

Simon Smith, Russ's law clerk, was young and hungry. The diligent young man was another one of Will's projects. The mayor had sent the boy to law school, and he'd tasked Russ with offering the young man an apprenticeship during his breaks from school. Not that Russ minded. Simon did the work of three clerks.

He tipped back his head. "Maybe I should take the boys for an afternoon soon."

Having three nephews reminded him of all the fun he and Seth and Adam had had as children.

Susannah's untimely defection had him wondering if he'd ever have children of his own. He'd taken far too much in his life for granted. Seeing Seth and his happiness at being a husband and father had Russ yearning for something more.

His mother ruffled his hair as though he was a young boy and not a grown man. "They'd enjoy spending time with you. They deserve all the love they can get after losing their parents and being uprooted." Her voice grew stern. "Just don't make them sit around your law offices while you work."

"Would I do that?" Russ feigned innocence.

"Yes." She rose from her chair. "I'm going back to the opera house. I only have another hour before James returns with them from fishing. Let's hope they didn't catch anything. I'll have to sit with the smell of dead fish all the way to the ranch."

Despite her feigned surliness, his mother enjoyed every minute with the children—even the minutes that smelled like fish. After waiting years for grandchildren, she'd been gifted with a ready-made family, and she couldn't be more delighted.

"Now that you've satisfied your curiosity," Russ said, "let me walk you back to the opera house."

His mother assumed an expression of mock outrage. "I only came by for my papers."

"Tell the truth." Russ stood up and reached for his coat. "You wanted to check on my hard head."

"That too." She hooked her arm through his elbow and rested her head against his shoulder. "I worry about you."

"You shouldn't. There's nothing to worry about."

"I'm sorry about Susannah," she spoke softly. "It's easier sometimes to be angry than it is to be hurt."

"I'm neither. Merely resigned. I'm certain everything will turn out for the best."

"Enough of this melancholy talk." She patted his arm. "Tell me more about Mrs. Linford. The former Anna Darby. What brought her all the way to Cowboy Creek?"

"I don't know," Russ said. "But I was hoping you could quietly spread the word that she's not a prospective bride—despite traveling on the bride train. She's still mourning her husband."

"Poor thing. I'll do what I can. Perhaps you should visit her this evening."

"Do you think that would be appropriate?" He hesitated in pushing the boundaries of their tenuous connection. "She's had a difficult day. She's probably resting."

"All the more reason to visit. A familiar face is a comfort after an ordeal."

He puffed out his chest. He'd saved her life, after all. Surely that entitled him to at least check on her?

His mother waggled her finger. "I know that look in your eye. Don't let that lump on your head affect your thinking. Just because you saved her life doesn't mean she's going to throw flower petals at your feet."

"That wasn't what I was thinking at all." He grinned. "I was hoping for a parade. Perhaps a banner across Eden Street."

"You're incorrigible."

"A statue, then? Something in bronze."

"I'm leaving this conversation."

"A gentleman caller is bound to be noted." He considered Anna and sobered. "I don't want people to get the wrong idea."

"You're a respected man in the community." His mother tightened the bonnet ribbons beneath her chin and adjusted the strings of the dangling reticule at her wrist. "Letting everyone think she's spoken for by the next mayor will keep the wolves at bay."

"For a time."

"Wouldn't hurt for Millie and Minnie to think you're off the marriage market."

"Ugh." Russ threw back his head. "In all the excitement, I'd forgotten about Minnie and Millie. You met them?"

The two cousins were the latest brides to arrive on the train that morning. They were nearly identical, right down to their penchant for overly flounced dresses. They each had matching brown eyes and hair and appeared inseparable. They spoke over each other and completed each other's sentences. Whoever married one of them married both. Russ didn't envy the men.

"Tomasina introduced me to the merry cousins," his mother said with a smile. "They made quite an impression."

"Is there anything Tomasina doesn't know?"

"No."

"I didn't think so. Neither Millie nor Minnie ceased

giggling from the moment they stepped off the train. I'm all for a good laugh, but those two are beyond the pale."

"Shall I scratch them off my list of potential daughters-in-law?"

Russ grimaced. "I've given up on the marriage market for the time."

Anna's name sprang to mind. He admired her. She was witty and smart, and she'd make any man a fine bride. He simply couldn't stomach spending the rest of his life competing against her late husband. Besides, she didn't want to marry anyone, let alone him.

"See?" His mother squeezed his arm. "It's all settled. Visit Anna as a friend. If people draw the wrong conclusion, that's none of your affair. No harm done to either of you."

"You make a sound argument."

He had no romantic interest in Anna, and she certainly wouldn't mistake his intentions. The innocent ruse suited both of them. He'd lost two fiancées to other men already, he wasn't about to lose out in love to a dead man.

His presence would chase away the less zealous suitors and discourage Millie and Minnie from setting their giggling sights on him. They'd done quite of bit of uncomfortable pointing and whispering at the train station this morning.

"Don't sound so surprised." His mother tilted her head. "I make sound arguments quite often, except you and your brothers are too headstrong to listen most of the time. You seem awfully concerned about Mrs. Linford. You're certain you're not holding a candle for Charlotte?"

"Absolutely not."

When he looked back at that time in his young life, it wasn't Charlotte's face he pictured.

He pictured Anna's laughing smile.

Chapter Five

Anna gaped at her surroundings. "Surely there's been a mistake."

Russ had accompanied her to the hotel after the shoot-out. They'd signed in at the desk, and he'd tipped his hat, urging her to rest and promising to check on the doctor. The porter had shown her to a perfectly lovely room in The Cattleman. She'd freshened up and was considering a nap when another flustered porter had appeared, insisting she'd been given the wrong room.

He'd obviously been mistaken.

The grandiose suite he'd insisted was the correct room featured an enormous sitting area and a separate bedroom. Fringed curtains the color of pine needles draped leaded glass windows, and tufted burgundy velvet furniture flanked the fireplace at precise angles. Plush oriental rugs in exotic shades of tangerine and burnt umber covered the floor.

She brushed her hand over a marble-topped table. "This is definitely a mistake."

Turning to correct the error, she discovered the porter had already deposited the key on a side table and disappeared with silent footsteps. She hovered in the archway separating the bedroom and the sitting area, hesitant to move farther into the room lest the rightful occupants suddenly appear.

A knock sounded, and she stifled a yelp. Pressing a hand over her rapidly beating heart, she crossed the room and opened the door to a carnival of blue, yellow and pink flowers set in an enormous glass vase.

"Oh, uh, dear," Anna stuttered. "I am definitely in the wrong room."

"This is the place."

A robust, middle-aged woman in a black dress with a crisp, starched white apron wrapped around her ample waist charged into the room. She set the vase on the marble-topped table and adjusted a few petals before stepping back.

"Perfect." She dusted her hands. "I'm Mrs. Foster. If there's anything you need, anything at all, just send for me. All the rooms are equipped with a bell that rings in the kitchen."

"I'm afraid there's been a mistake," Anna said. "This room is far too grand. I should be in the other room. I don't know why I was moved."

"This is your room all right, no mistake. Poor Nigel is in for a tongue-lashing when the boss finds out what happened. There was a mix-up with the names, you understand. It's all cleared up now. This is the room Mayor Canfield specified, and I never argue with the boss."

"The mayor owns this hotel?" He'd arranged the finest room for Russ's bride. Perfectly acceptable considering the two were friends. Except she wasn't Russ's bride. "I can't take advantage of his hospitality."

"He can afford it. He owns half the town. He's a town founder, after all."

"I'd prefer a smaller room." Something more suited to her status. "I prefer less expensive…accommodations."

"Oh pshaw." Mrs. Foster flashed her palm. "After what you've been through, you deserve a little pampering. He sent along the flowers."

Anna opened the card and scanned the contents. The mayor wished her a speedy recovery and repeated his invitation to dinner along with Russ. She held the card against her chest. Now to find a polite way of refusing. People might read more into her relationship with Russ if they appeared together socially. Not to mention dinner with the mayor was out of the question since she planned on becoming one of his employees.

"Mrs. Foster," Anna said, "do you happen to know who oversees the hiring of the hotel staff?" Perhaps she didn't need Russ's help after all. He'd done so much for her already, she mustn't trouble him further.

"That would be me," Mrs. Foster said. "I do all the hiring."

"I was hoping to find a job. Is there anything available?"

The housekeeper heaved a great sigh and rolled her eyes. "Oh no. Not again."

"I'm a hard worker," Anna rushed to say. "I promise you."

"I'm sure you are, but you're also young and pretty. You'll be married by the end of the year, and I'll be out another maid again. They all leave just when I get them trained. I can't afford the lot of you. I spend most of my salary on wedding gifts these days."

"I'm not one of the brides. I'm not looking for a husband. I'm widowed, you see."

"You poor thing." Mrs. Foster patted Anna's clasped hands. "I lost my own Mr. Foster. Still, you're young. You have plenty of time ahead of you. There are lots of good men in Cowboy Creek. Plenty of scoundrels, too, but I'll steer you right."

"I promise I won't let you down." She'd stay as long as she could, that much was true.

"We'll see." The housekeeper glanced around the room. "Is your trunk arriving later?"

Anna recognized her battered carpetbag. "I left my luggage on the train." She pressed her palm to her cheek. In all the excitement, she'd forgotten all about her trunk. "I'll only have the two dresses until it's delivered. It's probably still at the station."

"Then let's get your dresses aired and pressed." To her credit, Mrs. Foster didn't show any judgment of her meager belongings. "I'll have a tray sent up. Mayor Canfield said you weren't feeling well. What should I tell visitors?"

"Visitors? I won't be having any visitors. I don't know anyone."

Her heart did a little leap, and she mentally chastised herself. There was no reason for Russ to bother on her account. He obviously had much more important things to consider, yet she couldn't stop thinking about him. She hadn't been prepared for the changes in him the years had wrought. If only he'd turned to fat and grown an enormous wart on his nose. If only he'd been nasty and unhelpful and condescending.

She didn't want to like him. She didn't want to remember the naive girl she'd been all those years ago. That girl was gone, and the memories were too painful.

Mrs. Foster grasped a pillow from the settee a slapped some air into the feathers. "There's always a welcome wagon in Cowboy Creek. You'll have visitors. New folks in town are a novelty. I'll tell them you're resting."

"I'd appreciate that."

Anna's stomach rumbled. Despite being ill earlier, she was famished.

"Come along. Everything is ready for you." The housekeeper took Anna's hand and led her toward the bedroom. "You're as pale as a sheet on bluing day. You've had an ordeal, and you need to rest. I'll send up some toast and tea to soothe your stomach."

"That sounds marvelous," Anna said. She'd have preferred something more substantial but hesitated to ask.

"For dinner, I'll order up some stew," the housekeeper continued. "There's a fine stew today. And dessert. Oh, my word. There's a new miss in town, and she bakes desserts that would make a grown man weep. She's sent over a chocolate cake with cherry filling. I'll send up a slice with dinner. Do you like chocolate?"

"I adore chocolate."

"Then you're going to have a delicious experience." Mrs. Foster grasped the door handle. "Rest. You've had a terrible ordeal, and you look as though you haven't had a proper night's sleep in a month of Sundays. I'll take care of everything."

As the door shut, pressure built behind Anna's eyes. She couldn't recall a time in her life when anyone had pampered her. And that's exactly how she felt. Pampered. The experience was heady, and one she'd best not grow accustomed to.

She ran her hand along the embroidered counterpane. While she was grateful to both Will Canfield and Russ for the solitude to recuperate, guilt gnawed at her. She was living a lie, taking advantage of the mayor's hospitality while allowing people to make assumptions.

She sat on the bed and pressed her palms into the firm mattress. Since this room had already been arranged, she might as well stay the night. Tomorrow she'd start her search for a job. Mrs. Foster had been kind, and Anna loathed making more trouble. If she convinced Russ of her sincerity, he could assure the mayor and the hotel's housekeeper of her suitability.

Though inexplicably exhausted, sleeping during the middle of the day felt like a luxury she didn't deserve. She stood and crossed to the sitting room. Perhaps she'd make a list of things to do. With that in mind, she took a seat on the settee and rested her head against the tufted bolster.

Appealing to Russ about her future employment meant an excuse to see him again. Her stomach flipped, and she gave up trying to control the reaction. Somewhere along the way, her emotions had careened out of control, and she'd best get ahold of herself. She was nothing to Russ, and he was nothing to her. He was a girlish infatuation that had long since died. She didn't believe in love.

She certainly didn't trust her own heart.

If her time in Cowboy Creek was limited, she needed another destination. Perhaps somewhere in California. As she considered the cities along the west coast, her eyes drifted shut. She didn't know much about California beyond what she'd read in books, but at least she'd be far from Philadelphia.

A soft knock jerked Anna awake, and her heartbeat kicked.

Bolting upright, she checked the clock and gaped. Gracious, she'd slept for nearly two hours, and she felt as though she'd hardly blinked. The knock sounded again, this time more insistent. She rushed to the door and paused, patting her hair in the mirror and smoothing her rumpled skirts, then pinched her cheeks to add some color.

"Who is it?" she called.

"Russ Halloway."

Her breath caught, and her fingers quaked on the ornate brass handle as she opened the door. Russ stood on the threshold, a tray crowded with silver-domed dishes in his outstretched hands, his hat hanging from his fingers.

He'd combed his hair over his temple, but the purpling bruise near his left eye had nearly swollen shut the lid. His suit and tie were crisp and expensively tailored, yet even with the wainscoted corridor framing him, there was still that same touch of uncivilized power she'd sensed this morning.

"I offered to bring this up myself," he said.

"Come in." She swept her hand aside. "I didn't realize how late it had gotten."

Her stomach rumbled, and Russ laughed.

"Just in time, I see." He stepped into the room and set the tray on the low table before the burgundy velvet settee. His hat he put on the side table. "Mrs. Foster said she tried to deliver toast and tea earlier, but she didn't want to wake you. You'd best eat this offering, or she's going to be in fits. How are you feeling?"

"Much better, thank you. I had a rest."

"Excellent. I checked on the doctor before coming here. She's still assisting the midwife. The case appears dire, and I didn't want to pull her away."

"You did the right thing. I'm fine. Only shaken. How about you? How is your head?"

"Not even a twinge. Looks far worse than it feels." His smile was sheepish. "I'm not going to turn any heads this way."

"You look quite rakish."

"I suppose that's something." He stuck his hands in his pockets. "I'll go now. I wanted to ensure you were settled after all the commotion this morning. I should have known that Will would take care of everything."

"He even sent over flowers."

Russ scowled at the flowers. "He's a good man. Too good sometimes. I should have thought of that myself."

"Don't bother on my account." Anna gazed longingly at the stew on the tray. Though famished, she had something else she needed to do. "I spoke with the housekeeper, Mrs. Foster, earlier but she was reluctant to hire me. She fears I'll marry and leave her in the lurch. Is there any way you could put in a good word for me?"

"I'd be happy to assist, but surely there's something else you'd rather do? You shouldn't be extending yourself so soon after your illness."

"The exercise will do me good."

"If you insist." He crossed toward the door. "I'll leave you to your dinner."

"Stay if you like. I'd prefer not to eat alone."

"Are you certain?"

"Quite." She'd had far too much time alone lately. No one had been certain what to say after her husband's death, even before the rumors had started. She'd become something of a pariah following his shocking murder. "Should I have them send up another tray? I suppose it's rude to eat in front of you."

"Not rude at all." Russ took the seat opposite her and rested his ankle on his bent knee. "My mother is staying with me for a few weeks. She normally lives with my brother Seth, but he recently married. She's giving the newlyweds some time alone. Not that Seth and Marigold will ever be alone, with all those children." He rested the back of his head on the domed edge of the settee. "While I enjoy having a hot meal prepared for me each evening, my mother is under the mistaken impression that I have the appetite of a farmhand."

"If she lives on a ranch, I suppose she's accustomed to feeding farmhands."

"I suppose," Russ said. "She's going to call on you tomorrow. I hope that's all right."

"She needn't trouble herself. I'm not... Well, we won't be traveling in the same social groups. No one wants their maid as a guest at dinner. I don't want there to be any awkwardness."

"You'll find society is much less strict west of the Mississippi. We don't stand on ceremony." He lifted his head. "Especially when eating. Stop staring at your dinner. You must be famished."

"I am." She took a bite of her stew and nearly swooned. "This is delicious. Tell me about your work here in Cowboy Creek."

For the next twenty minutes, Russ carried the weight of conversation. He regaled her with stories of the unique court cases he'd encountered and offered tidbits of insight into his friends and family. Anna finished her stew and took a bite of the enormous slice of chocolate cake that accompanied it.

She collapsed back onto the settee with a sigh. "Mrs. Foster was right. That is a delicious experience."

Russ grinned. "I've never seen anyone so enamored of chocolate cake."

"Then they've never eaten this particular chocolate cake."

"Must be Deborah's work. I've only seen that reaction from people sampling Miss Frazier's baking. She's only been here a month or so, and her baking skills are already legendary around town."

"If this cake is any indication, I can see why." Anna paused. "Would you like a bite?"

"No. Thank you." He patted the flat plane of his stomach. "I'm still suffering through my mother's attempt to fatten me up."

Though Anna had only meant to eat half of the gargantuan slice, she soon found herself pressing the tines of her fork against the plate, gathering the last of the crumbs.

Russ stood and adjusted the wicks on the lamps.

Though she'd slept most of the afternoon, with her stomach full and the sun setting in the distance, her eyelids drooped once more. "Thank you for what you did this morning. I'm sorry you were hurt."

"It wasn't your fault."

"I'm afraid it was." The cake settled like a rock in her stomach. "The holdup was entirely my fault. The porter offered to carry my bag at the train depot, and I declined. I told him that I had precious cargo inside. It was an offhand comment. I had no idea anyone was listening, and the outlaws mistook my words." She choked back a sobbing breath. Crying didn't solve anything. "Poor Mr. Ward might have been killed."

Russ took the seat beside her, and the cushion dipped. He rested his hand on hers. "You are not responsible for the criminal behavior of others. Trust me. I'm a lawyer. I know these things."

"But none of this would have happened."

"They'd have simply held up someone else. Which means you did a great service to a complete stranger. I might not have been around to save the day had they targeted someone else."

"You very much saved the day." She desperately wanted to smooth her hand over his bruised temple. "I'm extremely grateful."

"You'll give me a big head." He touched the lump on his temple. "Bigger than I already have."

"I can't help but feel responsible."

He frowned, the stern effort thwarted by his swollen eyelid. "Had you announced that you were carrying the crown jewels in your trunk, that doesn't give outlaws or anyone else the right to steal from you."

"I'll be more careful in the future."

"That's a sensible enough reaction." A half grin softened the harsh lines of his face. "And speaking of being sensible, I certainly don't recommend that you announce you're carrying the crown jewels."

She offered him a reluctant smile in return. "Yes, one must be sensible."

He stood and then hesitated, as though he wanted to say something but couldn't find the words. The silence lengthened, and her pulse picked up rhythm. Had he discovered the truth already? Had Susannah said something in her letter?

"Anna," he said at last, "I hope you find what you need here in Cowboy Creek."

She exhaled a relieved breath. "Me, too."

"Lock the door behind me. I'll stop at the front desk and tell them you're not to be disturbed."

He grasped his hat from the table and stepped into the corridor. She closed the door behind him and turned the key, then leaned against the wooden frame. For the time being, all she needed to do was survive. One hour, one day, one month. One foot in front of the other.

Anna had sided with Charlotte all those years ago, yet Russ didn't seem like the sort of man who'd jilt someone without a good reason. Charlotte, on the other hand, had left Philadelphia behind, never to return. Not even after their father's funeral. She might have at least written or sent a telegram. *Something*. Instead, she'd walked away from her only sister without a backward glance.

Between Charlotte and Russ, her sister's behavior had proved more questionable in retrospect.

Anna's world wobbled, and she clutched the doorknob behind her, letting it dig into the palm of her hand. All this time she'd painted Russ as the villain, but now she didn't know what was true.

She didn't know whom to trust. Especially when she couldn't even trust her own heart.

Russ loped down the stairs and stepped onto the boardwalk. A light caught his attention, and he turned left, toward his office.

The door was open to catch the evening breeze, and he discovered Simon hunched over a stack of papers.

"It's late," Russ said. "You should be home."

His law clerk rubbed his eyes with fisted hands and stifled a yawn. Simon was young with jet-black hair slicked over his ears and dark eyes. His swarthy good looks had earned him a bevy of female admirers. Though Simon could have his pick of the young women in town, he worked relentlessly, ignoring their advances. He was driven by unknown forces. Russ only knew that Simon had been orphaned at a young age. He simply accepted the younger man's compulsion to excel. Sometimes the only way to escape the past was by building a new future.

Simon had been a porter at the Cattleman Hotel until Will sent him to law school. Russ had never asked his age, though he suspected Simon was far too young for the work he'd undertaken. The law clerk was smart as a whip and tenacious. He might be young in years, but he possessed an old soul. Simon accomplished more work on his breaks from school than most men achieved in twice the time.

The younger man indicated the stack of papers. "Jason Mitchell dropped these by."

Russ gave the papers a cursory glance. "Jason Mitchell of the Mitchell Coal & Mining Company, I presume?"

"That's the one." Simon pinched the bridge of his nose and yawned again. "He's buying the Henriksens' farm."

Russ set the papers aside and thumbed through a stack of mail. "I spoke with Artie Henriksen a while back. He was looking for signs of coal on his property. I guess he found it."

"Everyone is looking for coal. The whole county has coal fever. Jason Mitchell is paying good money for the land."

"Is that what we want?" Russ held an envelope to the light. "Do we want to turn Cowboy Creek into a coal mining town?"

"You're going to be the next mayor. What do you want?" Simon asked.

"I want the best for the town." Russ tossed the letter back onto the stack. "Coal mining is hard work. Dangerous. Men die young when they work in the mines." He took the chair on the opposite side of Simon's desk. "Then the mines dry up, and the town dies."

"That's a grim picture."

"That's why good leadership is important. Someone has to be on the lookout for the next opportunity. Nothing lasts forever." He rubbed the back of his neck. "In the end, my opinion doesn't matter. I can't stop people from selling. They have to do what they think is best."

"Not everyone is selling. Your brother is staying."

"He's a rancher at heart. It's in his blood. Not everyone has that kind of fortitude."

Simon stood and crossed to the potbellied stove in the center of the room. He grasped the blue-speckled kettle and poured a mug of tepid coffee. "There's more. Someone else is buying land outside of town. He's going after the same plots of land in Jason's path."

Instantly awake once more, Russ's attention sharpened. "Who?"

"I'm not certain. When I was filing the deeds for the Henriksen sale, the clerk was complaining. Said it was the third sale he'd recorded this week. I've only recorded two for Jason Mitchell."

"Maybe Jason is working with another lawyer. Playing us at both ends, perhaps?"

"I don't think so. He isn't that sort of fellow. Besides,

the clerk was muttering about a girl. He kept saying, 'she' was very annoying."

"Then who is buying up the land?" Russ drummed his fingers on the desktop. "I'll do a little digging."

"I can do the digging. You'll be busy." Simon tossed him a knowing look. "Weren't you expecting someone special on the train today?"

A flush swept over Russ's face. "You weren't supposed to know about that."

"Are you going to introduce me?"

"She didn't arrive."

Simon's expression sobered. "I'm sorry. I didn't mean to pry. Except you're not very neat. Your desk is a mess. Some of your letters smelled like perfume. That's difficult to ignore."

"It wasn't a secret. It just, well, it just wasn't news either."

"That's not how a man in love acts, if you don't mind my saying."

Russ offered a wry grin. "And you know a lot about being in love?"

"It's in the air. Have you seen Walter lately?"

"Walter Kerr, the photographer?"

"Yes. I ran into him at the newspaper offices. He must have mentioned Sadie's name four times in a ten-word conversation."

Russ stroked the neatly trimmed whiskers on his chin. "He took Sadie's photo recently. He's become our local photographer these days."

"They've been seen twice dining at The Lariat with their heads bent together."

"We shouldn't gossip." Russ stored the tidbit of information in case his mother tried her hand at matchmaking him with Sadie Shriver. He could safely tell her the bride was spoken for. "Have you finished up all the paperwork for the Mitchell Coal & Mining Company?"

"I've gotten as much done as I can until the clerk files the deeds." Simon took his seat once more and set his coffee cup on his blotter. "Maybe I'm wrong about Jason Mitchell. He's a handsome sort of fellow. I can see him asking a girl to do his bidding. Especially if he doesn't want us to know what he's doing."

"Maybe," Russ said. "You're right, Jason doesn't seem like the sort of man who'd play both sides, but it's worth checking."

"If you don't mind my asking, why represent him at all? If you don't want a coal mine taking over Cowboy Creek, maybe we shouldn't be doing business with him."

"Because he's going to buy the land whether I like it or not. I'd rather be the solicitor on record. Someone has to make sure the ranchers are getting a fair price for their land."

"True." Simon sipped his coffee. "I almost forgot to mention, someone came by looking for you."

"Who?"

"Didn't leave a name. Said he was new in town and wanted to inquire about some legal work. Asked questions about you."

"About the law offices?"

"No. About you personally."

That got Russ's attention. "What did you tell him?"

It wasn't unusual for people to solicit business unannounced. Personal questions, however, were highly irregular. No one cared what their lawyer did outside of working hours unless he was caught doing something illegal.

"What's there to tell?" Simon shrugged. "He asked me if you had family in town."

Russ leaned forward and braced his hands on the edge of Simon's desk. "Didn't you find that odd?"

"Of course I did. That's why I remembered him. Don't worry, though. I didn't tell him anything he couldn't find over at the courthouse."

Russ let his hands drop. The kid had a point. The town kept a registry of names. Perhaps the man was looking for Seth.

Or Adam.

The jarring thought shot him upright. Adam was often involved in shady dealings while doing work for the Pinkerton Detective Agency. Though his brother rarely spoke of his occupation, Russ was aware that his brother often changed his identity depending on his current case. If someone had discovered Adam's true identity and wanted to track him down, questioning relatives was an obvious means of gaining information.

Russ made a mental note to speak with Seth. They'd best be on their guard until they knew for certain what information this mystery man was after—and why. "Did he say if he was coming back?"

"Nope. Just left."

Russ fisted his hand. "Sounds like an odd fellow. What did he look like?"

At least he could tell Seth who to look out for.

"He was older. Had gray hair. Had one of those faces that looks young even with wrinkles. Boyish. Kind of like the sheriff."

The term *older* didn't help much. Sheriff Getman

was in his fifties. Then again, to someone as young as Simon, everyone probably appeared old.

"If you see him again, point him out to me. Better yet, see if you can get his name." Unease skittered along Russ's nerve endings. They hadn't had a letter from Adam in ages. The more he thought about it, the more logical it seemed. Was Adam in some sort of danger? "Can't be too careful these days," he added.

"Something wrong?"

"No. Nothing. Just sounds like an odd fellow," Russ said, lest Simon let something slip and spook the man. "Best to keep an eye on him, just until we have more information. He might be good business for us."

Or he might be a danger to Adam.

Simon nodded. "Will do."

Despite his feigned indifference, Russ vowed to speak with Seth as soon as possible. The two problems nagged him, dominating his thoughts. A woman was buying up land, and someone was asking about his family. Were the two people connected?

Adam had vowed that his job would never put the lives of his family in danger.

Had his brother lied?

Chapter Six

Anna awoke the following morning long past dawn. Though she rarely slept late, the extra rest left her feeling rejuvenated and optimistic. Dressing quickly, she discovered a note from Russ slipped beneath the door. Her seeds had been delivered to the lady doctor, and she'd offered to assist in organizing the collection.

Anna glanced at Russ's carefully drawn map with a grin. The town wasn't so large that she couldn't recall the place they'd visited only yesterday.

Anxious to assess the damage to her seed collection, she soon found herself standing before the door of Dr. Mason's office. The woman who answered her knock was not at all what Anna had expected. The lady doctor was young, in her mid-twenties, and wore her chestnut hair loose, the strands barely brushing her shoulders. Shorter than Anna, she wore a sturdy, white cotton apron over her beige calico dress. The apron flared over her stomach, indicating the early stages of a pregnancy.

"You must be Anna Linford." The woman stuck out her hand and gave Anna's fingers a quick, firm shake. "I'm Dr. Marlys Mason. I apologize for missing your visit yesterday. I checked with the hotel when I returned from my case, but you were sleeping. Since you'd finished your dinner tray, Mrs. Foster and I decided not to wake you. A good appetite is an excellent sign of health."

"I'm doing quite well," Anna replied cheerfully. "No ill effects from my encounter with the outlaws."

"Excellent. Come this way. I'm grateful you're feeling better this morning. I've been curious about your collection." She pivoted on her heel and swept through an inner door.

Taken aback by the woman's brisk speech, Anna paused a moment before following. The doctor led her into a large room that looked more like a laboratory than a physician's office. Two large raised tables dominated the space. Cupboards lined the walls from floor to ceiling, the expanse broken only by a smooth countertop. The entire room gleamed as though every surface had been recently polished. A crisp, clean, almost metallic smell permeated the space.

One of the tables held a row of familiar burlap sacks along with a larger bag secured with twine.

Her seeds.

A flush of excitement swept through Anna. "The mayor kept his word."

"Why wouldn't he? But first we should see to that cut on your arm." The doctor crossed her arms over her chest. "Mr. Halloway also mentioned you've been feeling ill."

"A relapse. I had the flu before I left Philadelphia."

"I read about the outbreak in the newspapers." Marlys dropped her hands to her sides. "My husband, Sam, runs the local gazette. He subscribes to newspapers all over the country. I watch for outbreaks. Smallpox, measles, influenza and the like. The pattern of a disease can be quite fascinating and often predictable."

"You don't say," Anna replied noncommittally, her ears buzzing. "Your husband receives the *Philadelphia Gazette*?"

"No. I don't believe that's one of his newspapers." Dr. Mason grasped a low, wheeled stool. "Have a seat. I assumed you wanted to ensure your collection was safe before I examined you."

"That's very kind of you."

Dr. Mason took another low stool for herself, then took Anna's wrist. "Your pulse rate is slightly accelerated."

"Brisk walk here." Anna swallowed hard. "From the hotel."

There was no safe corner anywhere. She should have changed her name. She should have gone by Darby instead of Linford from the beginning. She hadn't been thinking about newspapermen and running into other people from Philadelphia. Escaping had been her first and only goal. For the past three months, debtors had been pounding at her door, demanding payment on her late husband's credit. She hadn't been able to waste time thinking about the finer details of disappearing.

"Walking is excellent exercise," Dr. Mason said. "I highly recommend at least thirty minutes a day. More if you can manage. There's a lovely path following the Cowboy Creek."

"Mmm-hmm."

"I'll point you the way before you leave."

Anna wouldn't have much time for strolls through the countryside once she started work, and she'd get plenty of exercise going up and down the hotel stairs.

The doctor rattled off a series of questions that Anna dutifully answered. After jotting down a few notes, she checked the cut on Anna's arm, applied a salve and re-wrapped the wound. Then she plucked a second tin of salve from the counter at her elbow.

"Apply this morning and evening," the doctor said. "If there's any redness or swelling, contact me immediately."

"Thank you," Anna said. "Is there anything you can give me for the fatigue?"

"You're sure you're not expecting a child?"

"I'm certain." Anna blushed at the blunt question. "I had an examination in Philadelphia before I traveled to Cowboy Creek. Having children isn't possible."

She'd seen numerous doctors over the last year, and they'd all given her the same answer.

"Why?" Dr. Mason tilted her head.

"Why can't I have children? Well, um, I was married for two years. We didn't have any children. The doctors all had different diagnoses, but the conclusions were the same. My cycle has never been regular, and nothing I've tried has ever regulated the effect. I'm barren."

"That's flawed deductive reasoning. Many women with irregular cycles have been known to bear children." She patted her stomach. "I have a few more questions, if you don't mind."

"Go right ahead."

Dr. Mason asked several more personal questions, before inquiring whether or not Anna wanted children in the future.

Anna held up her hands. "There's really no need to speak of this anymore. I'm widowed now."

"My apologies, Mrs. Linford." Marlys penciled another note, a deep crease between her dark eyes, then stood. She mixed an herbal concoction from the glass jars lining her counter. "Add a teaspoon to your morning tea once a day. If you don't feel better in another week, come back for another examination. There are several things that might be causing your symptoms."

"What kind of things?"

"Any number of things. The body is attuned to mental stress as much as physical stress." Marlys turned to take down another apron from a peg on the back of the door. She held it out to Anna. "You'll want to wear this to protect your clothing while you tend to your seeds."

As Anna knotted the strings around her waist, Marlys produced a basket with a tight mesh lining stretched over the open bottom.

"It's used for panning gold, but I believe it will suit our purposes. Mr. Halloway thought it might be useful to sort your seed collection."

"How is Mr. Halloway?" Anna kept her gaze fixed on the mining pan. "No lingering effects from his injuries, I hope?"

"You may ask him yourself. His mother assured me on her morning walk that he'd visit before noon." Dr. Mason replaced the box of bandages in the cupboard. "Have you come to Cowboy Creek because of Mr. Halloway? He's an excellent prospect for a suitor. Nice home. Good health. Stable job."

"No! We're friends." Anabelle opened and closed her mouth. "Acquaintances really. He assisted during the robbery yesterday. We knew each other from Philadelphia. Not well! He was engaged to my sister. A long time ago. A long, long time ago."

Dr. Mason kept her expression carefully neutral.

"As you probably guessed, things didn't work out between them," Anna rushed ahead. "I haven't seen him in years."

She wasn't quite certain how to explain her current status in town.

"I didn't mean to pry," Dr. Mason apologized. "Sam, my husband, says I'm far too direct."

"That's all right, it's simply—"

The bell over the front door rang. A feminine voice sounded, and another woman entered the room. She was taller than the doctor with straight, gold hair that dusted her shoulders and cornflower blue eyes dominating her lovely features.

Marlys warmly greeted the new arrival. The two must know each other well. "Mrs. Gardner," the doctor said, leading the newcomer toward Anna, "I'd like you to meet Mrs. Anna Linford, Russ Halloway's friend."

"Acquaintance," Anna corrected. "I barely know Mr. Halloway."

"Call me Leah." The blond woman's smile was warm and friendly.

Dr. Mason reached for a ledger on the counter. "I don't have your mineral bath ready, Leah. I didn't expect to see you after such a late evening."

"I know I'm early, Marlys, but Evie went down for a nap, and Mrs. Ewing offered to sit with her. I couldn't pass up the opportunity. I checked on Mrs. Kluender. She's doing well, despite the difficult delivery. Thank you so much for helping. Without you, I fear we would have lost both her and the baby."

"I'll visit Mrs. Kluender during my afternoon calls. She owes you a debt of gratitude. If you hadn't correctly diagnosed her condition, we'd be having a very different conversation this morning. I've never seen a case as dire as hers before. If you'll excuse me for a moment, Mrs. Linford, Leah is here for a mineral bath. I won't be long if you want to get started on your seeds."

"Take your time," Anna called after the retreating doctor.

Leah flashed an amused grin. "Don't worry. She's always like that. Her brain works faster than her muscles. You and Russ must come to dinner. My husband, Daniel, and I always host the new brides. We're having Minnie and Millie next week. They are quite, um, joyful."

"Yes. One will start giggling and the next thing you know, they're both giggling."

"I noticed. Don't get me wrong, they seem like lovely girls." Mrs. Gardner's expression sobered. "Daniel mentioned you had quite an ordeal yesterday."

"He and Russ—er, Mr. Halloway—were quite brave. You must thank your husband for his assistance."

"You may thank himself yourself at dinner. I'll invite Russ, as well, since the two of you are already acquainted."

"Barely. I hardly know him."

Anna's heart sank. She couldn't stop fretting. What if Sam had read about her in the newspapers? Her husband's death had made the front page in Philadelphia. For all she knew, they were still running headlines there and elsewhere. She'd already involved Russ by traveling on Susannah's ticket. She didn't want her name linked to his any further. People turned their backs when their reputations were at risk, even by association.

If news that she'd been suspected of her husband's murder reached Cowboy Creek, she didn't want to put Russ in an awkward position. Until Edward's real murderer was discovered, she'd always be a suspect in the minds of the public. And no one wanted to associate with a potential murderess.

Leah doffed her hat and set the flowered brim on the counter. "It's nice to have someone familiar around when one is new to town."

"I appreciate the offer, but I can't possibly accept. The mayor has been very kind, but I fear I'm taking advantage of his hospitality. You must understand, I'm not one of the brides. I don't want people getting the wrong idea."

"Don't worry," Leah said. "No one takes advantage of Will Canfield. He's always been an advocate for the town." She lowered her voice. "Rumor has it that he's been grooming Russ to take over as the next mayor."

"Mayor?" Anna said faintly.

The past came rushing back, and she fought a tide of dread. Her late husband had been viciously ambitious. He'd run through her inheritance in a bid for city council, and the loss had infuriated him. Nothing made a man more dangerous than unchecked ambition.

"Rumors of my political career have been greatly exaggerated," a familiar voice spoke.

Neither of them had heard Russ's arrival. They both spun toward the sound of his voice.

Anna's lungs constricted, and she felt as though she couldn't breathe. Russ was the same man she'd seen last evening. He was still dashing and somewhat rakish with his bruised eye. Yet everything *had* changed. He wanted to be mayor. He wanted a job that thrust him into the fickle spotlight of the public.

She'd seen how politics worked in Philadelphia. If

people discovered her secret, they'd use it against him. The risk was far too great.

She had to escape Cowboy Creek as soon as possible or jeopardize the future of the one man who'd tried to help her.

The two women had spun toward Russ in startled surprise.

Leah recovered first. "Marlys will be right with you, Russ. She's preparing a treatment for me."

Leah offered a brief wave and a conspiratorial wink as she exited the room, and Russ rolled his eyes. He'd dropped some papers by her house that morning, and Leah had interrogated him about his encounter on the road. Apparently, Tomasina's tale of the outlaws had grown to epic proportions.

"Sorry about that." Russ cleared his throat. "Word of our previous acquaintance has spread. I'm afraid they've already started matchmaking. Logical, I suppose."

"I suppose." Anna glanced up from her collection of seeds. "Leah is the local midwife, I presume? She and Dr. Mason spoke of a difficult case last evening."

"Yes." Russ blew out a breath, grateful Anna had smoothed over the awkward moment. "I work for Leah's husband on occasion. He owns the stockyards in town. They have a baby girl named Evie. The way the two of them gaze at each other, Evie will soon have a sibling."

Leah and Daniel had known each other before the war and had rekindled their friendship when Leah arrived in Cowboy Creek as a prospective bride. Romance had soon followed, and the two of them obviously adored one another.

A becoming wash of color stained Anna's pale cheeks. "Leah appears very kind."

"She's blissfully happy in wedlock and wants everyone else to be the same."

"Hence the matchmaking. I can't say you didn't warn me."

An inspired thought struck him. "You know, there's a way we can solve this problem for the both of us. If everyone believes we're already courting, they'll leave us alone."

"No!" Anna appeared positively stricken by the suggestion. "We shouldn't lie to people."

Russ shrugged. "We can always drift apart later and say we didn't suit."

"I don't think that's a very good idea. We probably shouldn't even be seen speaking to one another. We've already been seen together at the hotel. If we start walking together in public too, we'll fuel more rumors."

"I retract the suggestion." He leaned one shoulder against the cupboard. He hadn't expected her to be quite so repulsed. "How are you feeling this morning?"

Probably she thought him a cad for even making the suggestion so soon after his engagement to Susannah. How did he explain to her that what he and Susannah had had was nothing more than an agreement? Neither of them was heartbroken over the matter.

"Dr. Mason says I'm as fit as a fiddle." Anna flourished the mining pan he'd purchased the previous evening. "I'm going to see if I can separate the seeds."

"Need some help?"

"I'm sure you have more important work to do." She tossed a furtive glance over one shoulder. "I don't want to keep you. Dr. Mason will be finished soon."

She'd probably grease the floor if she thought she could slide him out of the door any faster. Russ stood his ground. "I'm helping out an old friend. That's the truth, isn't it, Anna? Surely our past connection in Philadelphia counts for something."

"I don't want to impose on you."

Why was she so eager to be rid of him? He wasn't that bad of a fellow, was he? Perhaps he simply needed to show her that she could trust him. He hadn't parted from the Darby family under the best of circumstances. He didn't know what had been said after the business with Charlotte. Except there was no way of politely broaching the subject.

"I need to step away from my work for a while," he said. For once, the teetering stack of papers on his desk held no appeal. "My law clerk, Simon, has been requesting more responsibility." Russ slipped out of his jacket and rolled back his sleeves. "How can I help?"

Anna hesitated. "You can start by separating the bags that haven't been broken. I hope Marlys doesn't mind. This could get messy."

"Dr. Mason wouldn't have offered her workspace if she minded. I believe she's quite fascinated with herbal remedies. She'll be curious about your seed collection, I'm certain."

Anna shook a bucketful of dirt onto the table and sifted through the pieces with her index finger. "Good. The primula didn't spill. Those seeds are hardly more than dust."

"What's a primula?"

"It's a flower."

"I was never much for working outdoors," Russ said. "We had a kitchen garden growing up, like most families, and my mother kept a rosebush." A genial rush of memories flowed through him. "She had a cut-glass vase that she kept on the mantel, and she always had a rose on display. I don't believe she's grown roses since we left Missouri."

"There are several varieties that thrive in this climate. I saw some outside of that palatial house on the way over. She could ask the owners for a cutting."

"Did that palatial house have columns out front?" Russ asked.

"Yes. That's the place."

"The mayor used to live there."

"Gracious." Anna brushed her hands against the front of her apron. "Mayor Canfield lived in that monstrosity?"

"Not for very long."

"No doubt. That house looks brand new. I can't imagine having that sort of wealth. How large is his new house?"

"Nothing so grand. He's wealthy, to be sure. He married last year, and his priorities have changed. You'll meet his wife, Tomasina, at a dinner soon, I'm sure. Be prepared. She's a unique character. Came into town on a cattle drive and stole Will's heart."

"A cattle drive?" With the back of her hand, Anna absently brushed the hair from her forehead. "I can't imagine the mayor falling for a drover. I pictured him with one of those society ladies who always decorates her hat with too many feathers and pronounces the word schedule as shed-u-al."

"Tomasina is the exact opposite of a society lady." Russ chuckled. "Trust me, they adore each other. Will originally built the house in the hopes of making Cowboy Creek the county seat, but now he's set his sights on Washington. He's campaigning for the Senate, and if he wins, he and Tomasina will be spending much of the year out of state. They've built a smaller house in town. He sold the original house to Daniel Gardner, Leah's husband, who in turn donated it to Cowboy Creek for a library. The town is planning a fund-raiser to make the necessary renovations and purchase books."

Anna held a seed to the light. "I'll assist in the fund-raising long as they add a few books about gardening." With exacting precision, she separated two seeds that appeared remarkably similar.

"How can you tell them apart?" Russ tilted his head and looked closer. "They look exactly the same to me."

"Years of practice." She shook a dusting of soil through the mining pan. "Once you know what to look for, telling them apart isn't that difficult."

Russ considered the array of different varieties. "Do you collect all seeds or just flower seeds?"

"Vegetables and flowers. I've been developing a drought-resistant strain of pumpkin."

"Why pumpkin?"

"Because I enjoy pumpkin pie."

Russ threw back his head and laughed. "I thought you were going to say something extremely perplexing and scientific. I much prefer a culinary response." He leaned back and studied her. "So, you enjoy pumpkin pie and chocolate cake."

She laughed, and he caught a hint of the girl he'd known before.

"That was a delicious cake," she said. "You should have tried a bite."

"You have a sweet tooth."

"It's a terrible weakness. Much as I enjoy vegetables, I've never had an overwhelming craving for cucumbers."

"Nothing wrong with an indulgence," he said. "I wonder what dessert Miss Frazier is concocting today."

"After sampling her chocolate cake with cherries, I'm willing to try anything she makes. I'll have to be careful around here. With all those delicious desserts available, I'll be looking like Old Jack Sprat's wife before long."

"You have nothing to worry about."

Anna pressed a hand against her stomach with a humorless laugh. "That's what the outlaw said. 'The men of Cowboy Creek—'" she added a twang to her accent "'—must be really desperate to send for a skinny gal like you.'"

"He never." A fist tightened around Russ's heart. "You're beautiful, Anna. Don't let anyone tell you different." The outlaws were dead, yet his anger at the men simmered.

"I've heard far worse," Anna said.

"When?"

"Never mind." She shrugged. "I just mean that people are cruel."

The world abounded with malice, yet Anna seemed merely resigned to the slur. There hadn't even been a flicker of anger in her countenance. The reaction struck him as odd.

"Here." Anna plucked an oblong seed from the dirt on the table and held it to the light. "See if you can find any more like this. They should be easy to spot. They're the largest."

The subject hardly seemed to faze her, and he accepted the change of topic. "What do you plan on doing with all these seeds?"

"I'll grow them. Save them. See if I can cross-pollinate some of the species. Eventually, of course. I don't have a place for a garden now."

"You must have had an enormous garden in Philadelphia."

"Our townhouse didn't have much of a yard, but I made use of every inch." A melancholy shadow drifted over her eyes. "There were even vines growing up the side of the house. After two years, I saw progress. I miss that garden terribly."

"I didn't mean to bring up a sad memory." He was forever reminding her of her recent loss. What was wrong with him?

"That's why these seeds are so important, I guess. I can create a new garden."

"I don't have anything in my yard but a tree my mother insisted I plant for shade." Perhaps he could persuade her to fill out the space. That might cheer her up and take her mind off being a recent widow. "I would appreciate your advice on any new additions."

"What kind of tree did your mother plant?"

He shrugged. "A redbud, I think."

"That's an excellent tree for the area, but you should add something larger. For shade. Perhaps a poplar. They're a fast-growing tree."

He gestured over her collection. "You don't happen to have a poplar seed in the bunch, do you?"

"No, I'm afraid I don't." The smile returned to her expressive face. "But perhaps we can discover a seedling along the banks of Cowboy Creek. I saw a few that first day, when…when…"

"When you were recovering from your ordeal with

the outlaws," he interjected with as much finesse as he could muster.

For a man who made his living with straight speaking, he certainly didn't excel at small talk. He struggled to find topics to discuss as they worked on the seeds for the next fifteen minutes. Though many of the seeds were remarkably similar, the more they worked, the easier the sorting task became. Anna's earlier words proved correct; there were subtle variances that separated the batches.

When he triumphantly discerned the difference between a zinnia and a black-eyed Susan, Anna's warm praise felt like a rare prize.

He labeled her late husband a blessed man to have no doubt received those kind words and smiles. As much as Russ wanted to know about him and their marriage, he kept his questions unasked. He already knew she didn't speak much of him. She must miss her husband a great deal, and wanted to keep his memory protected.

Her concern was more than understandable. Russ didn't want to replace the man's memory in any way. He only wanted to be a friend to Anna as she settled into her new life. She'd apparently suffered a financial devastation, and he wanted her to know she could count on him. Yet a polite way to put her at ease without further embarrassing both of them eluded him.

Marlys hustled into the room, inquiring about their progress before barreling down on Russ. "Let me look at that head," she ordered.

Arguing was pointless. He'd been in town long enough to realize that once the doctor was set on a path, she rarely diverted.

Anna caught his gaze with a triumphant gleam in her

emerald eyes, and he conceded the fight. He'd promised her he'd sit for an examination, and it was time to pay up.

"I'm fine." He crash-landed onto a chair. Agreeing didn't mean he had to be happy about the unnecessary attention. "It doesn't even hurt anymore."

"No headaches?"

"Yesterday," he grudgingly admitted. There was no lying to Dr. Mason. "Not much today."

"A blow to the head is often deceptive in its gravity. Be careful of reinjury for the next few weeks. Your body is healing, and another blow to the head will compound the initial damage."

"Don't worry," Russ said. "I don't plan on encountering outlaws in the area."

Anna glanced up, her expression stricken, and regret dropped like a rock in his stomach. Her guilt over the encounter obviously lingered, despite his directions to the contrary. Why was it that where Anna was concerned, he always managed to say the wrong thing?

Dr. Mason kept up her examination. "Why wasn't one of Sheriff Getman's deputies patrolling the road? He has a duty to protect the traffic between here and Morgan's Creek."

"The mayor was none too pleased. He'll set the sheriff straight."

"If anyone can, it's Will Canfield." Dr. Mason gently inspected his eye, and Russ winced. "This should have been stitched yesterday. It's too late now. The healing has already begun. You're going to have a scar."

"I have it on account that scars are quite rakish these days."

He winked at Anna, and she glanced away, but not

before he caught a hint of a smile. She was starting to soften toward him.

Marlys tsked. "You're worse than my husband. Why don't men ever take their injuries seriously?"

"Speaking of your husband, how is the newspaper business these days?" Russ asked. "I wanted to speak with him about some advertising. The *Webster County Daily News* is flourishing. I've gotten business from as far as Wichita from my last advertisement. And I noticed Sam added a column about local crime."

"The newspaper is thriving," Dr. Mason said. "Especially the new column, Boom Town Bulletin. This week alone a toy train has gone missing from the mercantile, and the cook at The Lariat claims a whole side of bacon was stolen off his counter."

"A real crime spree."

"It gets worse." Dr. Mason lowered her voice to a dramatic hush. "Deborah placed a pie on the windowsill to cool, and when she came back an hour later, the pie was gone."

"Now that's serious," Russ declared with mock sincerity. "I'm willing to overlook a toy and some pork, but Miss Frazier's baking is another story. What's Sheriff Getman doing now that the town is overrun with thieves? Perhaps we should call in the Marshals?"

Dr. Mason snorted. "The sheriff won't do anything. He doesn't think there's a problem. Which appears to be his natural state. I have a prime view of the sheriff's office from my front window. He was snoozing in his chair on the porch outside his office when he was alerted to the outlaws yesterday. After spending a minimum amount of time at the scene of the incident, he returned home and took the rest of the afternoon off to recuperate. Can you imagine? One shoot-out and he needs a vacation."

"It was morning when the outlaws struck," Anna said gently. "I don't suppose there's usually much crime that early."

"You're probably right," Marlys conceded the point. "But he's got other problems, as well. As much as I'd like to scoff at the petty crimes, someone stole two cords of wood right out of our shed, easy as you please. They might be small things, but if the sheriff doesn't take care of the minor indiscretions, folks are going to think they can get away with more, and then we'll have a real problem." She dabbed a salve onto his head. "The sheriff managed to rouse himself for dinner at Aunt Mae's, the boardinghouse where the prospective brides usually stay. He can always be relied upon for dinner. And he manages to rouse himself after a bride train. Perhaps he'll be more focused if he finds a wife."

"Millie and Minnie are both good candidates," Russ said. "No one deserves one of the cousins more than Sheriff Getman."

Dr. Mason grew stern. "Russ, be kind."

"I am being kind. His house would always be filled with laughter."

"Sometimes people giggle when they're nervous," Marlys said. "Leah mentioned the two cousins were rather jocular."

"That's an understatement," Russ murmured beneath his breath. "Have you met them?"

"Mrs. Linford is the only person I've met from the bride train," Marlys replied.

"As I said before, I'm not a bride," came Anna's startled reply.

"Merely a turn of phrase."

"I mean, I traveled on the bride train, sort of. Most of the way. I only borrowed the ticket."

Russ jerked his thumb over his shoulder in the general direction of Eden Street. "She's not staying at the boardinghouse. Cowboy Creek is a fresh start for Mrs. Linford."

"I prefer my solitude." Anna touched her pale cheek. "I mean, I'm not looking to get married. I can't imagine I'll attract much notice."

She had no sense of her appeal. There was a delicate, subtle beauty to her features and a natural elegance in her figure. She was intelligent and kind. There was a sorrow about her that incited a primal need within him to safeguard her from further harm. She may not want his protection, but that didn't stop him from caring.

"You might be surprised by the attention, but the rest of us won't be." Marlys glanced between them with a knowing smile. "Don't worry, Mrs. Linford. The excitement should wear off soon."

"Call me Anna."

"Then you must call me Marlys. Do you have any chamomile seeds? The Shawnee medicine man assured me that a mixture of lavender and chamomile oils is a soothing balm for skin burns. I'd like to experiment with the mixture."

"I have some," Anna eagerly replied. "You'd be doing me a tremendous favor if you grew the plants. I've never stored those seeds beyond a year, and I don't know if they'll be viable next summer."

"You're welcome to grow anything you like alongside my own herb garden." A rare passion exuded from Marlys. "The Shawnee have introduced me to several plants that have previously gone unnoticed to Western medicine."

Russ grinned at the pair. Though his contact with her was rare, Russ had come to realize that Marlys was brisk and efficient until her curiosity was piqued, and then she came alive. Anna was obviously the same. The sorrow disappeared from her eyes when she spoke of her gardening.

Anna sparkled with enthusiasm. "Do you think the medicine man would speak with me? I'm curious to learn about indigenous plants in the area."

"I can introduce you. Mind you, I can't make any guarantees. The local tribes don't have much reason to trust us."

"I'd appreciate anything you can do to help."

"The medicine man is called Touches the Clouds. He's due to visit this week. I never know when. He doesn't keep track of days."

"Did you hear that?" Anna rested her hand on Russ's shoulder. "This is marvelous." She flashed a radiant smile, and his breath caught.

Marlys tapped her chin. "I almost forgot. Touches the Clouds mentioned something last week that disturbed me. Someone has been speaking with the local tribes about selling their land."

Russ leaned in. The Shawnee were often considered vulnerable targets. The United States government didn't consider the protection of the Native American population a high priority.

"I thought the government owned their land," Anna said. "Don't they live on a reservation?"

"Not this group. There are Eastern Shawnee in the area who were allowed to purchase their land. Although the parcels are managed independently, the entire tribe must agree to any sale of a property." The doctor pursed her lips. "According to Touches the Clouds, someone attempted to convince the tribe their land was worthless. Foolish man. The tribal elders were able to intervene."

Unease skittered down Russ's spine. "When did this occur?"

"A few weeks ago."

Russ mentally ticked off the days. "That's about the time someone started purchasing land from the settlers on the outskirts of town."

"Are you speaking of Mr. Mitchell?" Marlys titled her head. "The gentleman with the coal mining company? I heard he was giving top dollar for the land. Then again, perhaps he thought the Shawnee were gullible. He wouldn't be the first to underestimate the Native Americans."

"Not Jason Mitchell," Russ said. "A woman filed the deeds."

"The Shawnee didn't mention a woman when they spoke to me."

"Perhaps she's working with someone. I haven't tracked down the name yet. I've only heard rumors."

"Speaking of rumors." Marlys opened a cupboard and considered the contents. "I heard Dora Edison is back in town."

Anna glanced between the two of them. "I haven't met Dora yet. She's local?"

Russ threaded his hands behind his head "Dora, shall we say, has an opportunistic streak."

"She prefers rich and powerful men," Marlys added with a flick of her eyelashes. "She's a fortune hunter. There's no tiptoeing around the truth. Before I came to Cowboy Creek, I hear she had her eye on Will Canfield, but he wised up before she could get him to the altar. She never made any secret that she wanted him for his money. I'm being candid for your sake, Mr. Halloway. As the next mayor, she's bound to set her sights on you soon."

Russ shook his head. "I doubt she'd settle for me after Will's wealth."

"Consider yourself fortunate." Marlys toyed with a length of the bandage. "In any case, she's been bragging to anyone who will listen that her latest beau has more money than Vanderbilt. I never trust people who have to brag about their wealth. Sounds like a snake oil salesman if you ask me."

"I'll ask the clerk at the land registry if he knows of any suspicious activity," Russ said. "I don't like the idea of someone taking advantage of the locals in the area."

Leah returned at that moment, her cheeks flushed from whatever treatment Dr. Mason had prescribed.

She stifled a yawn behind one hand. "My apologies. It was a rather late night." She looked from Russ to Anna. "I was hoping you two could come by for dinner next Friday."

"Your officer is generous," Anna said. "But as I said before, you don't have to put yourself out for me."

"Don't be silly. I recall quite clearly when I first came to town from back east. It's overwhelming. We ladies have to stick together, especially in a town like Cowboy Creek."

Anna tugged her lower lip between her teeth. "I don't know…"

"We'd like that," Russ interrupted. "What time?"

They could stand here arguing politely with one another, or he could agree and save them all some time. He chose the latter.

"Seven. And just bring yourselves. I have it on good account that Will is going to ask you to dinner tomorrow evening." Leah sucked in a dramatic breath and splayed her hands. "Be warned, Tomasina is cooking. You might want to have a snack beforehand."

Russ chuckled. "Duly noted."

Marlys walked Leah to the door, and Anna bent her head close. "I don't think we should be seen together. I thought we agreed. People will get the wrong impression."

"She's only trying to help you get settled in a new town. There's no harm in that."

"But we're already having dinner with the mayor."

"I'm not that noteworthy, Anna. Being seen with me twice is hardly likely to make the papers."

She eyed him as though she didn't believe his words. "Someone is bound to notice."

"You're far more likely to attract attention than I am."

"Me?" She backed away, bumping into the table and toppling a bag of seeds to the floor. "No one knows me here."

"Yet." He knelt and reached for the bag. "There's still time to become notorious."

With trembling fingers, she swept up the seeds. "I just want a little peace and quiet."

He pressed his hand over her chilled fingers. "I was only trying to lighten the mood. Neither of us is likely to incite comment."

"If you say so."

Russ resumed sifting seeds, his thoughts troubled.

He certainly didn't expect everyone he met to take an instant liking to him, but he'd thought he and Anna shared a certain comradery given their history.

Since her arrival in Cowboy Creek, she insisted on treating him as though his every deed was suspect. He didn't know what to make of her behavior. Should he cancel the dinners and simply let her be? Yet canceling was liable to provoke more curiosity, and as far as he could discern, Anna loathed attention of any kind.

The memory of the carefree girl she'd been all those years ago lingered. Surely there was something he could do to bring back that mischievous twinkle in her eyes once more? She needed a few new friends, and Tomasina and Leah were ideal candidates. They were both well-respected and well-connected in town.

He was doing the right thing. He simply had to convince Anna that his intentions were honorable.

Perhaps if he knew more about her life, more about her time in Philadelphia, he'd have a better chance at avoiding potential hazards in their friendship. Five years was a long time, and a lot had obviously changed for Anna.

Not all of it for the better.

Chapter Seven

After hearing extravagant tales of Tomasina, Anna wasn't certain what to expect from the evening. She checked her reflection in the mirror hanging in her suite and turned to the side. Her trunk had yet to be delivered. There'd been a mistake at the depot, and the luggage hadn't been unloaded. The porter had wired ahead along the route, and he'd assured her they'd locate her missing trunk soon.

Until then, she was forced to wear either her traveling suit or the second dress she'd stowed in her carpetbag for emergencies. Neither of which was suitable for a more formal engagement.

Everyone kept assuring her that folks didn't stand on ceremony in town. Adjusting her collar once more, she gave a silent prayer their words were true.

She pinned her hat in place and plucked her reticule from the side table. A knock sounded, and she sensed Russ had arrived a few minutes early. He didn't have the hesitant scratch of a porter.

"Mr. Halloway," she greeted him as she opened the door.

He tipped his hat. "Mrs. Linford."

Despite her best intentions, her heart gave an unwelcome jerk. She'd thought all the pesky feelings of love and affection had shriveled inside her, wilted from lack of attention. Russ was like the sun, his smile filled with kindness and warmth, inspiring an unwelcome stirring of attraction.

His suit was an expensive cut of superfine wool, and a gleaming watch chain stretched across his flat stomach. The swelling around his eye had lessened, and the edges of the purple bruise had faded, though he'd kept the bandage Marlys had placed over the wound earlier.

Catching her interest, he touched the spot. "I didn't want to ruin anyone's appetite."

"Never," she said, her voice barely more than a whisper.

Impressions of him warred in her mind. She'd wrapped him in a villain's cloak after he'd broken his engagement with Charlotte, and the costume didn't fit. He was the same man she recalled as a young girl—handsome and charming with a ready smile and a razor-sharp humor.

Why must the heart be such a fickle and untrustworthy thing? Susannah had forsaken the chance of this man's love for a doughy banker with loose jowls who'd treated her poorly in the past. Susannah would rather settle down with a man who'd already disappointed her than risk a future and the chance at real love.

Susannah was a fool.

Russ brushed his hair over the bandage. "I thought about borrowing an eye patch from the opera house costume collection."

"I'm sure you would have worn it well."

Susannah didn't even realize what a poor choice

she'd made. Russ Halloway was everything one expected of a suitor.

More and more Anna realized that what happened all those years ago wasn't completely one-sided.

With the filter of youth dissipated, Anna considered her sister's husband, the man she'd eloped with, in a new light. Her brother-in-law worked for a publisher and took simpering pride in his appearance. Though not more than twenty when they eloped, he'd carried a silver-topped cane. His collars had been painfully starched, and the precise way he took his seat had been designed to inflict the fewest creases in his trousers.

Charlotte had found him dashing. Anna had thought him dandified and vain. Then again, Charlotte had been obsessive about looks. And money. The two suited each other. No doubt their walls were papered with looking glasses.

"You're smiling," Russ said, startling her from her thoughts.

"You act surprised."

"You've had little enough to smile about since your arrival."

She swallowed around the lump in her throat. "No."

Turning Charlotte into the villain didn't make Anna the heroine of the piece. Even if she'd been a few years older when Russ had lived in Philadelphia, Anna paled in comparison to Charlotte. Her hair was not as blond and her eyes were a weak shade of green. She didn't have Charlotte's soft voice or retiring manner. She wasn't the sort of girl who provoked passionate, romantic interest.

Even if her past wasn't tainted, she didn't stand a chance with someone like Russ. He was being kind to her because of their past connection. Once a prettier, more accomplished woman caught his eye, he'd forget all about her. She wouldn't have to worry about people associating them together.

As much as she told herself that would be for the best, the thought didn't settle well.

He doffed his hat and brushed his fingers through his thick, dark hair. "I hope you don't mind, I'm a little early. I wanted to ensure you were feeling well enough for dinner."

"I'm fine." She touched his sleeve, marveling at the play of muscles beneath her fingertips. "You mustn't worry about me. I'm fit as a fiddle and ready to start working."

She desperately needed a job, and she couldn't be seen as sickly in the eyes of a man who could secure her a position.

Appearing sheepish, he said, "You can't blame me entirely. Our first encounter was rather dramatic."

"I appreciate your concern," she said. "But there's no need to treat me with kid gloves. I'm ready to find work and move out of this suite." She flourished her arm. "I was hoping to speak with Mr. Canfield tonight about working at his hotel, if you don't mind."

"Why should I mind? I'll put in a good word for you, as well."

"Thank you." The tension eased from her shoulders. "You have no idea how much your assistance means to me." He stuck out his elbow, and she looped her arm through his. "I didn't mean to be cross."

"Were you being cross?" His mouth quirked in an endearing grin. "I didn't notice. How are you enjoying Cowboy Creek otherwise?"

A sense of hope filled her spirit. "Wonderfully alive and free. After my father died, I lived with my aunt for a few months and married shortly after. This is the first time I've ever been completely independent. It's frightening, but it's exhilarating, as well."

There was always a sense that she was living on borrowed time, and her good fortune was bound to end. Even with the threat of storms on the horizon, she was determined to store what bit of sun currently shone through the clouds. She had today. She had this moment. There was no one to berate her, and no one in town who knew her secret shame. She could live, just for the moment, like anyone else.

She'd been at the mercy of the men in her life for as long as she could remember, and she was determined to savor this glimpse of freedom.

"I remember that feeling," Russ said. "I was all of seventeen when I boarded a train alone for the first time. I was terrified and euphoric in the same moment. At the first stop, I bought an entire bag of licorice and ate every piece. Made me sick, but it was totally worth the suffering."

"That's exactly how I feel. Childishly jubilant. There's no one to scold my faults. All of my choices, even the poor ones, are my own."

"I'm glad to hear you're happy." His gaze deepened, and beyond the small smile, she thought she saw questions in his eyes.

She ducked her head. "We should go. I don't want to be late."

He led her down the three flights of hotel stairs, and they crossed the ornate lobby. A porter in a smart green uniform with a matching cap tugged on his forelock in greeting.

Russ held the door, and they stepped into the cool evening air.

Anna inhaled the spring breeze, letting her lungs expand until the feeling was almost painful. "It's beautiful here. The sky is endless. Sometimes it's almost frightening."

She was normally afraid of looking to the future, afraid of feeling optimism. But tonight, for a brief, beautiful time, she was filled with hope. Surely if God had created a sky this ferociously blue, anything was possible? As one of God's creatures, even she was afforded a modicum of happiness.

Russ followed her gaze. "It's overwhelming, sometimes. I recall the first time I watched a storm approaching over the horizon. The clouds were astonishing. Beautiful and incredibly humbling. Back home in Missouri, I'd never seen a storm with that sort of power."

"I felt that way when I stepped off the train. The colors were too bold and the scenery too overpowering."

"After Philadelphia, everything is brighter. Do you miss home?"

"No," she said, emotion clogging her throat. The conviction of her words set her firmly on the path to freedom. "I'll never go back."

"Never is a long time."

Never wasn't nearly long enough. There was nothing in Philadelphia but melancholy reminders of the past. "What about you? Is Cowboy Creek where you'll settle permanently? Or are you like the mayor? Do you have your sights set on Washington?"

"I like it here. I have family here. I'm content to stay."

His words didn't entirely answer her question. What was Cowboy Creek when compared to the glamour and power of Washington, D.C.? Even considering a run for mayor marked him as ambitious, and she'd had her fill of ambitious, scheming men.

She set her chin and lifted her head. His future was none of her concern. In all likelihood, neither of them would stay in Cowboy Creek long. Which was probably for the best. No one could capitalize on their slight connection for political exploit.

Instead of worrying about the future, she told herself to enjoy the evening. "I have to admit, I wasn't expecting such a fine town."

"You were expecting gunfights and loose cattle wandering the streets?"

"Something like that."

"We've had our fair share of excitement, that's for certain. Not to mention the occasional cattle drive down Eden Street. But we also have a lot of amenities. Two beautiful hotels, several excellent restaurants, stockyards and lumberyards, even an opera house. Soon we'll have a library."

"You don't have to sell the town to me. I'm quite fond of Cowboy Creek already."

Though not as crowded as the previous day, the boardwalk teemed with activity. She recognized two elderly men sitting outside the mercantile. She'd seen them sitting in the exact same spot the previous day.

She gestured discreetly. "Do they ever move?"

Russ threw back his head and laughed. "It's time I introduced you to Gus and Old Horace. The town wouldn't be the same without those two."

With an outstretched arm, Russ held back the passing

wagons as they crossed the road. "Horace and Gus, I'd like you to meet the newest resident of Cowboy Creek. Mrs. Anna Linford."

"Pleasure to meet you, ma'am," Horace declared, a slight twang in his booming voice.

Horace wore his long gray hair pulled back with a leather strap from a weathered face dominated by rheumy eyes. Though he sat slightly hunched, she guessed from his frame that he would stand tall and lean. The nub of a cheroot hung from the side of his mouth, and the odor made her stomach rebel.

"That name sounds familiar," he said. "Are you staying at the boardinghouse?"

"No." She tamped down a twinge of guilt. There was no reason he might have heard of her. "I'm staying at The Cattleman."

"That's a nice hotel. Will Canfield even put carpet on the stairs. Have you ever seen such decadence?" Horace asked. "I heard The Lariat is even nicer. What could be nicer than carpeted stairs?"

"She came with ol' Ward," said the second man, Gus. "You remember. He was telling us all about how he stopped those outlaws with nothing but his bare hands and his wits."

Gus appeared shorter than Horace, with dark eyes, a shocking tuft of snow-white hair and a matching beard.

"He didn't do nothing but get hisself tied up and thrown in the ditch," Horace argued. "That's what I heard."

"And I suppose you'd have done something different?"

"I coulda' taken 'em out blindfolded with one hand behind my back. These young fellers don't know the first thing about being a true outlaw." Horace cocked his thumbs and extended his index fingers as though brandishing a pair of six-shooters. "You gotta show 'em you're crazy."

Gus snorted. "You got that part down. We all think you're crazy."

"Mr. Ward acted quite bravely." Anna pressed two fingertips against her mouth, stifling a laugh. "As did Mr. Halloway. Although I'm certain he could have used your assistance."

Russ squeezed her arm. "It's true. They knocked me out cold. A couple of tough soldiers like you two would have saved me a headache."

"He's right, you know." Horace elbowed Gus. "I don't know what this town would do without the two of us."

"Me, either," Russ said.

"Oh go on, you old fool." Gus chortled at Horace. "At the end of the day, you can't hardly lift your backside from the grooves you've made in that chair, let alone take on a couple of armed outlaws."

"You're getting too old, Gus. Don't you remember the old days?"

"'Course I remember the old days. Cuz that's all you ever talk about. It's like your life ended forty years ago after the Battle of San Jacinto with old Sam Houston."

Horace nodded. "Now there was a man. Old Sam Houston never cracked. Not even when they drove him out of office. He didn't live to see the end of the war. They don't make men like that anymore."

Russ cleared his throat. "We'd best be going. Dinner at the Canfields'."

"Word around town is that Tomasina is cooking." Gus rubbed his stomach. "You'd best eat something

"4 for 4" MINI-SURVEY

We are prepared to **REWARD** you with 2 FREE books and 2 FREE gifts for completing our MINI SURVEY!

FREE
Value Over
$20!

You'll get...

TWO FREE BOOKS &
TWO FREE GIFTS

just for participating in our Mini Survey!

Dear Reader,

IT'S A FACT: if you answer 4 quick questions, we'll send you **4 FREE REWARDS!**

I'm not kidding you. As a leading publisher of women's fiction, we value your opinions… and your time. That's why we are prepared to **reward** you handsomely for completing our mini-survey. In fact, we have 4 Free Rewards for you, including 2 free books and 2 free gifts.

As you may have guessed, that's why our mini-survey is called **"4 for 4".** Answer 4 questions and get 4 Free Rewards. It's that simple!

Thank you for participating in our survey,

Pam Powers

To get your 4 FREE REWARDS:
Complete the survey below and return the insert today to receive 2 FREE BOOKS and 2 FREE GIFTS guaranteed!

"4 for 4" MINI-SURVEY

1 Is reading one of your favorite hobbies?
☐ YES ☐ NO

2 Do you prefer to read instead of watch TV?
☐ YES ☐ NO

3 Do you read newspapers and magazines?
☐ YES ☐ NO

4 Do you enjoy trying new book series with FREE BOOKS?
☐ YES ☐ NO

YES! I have completed the above Mini-Survey. Please send me my 4 FREE REWARDS (worth over $20 retail). I understand that I am under no obligation to buy anything, as explained on the back of this card.

❏ I prefer the regular-print edition
105/305 IDL GMYL

❏ I prefer the larger-print edition
122/322 IDL GMYL

FIRST NAME	LAST NAME

ADDRESS

APT.#	CITY

STATE/PROV.   ZIP/POSTAL CODE

ahead of time. That gal knows everything there is to know about cattle 'ceptin' for how to cook them."

Anna's stomach lurched, and her smile became strained. She generally had a strong constitution, but lately everything sent her stomach churning. Right now, she didn't want to consider the origins of her next meal.

Horace jabbed his friend and pointed. "Now look what ya done. You've gone and turned the lady green with sick. Don't you know any better than to talk about where your food comes from afore you eat it? Not everyone has an iron stomach like you, you old goat."

"I'm right sorry, ma'am," Gus mumbled an abashed apology. "I didn't mean to discuss butchering around a lady."

"It's been entertaining as always." Russ pressed a firm hand into the small of her back. "We'd best be going. Don't want to be late."

"Nice meeting you, Mrs. Linford," Horace called. "Tell Mayor Canfield I saw them two urchins again. I reported them to Sheriff Getman, but that old fool says I saw your brother's youngins. I told 'im I ain't blind, I know the difference between folks. I know they wasn't the Halloway boys."

Gus crossed his arms over his chest. "You couldn't see a bear if it was tapping you on the shoulder. You got the eyesight of a mole."

"I see just fine, and I'm telling you, I saw two boys that ain't the Halloways lurking around the back of the mercantile."

"Lurking, were they?" Gus shook his head, flapping his jowls. "Well, ain't you something, using them big fancy words."

Horace crossed his arms and leaned toward his

friend. "If you ever quit your yapping long enough to do a little reading, maybe you'd know some big fancy words, too."

"Don't you get sassy with me." Gus brandished an index finger in rebuke. "I'll tell them about the time you set out to rope a steer and wound up roping yourself."

"Did not."

"Did, too. You trussed yourself up like a Christmas goose."

Russ urged Anna toward the street. "I'll tell the mayor about the boys you saw." He tugged her along. "Nice seeing you fellows."

"Nice meeting you," Anna called over her shoulder.

Russ picked up his pace. "I should have warned you. Those two can talk your ear off."

"I liked them." She sent another wave at the two elderly men. "They're very funny."

"The town wouldn't be the same without them, that's for sure. They know just about everything about everyone around here. No one has secrets around those two."

"Really?" Anna shivered. "I don't have to worry then."

Much. As long as the two older men rarely strayed from their vigil outside the mercantile, there was little chance they knew anything about gossip from Philadelphia. Then again, Horace obviously liked to read. Or was it Gus? She couldn't tell them apart. Either way, she'd make a point to avoid those two. If one of them had read something in the papers, she didn't want them linking her name.

Distracted by the encounter, she passed the rest of the journey in silence, letting Russ carry the conversation.

He pointed out the local sights, including Daniel and

Leah's house, then indicated a two-story home painted a light shade of slate with a wraparound porch and turreted corner. "I moved here a few months ago."

Anna did a double take, and her footsteps slowed. The yard was enormous with a large patch of land on the south-facing side. True to his word, there was a single redbud tree standing like a lonely sentry in the side yard.

Her mind immediately went to work on the best place to plant a garden. With all the sunlight on the south side, she could sow nearly a quarter acre of herbs in the unused space. A well pump visible on the far side of the house was the perfect source for water.

"That's why I left it that way," Russ said, his voice seeping into her plans.

"Left what that way?" she quizzed.

"The yard. I bought both the lots when I built the house. The Fletchers lived on the other side at the time, and Dr. Fletcher had a voice like a foghorn. His whisper sent cattle stampeding. I figured it was best if we put some space between us."

He gently tugged her along, and she gave a last look over her shoulder. "Sounds prudent. A budding opera singer once lived next door to us in Philadelphia. She had a voice like a drowning pelican."

"God loves those who dream."

"It was a nightmare for the rest of us."

Russ grinned. "Then you understand. Dr. Fletcher and his wife moved, though. They retired to a warmer climate. Good thing I didn't sell the extra land yet. They may be moving back soon. There's coal in the area, and some of the ranchers are selling for quick profit."

"You don't sound pleased."

"There's no such thing as easy money. Sooner or later, someone has to pay."

Anna sniffed the air. "Do you smell that? I think something is burning."

"I'm guessing that's dinner. We're here."

Russ led her up the wide porch stairs and knocked on the door. Will and Tomasina's house sat near the edge of town, and the prairie stretched into the distance. The house was larger than Russ's and elegant, though not nearly as ostentatious as the Canfields' former home. The sprawling two-story home, along with the barn and side yard, took up nearly an entire town block. Leaded glass windows decorated the turreted window, and a pair of chaps flung over the porch railing added a touch of the commonplace.

A redhead with a mass of wild curls piled atop her head swung open the door. An acid-green dress perfectly fitted her frame, and her cheeks were flushed with hectic color.

She thrust a bundle into Anna's arms. "Can you hold Andrew for a moment? We've got a bit of a fire in the kitchen, and Will has his hands full right now."

Chapter Eight

Anna accepted the tiny bundle with a startled gasp. "I'd be delighted."

Tomasina grasped a towel she'd draped over her shoulder and extended her hand. "You'll need this if you ever want to wear that dress again. He's got the stomach of a seasick sailor."

Anna adjusted the tiny bundle before she accepted the cloth. "Thank you."

"Thank *you*. He's normally quite content. I don't expect you'll have a problem. Call if you need anything." The redhead pivoted on her heel and followed the cloud of acrid smoke drifting from the rear of the house.

Russ waved his hand before his face and turned toward Anna. "I'd best see if they need any help. Will you be all right for a few minutes?"

Staring down at the bundle in her arms, Anna wasn't too sure. But she looked up and nodded. "I'll be fine for a few minutes."

"Right then. I'll see if we need to ring for the fire brigade."

Following his hasty retreat, Anna hovered uncertainly

in the vestibule. With her index finger, she gently tugged the blanket free of the infant's face. Blurry, blue-black eyes stared back at her. The bundle was light, lighter even than a sack of flour, and smaller, too. Warmth radiated from the tiny mound of blankets, and the child's mouth worked, his tiny eyes blinking in drowsy curiosity.

"Hello, Andrew," she said. "It's a pleasure to meet you. I hope you don't mind, but your parents are a little preoccupied right now."

Andrew opened his mouth in a gummy yawn and smacked his lips.

"I think we're going to get along just fine."

She peered into the rooms flanking the vestibule and discovered a well-appointed parlor wallpapered in dancing blue peacocks. She perched on a tufted velvet chair and surveyed her surroundings. Much like the outside of the house, the room had touches of elegance alongside a bit of chaos. The patterned wallpaper lent an air of colorful cheer, at odds with an enormous painting of a grim-faced drover that hung above the mahogany fireplace mantel.

The infant stirred, and Anna focused her attention on her precious duty. Swathed in a pale blue dressing gown, a miniature pair of feet encased in crocheted booties kicked free from the enfolding blankets. The child remained blissfully unperturbed by the voices raised in panic echoing from the kitchen. A pot clattered, and Anna winced. Andrew barely blinked when the back door slammed. She peered around the corner and sat back again. She was only a few steps from the front door if the situation worsened.

Judging by the resigned expression on Tomasina's face earlier, this wasn't her first kitchen fire. "I'm assuming you're accustomed to a bit of ruckus around the house," she told the baby.

The child's eyes drifted shut, and a look of complete and utter peace settled over his pudgy face. An unexpected burst of sorrow robbed Anna of breath, and she blinked back tears.

Her eyes smarted, and she blamed the lingering curl of smoke escaping from the kitchen. She'd taken so much for granted in life. She'd assumed that once a woman married, children naturally followed. She hadn't realized how very much she wanted children until she was denied the possibility. Edward had not been a comfort.

Marking her two-year anniversary with Edward had been dismal. They'd dined with his colleague at an elegant restaurant in downtown Philadelphia. The man and his wife were celebrating the birth of their third grandchild. Their joyful celebration had been in sharp contrast to the grim diagnosis she'd received that morning from yet another specialist. Children were not to be. She'd tried several herbal remedies from well-meaning friends to no avail.

Edward had considered the prognosis her personal failure. He had spent the rest of the evening critical of her appetite, convinced her slender frame was the cause of her difficulties. When she'd reluctantly accepted a dessert in celebration of their anniversary, he'd criticized her poor nutrition. There was no winning. Looking back, her marriage had been irrevocably broken at that moment.

If they'd had a child, tensions might have eased between her and Edward. But that happiness was not to be.

What had seemed like such an easily bestowed prayer in the early days of her marriage had gradually turned into the center of her existence. She hadn't understood how much having a child would come to mean to her personally, to her identity and her sense of self, until that gift was denied.

She felt as though she'd come adrift from herself, two separate pieces floating through space and time. She was set apart from the other young wives in their social group. They had conversations to which she couldn't contribute; they made assumptions that didn't apply to her. Gradually, they began to treat her differently, as though they'd all joined a club and her membership had been denied. The future she'd taken for granted had been yanked from beneath her feet, turning the present into something unsafe and unpredictable.

She'd never considered herself a greedy person. She hadn't wanted much out of life beyond a roof over her head and a family to love.

Charlotte had been the ambitious sister. Charlotte had wanted the perfect man and the perfect house and the perfect life. All Anna had ever sought was someone to love her, a comfortable, safe home and a family of her own. Yet she'd been denied even those simple desires.

Though her husband had never been physically abusive, his sharp words and cruel comments had often cut her to the quick. In the early days, she'd been horribly naive, thinking that if she simply did everything correctly and on time, he wouldn't be so cross and disappointed in her. She soon realized that nothing she did was ever going to be good enough for him. He found fault in her cooking, in her housekeeping—even in her manners when they met with his business associates. The more she tried to change, the more he criticized her. Eventually, she gave up even trying, and they drifted apart. Barely twenty-four months married, and they were two strangers boarding in the same house. He made every excuse to stay away from home.

She might have reconciled her life more easily had it not been for her own culpability in the disaster. To others he was jovial and kind, the same man she'd *hoped* she'd married. Looking back, there'd been plenty of signs, but she hadn't wanted to acknowledge them. He'd belittle her under the guise that he was only trying to help her improve. He dictated every aspect of her housekeeping—the meals, the groceries, even her garden. When something went wrong, he'd blame her for his behavior, claiming she was somehow responsible.

There were times she was certain she was going mad. If only she'd trusted her instincts. Yet each time she balked in the early days of their relationship, he'd shower her with praise and attention or invent a plausible explanation for his behavior.

With Charlotte married and her parents gone, there'd been no one she felt she could ask for advice. Instead, she'd married the wrong man, and she'd paid a terrible price.

Pots and pans clattered from the deep recesses of the house, breaking into her memories. Brisk footsteps sounded, and Will Canfield strode through the room. He'd doffed his coat and rolled back his sleeves. A smudge of soot streaked across his left cheek, and his dark hair was disheveled.

He paused in the center of the room and spun on one heel, catching sight of her. "I'm quite sorry, Mrs. Linford. We're having some difficulty."

"That's quite all right."

"I was certain I left my glasses somewhere around here."

Anna spotted a pair of spectacles on the side table and gestured. "Are those what you're looking for?"

"Yes. Thank you." He placed the lenses on the tip of his nose and adjusted the metal frames over his ears before spearing his fingers through his tousled hair. Then he plucked a sheet of paper from his front pocket. "Still getting used to these new glasses. Apparently, Tomasina misread a step in the recipe. Fifteen minutes is very different from fifty minutes. A raging inferno of a difference, apparently."

"Is the fire under control?"

"Mostly. Russ is fetching another pail of water. Should be short work after that." He tucked the paper into his pocket and leaned over his son. "I hope you have a strong constitution, my little man. You're going to need it if your mother insists on cooking."

His smile was saturated with pure, unabashed adoration. The undiluted emotion stole the breath from her lungs. Her heart ached in her chest, and she ducked her head lest he note her distress.

Will crooked his finger and rubbed his knuckle along his son's cheek. "Be right back, little fellow."

With that, he strode from the room with long, purposeful strides.

Her throat closed, and tears threatened behind her eyes. She grasped an edge of the blanket and frantically dabbed at the moisture.

Russ appeared in the archway, and she dropped the blanket with a sniffle.

He was at her side in an instant, dropping to one knee

before her. "What is it? What's wrong? Has something happened?"

"It's nothing. The smoke. Is the fire under control?"

"Crisis averted." He didn't appear entirely convinced by her hasty excuse, but he was too much the gentleman to say anything different. "How's the little man?"

"Quite content." She glanced at Russ from beneath her eyelashes. "Is Mr. Canfield very angry? Should we postpone dinner for another time?"

Russ's expression turned questioning. "Angry at what?"

"At...well...at Tomasina. Isn't he worried about what people will think?"

Russ guffawed. "Will couldn't care less what the rest of us think. He's fiercely defensive of Tomasina. Not that she needs his protection." He snorted. "He wouldn't know what to do if one of Tomasina's dinners went smoothly."

Will strode past the door, pivoted on his heel, threw up his hands, and turned back toward the kitchen.

"See what I mean?"

"Oh," Anna said dumbly.

Tomasina had caused a crisis in the kitchen, yet her husband wasn't angry or berating her for her foolish behavior. He appeared resigned, even amused by his wife's antics. And he obviously adored his son.

Russ pulled his watch from his pocket and dangled the shiny, gold case just out of Andrew's reach. The child tracked the movement with his eyes, then pursed his lips and let out a gentle coo.

Anna's chest expanded. "He's fascinated. Have you been around babies often?"

"Nope." Russ shrugged. "I just figured he'd like something shiny."

Tomasina appeared once more, her volcanic curls having taken on a life of their own. They bounced around her head in cheerful abandon, independent of her movements.

She caught sight of Russ and Anna and smoothed the corkscrew tendrils before running a hand down the front of her apron. She needn't have bothered. The next instant, her curls sprang back to life with shocking fervor.

"I'm terribly sorry about that," their muddled host apologized. "Don't worry. No harm done. Unless you count the side dish. I never was fond of brussels sprouts anyway." She crossed the room and reached for her son. "All right, little fellow. First supper and then it's sleepy time for you. I'm Tomasina, by the way. I don't suppose handing you a babe on the front stoop counts as a formal introduction."

"Pleasure to meet you." Anna reluctantly handed over the warm bundle. "He's just precious."

"Isn't he? I never was much for babies until I came to Cowboy Creek. I thought they all looked like hairless little drooling monsters. I love this little fellow to bits, though. I guess it's different when you have your own. I'd like a passel more of them."

"Did I hear someone calling for more children?" Shrugging into his coat, Will appeared in the archway. He dropped a kiss on his wife's cheek and gazed at his son with that same unashamed reverence. "You won't get an argument from me."

Tomasina playfully elbowed her husband in the side. "I only wish I could skip the last few weeks before he was born. I was tired and cranky, and my feet swelled up something fierce. Looked like I was walking on two watermelons."

Will tucked his wife against his side. "That's because you wouldn't slow down. You needed to rest and put your feet up."

"I'll rest when I'm dead. There's work to be done. Fix these two something to drink, and I'll be right down for supper."

Will followed his wife's exit, a lopsided, somewhat bewildered expression on his face. He glanced at them and started, as though only just remembering he was supposed to be entertaining a couple of dinner guests.

"Sorry, sorry. That woman has a way of distracting me. Come this way. We've got everything laid out in the dining room."

He paused at the bottom of the stairs and glanced toward the second floor, his expression wistful.

Anna and Russ exchanged an awkward glance. There was such a breathtaking intimacy between the couple, it almost felt as though they were intruding on a private moment.

Finally, Russ shrugged and assisted her to her feet. He leaned near her ear. "Don't worry. You get used to those two. Will is head over heels and always seems slightly befuddled when Tomasina is around. I don't know how he manages to run the two hotels in town and serve as mayor."

"One hotel," Will declared, his gaze sharp. "As far as anyone knows, I only own one hotel. Which is mostly the truth. I'm only part owner of The Lariat." He slapped Russ on the shoulder. "You know how it goes, old boy."

Anna frowned. "Why don't you want people to know that you own two hotels? That sounds like a grand accomplishment."

Her late husband had shouted even his smallest achievements from the rooftops. She'd thought he was the highest-ranking member of the firm before she married him. He wasn't. He was simply the most vocal about his achievements. When he succeeded, the credit was his and his alone. When failure threatened, the fault rested everywhere *but* him. He was either the victor or the victim, there was no in-between.

"I prefer to remain a silent partner," Will began, leading them into the dining room. "People are odd. There are folks who think it's a personal affront if another man is too successful. Not to mention I've made a few enemies over the years. The folks who don't like me enjoy thumbing their noses at me by staying at The Lariat." He winked. "I'm better off if they don't know I'm still making money off them."

Footsteps sounded from the second level, and Tomasina's sweet voice drifted down the stairwell in a soft lullaby. Will showed them to their seats and disappeared into the kitchen, returning moments later with a covered dish.

Anna stared in mute shock. Her late husband had rarely graced the kitchen, and never when they were entertaining. She half stood from her chair. "Let me help."

"Not at all," Will replied quickly. "I've become quite adept at culinary duties since marrying a woman who cooks best over an open campfire."

Russ shook out his napkin and draped the fabric over his lap. "Perhaps we should have dinner outside next time."

"That's not a bad idea." Will stroked his goatee. "That's not a bad idea at all."

"That sounds quite fun," Anna said, surprising even herself. The two men turned toward her, and her chest seized. "You're making a joke, aren't you?" she mumbled, stricken by her faux pas. "I didn't realize."

This was precisely why she avoided social gatherings. She always managed to say or do the wrong thing. At least she wouldn't have to worry about Russ inviting her any longer. After tonight, he'd probably avoid her at all costs.

"No joke intended." Will slapped his hands together. "Our next party will be a barn dance. Why didn't I think of that before?" He patted his breast pockets with both hands, searching for a nonexistent pencil or a piece of paper. "I should write that down. Don't want to forget."

Tomasina soon joined them, having fed and put Andrew to sleep. Despite the inauspicious start, the meal was delicious. If the roast was slightly charred on one side, the potatoes a touch mushy, and the brussels sprouts missing altogether, no one mentioned the slight imperfections.

"Did you hear?" Tomasina directed the conversation. "President Grant refused to sit in a carriage with President Johnson. He didn't even attend the inaugural ceremonies. It's a disgrace. I think politicians should set their differences aside in public and settle them in private."

Will gave them a sidelong glance. "Mind you, this is coming from a woman who called Ulysses S. Grant a drunken boor."

"I'm from Texas. And I'm not the president," Tomasina defended herself.

"Yet. You'd make a fine president." Will winked, as though well aware he was about to start a controversy.

"You ignorant men won't even give us the right to vote." Tomasina half rose from her chair and pointed across the table at her husband. "While I applaud the ratification of the Fifteenth Amendment, it wouldn't hurt for Congress to pay attention to women's suffrage."

Will held up his hands. "Go easy. I'm on your side."

She dropped into her chair with a thud. "And don't you forget it."

As the sun sank low on the horizon and the candles dripped wax in lazy, rolling patterns, Anna sat back in her chair and drowsily watched the three friends. Clearly at ease with one another, they laughed and bantered, their rapid-fire wit volleying across the table at lightning speed. Tomasina was brash and charming, fiery and uncompromising. Her emotions hovered near the surface, and she shifted from anger to joy in a flash.

Will remained quietly indulgent throughout the dinner, interjected when appropriate, but mostly he cast admiring glances at his wife. His tolerance baffled Anna. Perhaps the political climate was different out west. In Philadelphia, a meek countenance and a quiet, retiring manner were the most necessary components in a political spouse.

As Tomasina and Will sparred over the benefits of a recent Kansas law, she leaned closer to Russ. "Is the conversation always this lively?"

He smiled. "They're being rather subdued for your benefit."

"Does Tomasina plan on accompanying her husband to Washington?"

"Yes. I can't imagine separating those two for more than a day."

"But you know what it's like. Aren't you worried about them? Shouldn't you say something to Will? His career…"

"His career is bound to thrive. Tomasina will bring her own, unique charm to the proceedings."

Her late husband would have loathed Tomasina. Moreover, he'd have been frightened of her. Edward had been intimidated by powerful women. Yet Will was at ease.

Anna sat up with a gasp.

The conversation silenced.

Russ tilted his head. "Is everything all right?"

Stricken, she glanced around the table. "I just remembered something. Sorry."

The enthusiastic conversation sparked to life once more, and her thoughts raced. Edward wasn't strong, he was weak. Weak and insecure. Will admired his passionate wife, and his admiration gave him strength.

The two men at the table were remarkably similar in many ways. Russ was charming, handsome and successful. Even in Philadelphia, when he was merely a young law clerk, there'd been something special about him, a quiet, steady ambition.

He belonged here. The wild, barely tamed land suited him.

Russ rested his napkin beside his plate with an amused grin. "What are you thinking? You're looking far too serious all of sudden."

Her heart sank. She didn't belong here, and she never would. Her miserable marriage and her husband's shocking death had tainted her. She felt as though she'd been poisoned with a slow, insidious tincture. As though the scandal had changed the very fiber of her being, and she was gradually rotting from the inside. Perhaps if they found the killer, she'd be free. Yet the detective's words rang in her ears. The longer the case dragged on, the less likely they were to find the killer.

These welcoming and kind people didn't deserve to be saddled with her reputation. Exhaustion seeped into the very marrow of her bones. Her timing was rotten, that was all.

She plastered a serene smile on her face and responded to his question. "I was thinking what a wonderful life you have here."

These people didn't deserve her troubled past interfering with their bright futures. She had to find a way to leave—quickly.

She'd seen how politicians were scrutinized. Even the slightest transgressions were leveraged for maximum damage. She risked Will's run for the Senate by simply being in his house, accepting his hospitality. What if word reached the voters that he'd entertained a suspected murderess? Russ's political career, too, would be over before it even began.

The walls closed in around her, and her lungs constricted. Her stomach protested, and she feared she'd have another mortifying episode like the one the day of the shoot-out.

Tomasina caught the attention of the table once more. "I met the other two brides at the teahouse on Friday. Millie Lewis and Minnie Dowie. They seem quite nice. They're cousins, but they could be twins. They're both petite, and they wear their brown hair alike—in braids wrapped around their heads. They've already generated quite a bit of attention, as I understand. They're nice enough, don't get me wrong, but there's a little too much giggling between the two of them for my taste."

"They seem very close," Anna said. "I hope they're able to live near each other after they marry."

"They asked about you, Anna," Tomasina continued. "They were quite worried when you missed the train departure. Millie nearly swooned when I told her that you'd been set upon by outlaws. That girl will never miss a train, I can assure you of that. She was so terrified during the telling, she'd never have survived the actual event."

Anna flushed. "I haven't seen them since I've arrived in town. I should apologize for making everyone worry."

"I wouldn't feel too bad. If I had to listen to those two giggle all day, I'd have jumped the tracks," Tomasina declared.

Anna fought a smile. "They were very enthusiastic about being brides. I hope everything turns out well for them."

"We'll be hearing church bells ringing before long, don't worry." Tomasina turned toward her husband. "I heard Pete Sacket had flowers delivered to a certain Minnie Dowie at the boardinghouse." She turned toward Anna. "Pete is a sign maker."

"Pete's a good man," Russ said. "He made the sign for my office. Steady hand and a sharp eye for detail, that fellow. I hope Minnie returns his affection."

"If not," Tomasina said, "he can always try for Millie."

"I must say I'm a little jealous," Russ joked. "I can't believe old Pete is going to find a girl before me."

"It's probably because you're so ugly." Will chuckled.

"Will Canfield!" Tomasina admonished. "You apologize this instant."

"It's all right." Russ grinned.

"Ah, c'mon." Will rested his hand on his chest in a placating gesture. "You grew up traveling with a bunch of drovers on cattle drives, Tomasina. You know how men talk to each other."

"I know. But we're having a nice dinner party. I expect better behavior from the two of you."

Russ needn't worry, Anna thought. He'd be married in no time. She was shocked he hadn't been inundated with flirtations already. She wanted him to be happy. He deserved everything he desired: a home and children. He deserved everything she couldn't have.

"Excuse me," she said, rising from her seat and tossing her napkin beside the plate. "I just need a little fresh air."

She wanted nothing more than to dart out the front door and never stop running, but she was trapped until she could earn enough money for a train ticket. Then she'd find someplace where no one knew her. Someplace where she could start fresh. It was better this way.

She could bear the disdain of strangers far easier than the pity of friends.

Instantly alert, Russ half stood. "I hope everything is all right."

Tomasina reached across the table and took his hand. "Give her a moment."

"Are you certain? She wasn't feeling well when she arrived. What if she's ill again?"

Will and Tomasina exchanged a glance.

"I always listen to my wife," Will said. "It's difficult

adjusting. Cowboy Creek is quite a change from Philadelphia." He straightened the fork next to his plate. "She
can't have been widowed for very long."

"Three months, I think. I'm not certain."

"Grief is different for everyone," Tomasina spoke
gently. "When my pa died, I was ornerier than a bum-
blebee in a late spring snow. It took me a long time to
figure out that I wasn't mad at Pa for dying, I was sad
that he was gone. I cried at the oddest times. I wanted
to pick a fight with everyone, even the people I loved.
It was easier, somehow, being angry. Other people's
emotions work differently."

Will cleared his throat. "You know her better than
any of us. Is there anything we can do for her? Anything to make the adjustment easier?"

"I don't think she's angry." Russ scrubbed a hand
down his face. "She must miss her husband something
fierce, but I've never even heard her mention his name.
It's almost as though she's frozen. She's not happy, she's
not sad. She wants a job, but that's about all I know.
I've tried to put her off because I don't think she should
be working. Especially not now. If she's still weak, she
could have a relapse."

"If she wants to work," Tomasina said, "then let her
work."

Russ leaned back and crossed his arms. "I thought
you'd agree with me. There's no reason for her to suffer. I can move her into The Lariat, and she can stay
for as long as she needs. My share in the hotel grants
certain privileges."

"Life is different for women," Tomasina said. "We
don't have as many choices as men. The poor thing is

probably terrified, wondering where her next meal is coming from and where she's going to sleep."

"But she has us." Russ yanked on his lapels. "It's not as though we're going to let her starve or go homeless."

"She doesn't know that. Not yet." Tomasina circled the table to sit on the other side of Will, her bright green eyes filled with compassion. "Why should she trust any of us? According to Will, you were engaged to her sister five years ago. She was little more than a child when you last met. She went from her father's house to her husband's, and now she's all alone. If working gives her a sense that she has some control over the outcome of her life, then let her work." Tomasina hooked her arm through her husband's elbow and leaned her head against his shoulder. "We'll arrange for a job at The Lariat. We'll assign someone to look out for her. Discreetly, of course. Someone who will ensure she doesn't work too hard."

Will glanced at his wife, and a smile spread across his face. "Remember when you worked for me? And you hogtied that guest? I thought poor Mrs. Foster was going to have an apoplexy."

"Served him right." Tomasina huffed. "He slapped my bottom."

Russ shot upright. "Anna certainly won't be working in a hotel if that's the sort of thing that goes on. I won't have her…abused by one of the guests."

"We can't wrap her in cotton, but we can keep track of the guests." Will splayed his hands. "We'll ensure that she's looked after."

"I don't like it." Russ shook his head. "I don't like the idea of her working, especially as a maid."

"Remember when you bought that roan horse from

me?" Tomasina asked Russ, a knowing sparkle in her vivid green eyes.

"Yes."

"And he bucked you off three times in a row?"

The sharp sting of humiliation lingered. "Twice. Twice in a row," Russ grumbled.

"And you tore your britches on the fence rail?"

"I get it, I get it. When you fall off a horse, you have to get back on. But what does that have to do with Anna? She's come this far on her own, she doesn't need a lesson from us in perseverance."

"It's my story and quit your interrupting," Tomasina scolded. "Think of how proud you felt when you finally got that beast under control. You worked hard, and you got the reward. That's a good feeling. Let Anna solve her own problems. Let her have that feeling."

Every fiber in Russ's body rebelled at the notion. He had the ways and means to support her as long as she needed the help, and his closest friends were advising against his assistance.

"Now," Tomasina stated abruptly.

Russ started. "Now what?"

"Now you can check on her. Tell her she can have a job at The Lariat. It's slow this week, and we'll make certain she doesn't have to work too hard. If she doesn't like the job, we'll find her something else to do."

"You've just lectured me on giving Anna her independence, but you're expediting her job search. How is that any different than what I'm proposing?" Russ demanded. "You're helping her, aren't you?"

"You're trying to rob her of her independence. We're giving her a sense of freedom."

"That doesn't make any sense."

Will gazed adoringly at his wife. "I agree with To-masina. Let Anna establish her independence if that's what she's determined to do."

He and Will rarely disagreed on a course of action. Then again, he and Will rarely discussed personal matters. Though Russ's instincts strained against the idea, he was outnumbered. Besides, he obviously knew nothing of women or he wouldn't be twice-jilted himself.

"All right, all right." He threw up his hands. "I still don't understand, but if the both of you agree this is the best decision, then I'll go along with it. For now."

"Excellent," Tomasina said easily, clearly anticipating a victory. "Tell her I had a very special chocolate cake prepared by Miss Frazier especially for this occasion."

"With cherry filling?"

"Mrs. Foster told me Anna adored the cake, and I ordered one special for the evening. I'd hate to see it go to waste."

"I'll tell her."

Russ reluctantly stood and pivoted on his heel. He crossed the vestibule and stepped onto the porch. The sun had dipped below the horizon, and Anna stood near the railing, staring into the distance. The moonlight shimmered through the clouds and cicadas called in the yard. A fierce sense of protectiveness filled him. She was achingly vulnerable, and he wanted to shelter her. Nothing more, nothing less. She was a friend from his past. A friend in need.

"I'm sorry," she said without turning around. "I shouldn't have run off like that. What must your friends think of me?"

"They think you're a strong woman who's been through a lot recently. If you don't mind my saying, you're pushing yourself too hard. There's no shame in taking a rest."

"Have you spoken with Will about getting me a job?"

"If you're worried about incurring costs at the hotel, you can always move to the boarding house. I don't mind carrying the cost until you're settled. It's the least I can do."

"I don't need your charity."

"It isn't charity."

"I was a burden to my father after my mother died. I was supposed to be a son, you see. I was a burden to Charlotte. She wanted to be a sister, but she was forced to take over the role of mother. I was a burden in my… I was a burden to my friends after my husband died. For once in my life, I want my independence. For once in my life, I don't want to feel as though I'm a burden to anyone."

"You could never be a burden to me." Russ stifled a sound of frustration. She was as stubborn as the day was long. "If you insist on working, then it's all settled. You may start at The Lariat whenever you feel ready."

"The day after tomorrow?" She spun around, and her expression radiated joy. "If that's not too much trouble."

"No trouble at all."

"I won't be a bother anymore, I promise. I'm sure you'll hardly see me after today."

There was so much more he wanted to say, but the words escaped him. What rights did he have with Anna? Their families had tangled half a decade before. That left his friendship with her tenuous at best.

Yet guilt nagged his conscience. Something wasn't all that it seemed with Anna. She was ill. She was alone when she should have had friends and family looking out for her. She refused his help beyond providing a reference.

"I hope we'll remain friends," he said after a lengthy pause.

"You needn't worry about me. I'll be fine."

He could easily walk away and never say another word. She acted as though she'd be more than happy if she never saw him again.

He didn't like that idea. He didn't like that idea one bit. Though he resented her independence, she wasn't the only one of them with a stubborn streak.

Chapter Nine

Anna tightened the bow of her bonnet beneath her chin and set out for her morning walk. The two other brides who'd been traveling with her, Millie Lewis and Minnie Dowie, had been kind to her and deserved an apology.

As she stood on the porch of the boardinghouse, the sugary sweet aroma of a freshly baked confection wafted from through the screen door.

A petite woman with dark brown hair appeared on the threshold. She opened the screen door, but her attention remained focused on something in the house.

"Not again, Sadie!" She turned, and her topaz eyes widened. "I'm sorry. I thought Sadie had forgotten her key again."

"I'm Anna Linford. I traveled part of the way on the train with Minnie and Millie."

"Pleasure to meet you. I'm Deborah." The woman glanced over her shoulder once more. "Deborah, uh, Frazier. Oh dear. I must apologize, I've got a cake in the oven, and I'm a bit distracted. Do you mind following me into the kitchen?"

"Not at all."

Anna had never considered herself tall, but she felt like an Amazon beside Deborah. Petite and pale with perfect waves sculpting her dark hair into an elaborately braided swirl at the base of her neck, Deborah was as perfect as an oil painting. Though her royal blue dress was cut in a simple style, even Anna recognized the expense of the luxurious fabric as she followed the other woman.

Deborah's footsteps were light, soundless and her movements elegant, as though she was floating down the corridor rather than walking. Without looking back, she scooted into the kitchen and opened the stove door. She frowned at the two pans inside, tilting her head this way and that before shutting the door once more.

"Two more minutes," she said. "It's quite challenging trying to judge the time on a chocolate cake. One can never discern whether or not the batter has browned."

Anna was grateful to finally put the name to the face. "I'm already a fan of your baking skills. It's a pleasure meeting the person who creates such wonderful confections."

"You're chocolate cake with cherry filling!" Deborah exclaimed. "Tomasina was very specific when she ordered the dessert for her dinner party." A wistful look drifted over Deborah's delicate features. "What was dinner like at the mayor's house?"

"Smoky." Anna smiled. "I don't think Tomasina is as accomplished a cook as you are a baker."

"Which is a diplomatic way of saying she set the dinner on fire."

"Yes." Anna laughed. "Although what was salvaged was quite delicious. I'm being embarrassingly impolite. One should never complain about one's host."

Deborah flapped her hand dismissively. "Don't worry. Tomasina would be the first one to laugh about her escapades. She's quite unique." She lifted a glass dome revealing a plate of delicate, flaky pastries. "Will you try one of these? I need your honest opinion."

Anna hesitated only a moment. "All right." It would be impolite to refuse, after all.

Morning sunlight filtered through delicate lace curtains, sending patterned shadows over the cheery gingham tablecloth. She sat at the table, and Deborah handed her a plated pastry and fork. The silver tines pressed through the crust with a crisp snap, and strawberry filling oozed from the flaky layers. Aware of Deborah's intense scrutiny, Anna took a cautious bite.

The filling melted on her tongue, an exotic mixture of sweet and tangy followed by a surprising snap of mint. "This is delicious. What's that unusual flavor I'm tasting?"

"I've been experimenting with mint and vinegar in the strawberry filling."

"Mint and vinegar? I'd never consider marrying such flavors together. You're quite talented and creative."

"Only with baking." A ghost of a melancholy smile hovered on Deborah's lips. "I don't have much talent for anything else."

"You don't need another talent when you bake this well."

As Deborah blushed, footfalls sounded on the stairwell, and another woman appeared on the threshold. She clapped her hands. "Is the cake ready yet?"

Buxom with medium brown hair, she wore an elaborately flounced dress in a shocking hue of fuchsia.

"Not yet." Deborah shook her head. "You have to be patient, Sadie. These things take time."

Sadie eyed the domed dessert on the table. "As long as I'm here, I might as well have a bite of that strawberry pastry. I hate to waste a trip." She caught sight of Anna and stuck out her hand. "I'm Sadie Shriver. I don't believe we've met yet."

"Anna Linford."

"There's something familiar about that name." Sadie tapped her chin. "Have we met before?"

Anna would definitely remember meeting someone as striking as Sadie Shriver. "I don't think so."

"I always remember faces. I'm not as good with names..."

Deborah glanced up. "You probably read about her in the newspaper."

Anna blanched, and her fork hit the plate with a clatter.

"Sam did a story about the outlaws on the road," Deborah continued. "You must have been terrified."

Reaching for her fork with trembling fingers, Anna nodded. "It was quite frightening."

Sadie gasped and pressed her fist against her ample bosom. "Tell me everything and don't leave out a single detail. I heard Mr. Halloway acted quite bravely. He's not quite as cute as my Walter, but there's something about that man that gives me the shivers."

A tremor of jealousy shook Anna. She shouldn't be surprised that other women had noticed Russ's unique appeal. She had no hold on him, and Sadie's observations shouldn't matter a bit.

"Sadie!" Deborah touched the other woman's shoulder. "Don't badger the poor woman. And what would

Walter say if he heard you talking about Russ Hallo-way in that fashion?"

The buxom woman stretched out her hand and stud-ied the tips of her fingernails. "He wouldn't say any-thing. Why should he care?"

"Because he's sweet on you, that's why." Deborah opened the oven and another delicious wave of mouth-watering aroma puffed through the kitchen. "He's here most every day calling on you."

Sadie rubbed a hand down her skirts. "He doesn't seem interested in Millie or Minnie. I suppose that's something." She patted her hair. "But I know how men are. As the youngest of four sisters, I learned that lesson the hard way. Men are fickle for a pretty face."

"Now you're talking nonsense," Deborah said. "If someone loves you, they love you for yourself and not your looks."

"Easy for you to say. Believe me, I've been through this before. I'd bring home a beau, and inevitably one of my three older sisters would breeze through the room and turn his head. It isn't fair they were born with our mother's blond hair and willowy figure while I was stuck with my aunt Livia's sweet tooth and bushy eye-brows. What man wants to court an overstuffed French pastry when there's a Greek goddess at hand?"

"Oh, Sadie. That's not true, and you know it."

"I thought if I went someplace where the men out-numbered the women five to one, I'd at least have a fighting chance."

Though she was quite lovely, Anna sympathized with having been overshadowed by a captivating older sister. Sadie didn't recognize her own, unique charm. "Older sisters can be a challenge. I have one myself."

"Try having three."

Anna grimaced. "I can't even imagine. Living in the shadow of one beautiful, older sister was plenty."

"I'd give anything for your figure." Sadie stabbed a generous bite of pastry. "Anything except starve myself, that is."

"With Deborah around, I won't have this figure for long."

"Enough about dessert," Sadie declared. "Let's get back to the outlaws. Don't leave out any details."

"Actually," Anna began, "I came to apologize to Minnie and Millie for causing them to worry. Are they here?"

"No. They're somewhere together. They're always together. Giggling. I think they've quite recovered." Sadie rolled her eyes. "Now tell me all about what happened. Were you frightened out of your wits?"

"Sadie." Deborah tsked. "Maybe Anna doesn't want to talk about what happened."

"It's all right," Anna assured the other woman. She might as well embrace her claim to fame. "We were set upon by two outlaws. Mr. Halloway and some of the men from town happened upon us. They rescued Mr. Ward and me."

"Rescued? That sounds simple and boring. What really happened? I want details. I heard Mr. Halloway disarmed the two men by himself after being shot in the leg."

"I heard he was shot in the arm," Deborah chimed in.

"He wasn't shot," Anna gasped. She never ceased to be amazed at how quickly false rumors spread. "Mr. Halloway rode into the ambush and created a distraction while the other men surrounded the outlaws. They hit

Russ, I mean Mr. Halloway, on the head quite sharply for his troubles."

"Does he have a scar?" Sadie braced her hands on the table. "Something that enhances his rough good looks?"

"I'm starting to have sympathy for Walter," Deborah spoke. "Gracious. Be careful if you're trying to make the man jealous. You're liable to frighten him off."

"How else will I know if he even cares?" Sadie blushed to the roots of her hair. "He's coming by this afternoon. He wants to take some photographs of the town."

"He wants to take photographs of you." Deborah clasped her fingers together and blinked rapidly.

Sadie stood, and her hands fluttered. "He could have any woman he wants. Why would he want plain old me?"

"You're not plain," Anna protested. "You're beautiful."

Sadie glanced at her with a frown. "Are you widowed? There was a woman in Philadelphia… No. That can't be right."

Anna's stomach twisted. "Lovely to meet you. I should be getting back. I only wanted to apologize for missing the train and causing everyone to worry."

Deborah slid a pastry onto a plate. "I'll let Minnie and Millie know you visited. Don't be offended if they don't return the call. I believe they've been quite distracted by the gentlemen in town. The Simms brothers, to be specific. Freddie and Billy."

"Pete Sacket is a better choice, but I don't know if Minnie has the sense to see that. They're a couple of giggling gooses." Sadie planted her hands on her hips.

"I hope they marry soon or I'll go mad listening to them day and night."

"Be kind," Deborah admonished. "Laughter is a joyful sound."

"Not the way those two gad about."

Anna backed toward the door. "Thank you for the enchanting dessert, Deborah. I hope we can visit again soon. It was a pleasure meeting you, Sadie."

Except Sadie didn't appear to be listening. She tapped her chin and gazed at Anna, her expression intense. Anna's stomach flipped. What were the chances? She didn't dare ask if Sadie was from Philadelphia. She didn't want to say anything that might spur her memory.

Deborah yelped and stumbled back from the counter. "I've spilled strawberry jam on my favorite dress. I'm going upstairs to soak this before the stain sets."

Anna seized the opportunity to leave. She ducked her head and rushed toward the door. But she was stopped by a sharp gasp.

"It's you!" Sadie exclaimed. "I knew there was something familiar about the name, but I didn't put it together until we were talking about the shoot-out. You're from Philadelphia, aren't you?"

Anna reached for the doorknob. "I have to go."

"And your husband." Sadie snapped her fingers. "He was a politician or something. It's all coming back to me. There was a front-page story in the newspaper." She dropped onto a chair with a thud. "Did you kill him? According to the gossip, you weren't the only one who had a motive."

"I didn't kill him. I was questioned. Briefly. A woman was noticed fleeing the scene. I had an alibi."

"But they never caught his killer?"

"No."

"I wouldn't blame you if you did kill him."

"I didn't. Please don't tell anyone what you know." Panicked, Anna stepped back into the room, swept her skirts aside and knelt before the stunned woman. "I was deemed innocent by the police in Philadelphia. Nobody here knows anything about what happened, and I'd like to keep it that way as long as possible. At least until I can earn enough money to move someplace else."

Sadie tilted her head, as though emerging from a torpor. "Oh, you poor dear. The things your husband did. And to have the scandal spread across the front page of the newspaper. That must have been awful."

Anna blinked rapidly. "Promise me. Promise you won't tell anyone what you know."

Sadie crushed her against her chest. "You've got nothing to hide, dearie. It's like you said, the police don't think you did anything wrong. Why go skulking around? It's your husband's fault, not yours."

Anna stumbled upright and touched her forehead. "Because not everyone came to the same conclusion as the police. There are still people in Philadelphia who think I killed him. Until they find his real killer, I'll always have a cloud of suspicion hanging over me."

This was a disaster. Sadie was kind, but she enjoyed a bit of gossip. How long before she slipped up and said something?

"If it were me, I'd hire a Pinkerton detective and find the murderer myself." Sadie reached for another pastry. "You can't shoot someone in the middle of the day without someone noticing something."

Anna had already considered that possibility, but after paying off her husband's debts, there was no money for a train ticket, let alone a pricey Pinkerton detective. "Maybe I will. Someday. But promise me you won't tell anyone what you know."

"I promise." Sadie drew an X over her heart with her index finger. "No one will hear a peep out of me." She cupped her cheek with one hand. "Say, you oughta ask that lawyer, Russ Halloway, for help. I heard his brother was a Pinkerton detective. Maybe he can get you a discount or something."

"No," Anna replied, stricken. "I can't involve him. He's running for mayor. He can't have any hint of scandal around him." She shuddered. Involving Russ was out of the question. She was already living on borrowed time in Cowboy Creek. She'd ask for extra hours and save every penny.

"I suppose you're right." Sadie harrumphed. "Still, it doesn't seem fair that your husband was the one cavorting around and getting himself shot, and you're the one who's suffering."

"Life is seldom fair."

"No. It isn't. I'll keep your secret if that's what you want, but you might be surprised by folks around here." Sadie cut through her second helping of pastry. "There are two kinds of people who live out west—the folks that were born here, and the folks who came here to escape something." The other woman caught her gaze. "I wasn't born here."

"Thank you," Anna said. "I owe you a great deal."

"Ah, you don't owe me nothing. We girls have to stick together."

"Yes," Anna replied weakly.

Sadie led her to the door, and Anna glanced over her shoulder one last time before starting in the general direction of The Cattleman. She walked with her head bent, her footsteps brisk. The fresh air was invigorating, and she soon lost track of where she was going or how long she'd been walking.

She'd bought herself a reprieve, but for how long? With each day that passed, she felt the steady ticking of the clock. She'd already discovered someone who knew her secret. How long would it be before someone else sought the truth?

The detective back in Philadelphia was relentless, but even if he caught the killer, something as wonderful as an exoneration of her name didn't guarantee an end to the gossip. Folks didn't always believe the facts, and they didn't always trust the newspapers. People stubbornly clung to their beliefs, even in light of evidence suggesting otherwise. Anna knew the pitfalls of trusting one's heart over one's head. She'd married Edward despite her misgivings, hadn't she?

Instead of being a possible murderess, she'd be the humiliated widow. She'd always bear the taint of his murder, of the immoral life he'd led and of the poor choice she'd made in a husband.

The boardwalk ended, and her footsteps slowed. Railroad tracks snaked into the distance, leading to another town, another future, another fresh start. She told herself again that she only had to survive a few more weeks, save some money and then she could run again.

This time, she'd change her name. She'd been too overwhelmed to revert to her maiden name before. This time, she'd be more thoughtful about her escape. This time, she'd disappear for good.

A school bell rang in the distance. Pail in hand, with

blond pigtails flying, a young girl dashed toward the sound. Anna barely recalled ever being that innocent.

Children should be protected from the cruelties of the world. Though she'd desperately wanted children during her brief marriage, she was reluctantly grateful she'd never been able to conceive.

She pivoted back toward the town and threw back her shoulders. She had a plan. Her health was gradually returning. Whatever happened, the burden was hers to bear alone.

At least she'd never have to explain Edward's shocking death to an innocent child, and that was a blessing she'd cling to when all else failed.

Russ propped the spade against the base of the house and swiped at his forehead with the back of his hand.

A voice called from a passing wagon, and he turned toward the sound. Seth held the reins for a team of horses. Beside him, three young boys, their heads stairstepped by age, sat on the wagon seat.

Russ's brother had inherited guardianship of the three Radner boys—now known affectionately as the Halloway boys—last month. They were seven, five and three respectively, with hair in various hues of blond. Since adopting them, Seth had taken a shine to fatherhood and rarely missed an opportunity to spend time with the children.

"Uncle Russ!" called Tate, the oldest. "How come you're stealing the mayor's rosebushes?"

Russ abandoned his labors and trudged toward the wagon. He braced his hands on the side of the center board with a grin. "I'm not stealing them, Tate. I'm taking a cutting to plant in my yard."

Tate grimaced. "Rosebushes? Did the heat addle your brain, Uncle Russ? What sort of feller goes digging up rosebushes?"

Seth rested his hand across the back of the bench seat. "You know better than to say that sort of thing, Tate."

Russ and his brother were nearly the same height, though Seth had more of their father's bearish build— he was broad-shouldered and lean-hipped with beefy arms and legs from manual labor around the ranch. They shared the same light brown hair and brown eyes, though Seth wore a mustache while Russ had sported a goatee since his time in the army. They'd drifted apart during the war, but Cowboy Creek had been a new opportunity to get to know his brother once more.

"Ah, Seth, I was only funning." Tate appeared suitably chastised. "Tell us about the outlaws. Did you shoot anyone? Did they die? Did their tongues stick out and swell up after they were dead?"

"Tate!"

"Ah, c'mon, you're curious too, ain't ya?"

Russ stretched out a hand and ruffled the boy's hair. "Where are the girls? They're brave, letting the four of you storm the town all alone."

"Marigold is finishing up some work at the schoolhouse with Violet. We're visiting the mercantile before we head home." Seth narrowed his gaze. "Now tell us about the outlaws. Ma didn't say much. She mentioned one of the Darby sisters was in town."

Russ stared at the top of his boots. "Yep."

"That's all you're going to say? Yep."

Harper, the five-year-old, tapped on Seth's shoulder. "Who are the Darby sisters?"

"Why don't you three boys run along to the mercantile ahead of me?" Seth offered, fishing in his pocket for loose change. "Stick together and don't bother the owner, Mr. Booker."

He gave each of the boys a nickel, even the youngest, Little John, who fisted the precious coin in his pudgy hand. The three boys climbed out of the wagon in eager anticipation. Once they safely crossed the street hand in hand, they took off in a dash. From his seat, Seth watched their progress until they entered the mercantile.

He shook his head. "If I had even a tenth of that energy, I'd be as rich as Vanderbilt by now. I don't remember any of us being that rambunctious when we were little. Even Adam."

"You heard from him lately?" Russ asked. "Ma is worried."

"Nope. Nothing. Marigold thinks I oughta do something about it."

"Like what? Hire a Pinkerton detective to find a Pinkerton detective?"

Seth offered a wry, half grin. "Maybe that's not such a bad idea."

"I don't want to get Ma's hopes up."

"What'd she say about him?"

"You know how she is," Russ said. "She doesn't talk about him much, but I know she's hurting."

"Adam never was one for writing. I'm sure he's fine." Seth adjusted the reins in his gloved hands, and the horses shifted, their tails swishing against the buzz of flies. "Say, you know people. Maybe you could ask around. Write some letters."

Russ had a few contacts. A few people he used when he needed information that wasn't readily available through the usual channels. "I'll do what I can, but don't expect much. Adam should at least let Ma know he's still alive once in a while."

Russ's influence only went so far. Depending on how deep Adam had gone into hiding for his current case, they weren't likely to find him unless he *wanted* them to find him.

"I'd feel better if we at least tried," Seth said. The brothers exchanged a knowing glance. Neither of them liked to see their mother upset. "How much longer do you think Ma will stay with you? Marigold was asking."

"Don't know. She's cooking up a storm."

Seth set the brake on the wagon, swung his legs over the side, then leaped to the ground beside Russ. "Yeah. She's used to feeding a man who works in the fields all day. Not someone who sits behind a desk."

Russ chucked his brother on the shoulder. "I hope Marigold makes you fat."

Seth patted his stomach. "She's trying, that's for sure." He gestured to the hole and the shovel. "What's the deal with the rosebush? Ma talk you into that?"

"Nah. Just figured I'd spruce up the place."

Seth pinched the brim of his hat, shadowing his face with his forearm. "Ma might have said something about Susannah when she picked up the boys yesterday."

"Susannah isn't coming out. Changed her mind."

"Her loss."

"Guess so."

"Didn't see that one coming." Seth hooked his index fingers through his belt loops. "Something will work out. It always does."

"Yep." Russ paused. "Maybe I oughta just give up. Maybe there's something wrong with me."

Seth guffawed. "Yeah, there's something wrong with you. You're stubborn, and you're too smart for your own good."

"Glad I asked."

"Ah, c'mon. If you can't let your brother rib you, then you're in a bad way. Why don't you have dinner at the boardinghouse? Meet someone new."

"Nah." Russ groaned. "I'm all full up on humiliation."

"Maybe next time you oughta try getting to know someone first."

"What's that supposed to mean?"

"I'm just saying that getting married is for life. Take your time. Find someone who suits you."

An image of Anna sprang to mind, and Russ shook his head, clearing his thoughts. His feelings toward her were jumbled and confused. He'd known her when she was younger, and he was protective of her, that was all.

"I figured you'd have a go at me," Russ said. "And a good laugh."

"I'm not laughing at you, Russ. I want what's best for you. That's all I've ever wanted."

"I know."

"But women are different. You can't just pick one off the shelf because you like the way she looks."

"When have I ever done that?"

"Never mind."

"I see," Russ grumbled, his annoyance sparking. "You're an expert on women now."

Truthfully, he was envious more than irked. Marigold and Seth had found each other through happenstance, and they'd fallen in love. Not everyone had it that easy.

"Someday you're going to fall head over heels in love," Seth said. "And it's going to be a real shock.

You're going to have to feel, and you're going to have to open yourself up to pain. I hope when that happens, you recognize that finding the right woman is worth the effort."

"I'm open." Russ splayed his arms. "Just the other day, Dr. Mason told me that I was a good prospect as a husband. She said I had good health, a decent job, and a nice house. A woman could do worse."

"Sure. Forget I said anything. You're a real catch. That's why we're having this conversation."

"I never thought I'd live to see the day you gave me advice about women."

"Well, I never thought I'd see the day when I fell in love," Seth said. "You just keep on picking the wrong girl and stay single. That seems to be working for you."

"You're not making any sense."

"I'm not arguing with you about it. You're too stubborn and thickheaded to listen, so I'm not wasting my breath."

"Stubborn and thickheaded? That's fine talk coming from you."

"I know what you think Pa did, but you're wrong." Seth's accusation exploded out of nowhere. "You're wrong about him, and you're wrong about yourself."

"What does that have to do with me?"

"I think you're afraid. I think you're afraid you're too much like Pa. I think you're afraid of letting people down."

"That's ridiculous." Russ's growing anger bubbled over. "I work every day to make sure folks don't fall for people like Ogden. I've seen smart, hardworking men and women fall for those types. I'm not afraid because I know a fraud when I see one."

"Yeah. But that's not the point, is it? Doesn't matter why you think Pa fell for Ogden's lies. You're still mad at him for leaving the rest of us to pick up the pieces."

"You picked up the pieces." The realization of all Seth had lost doused Russ's anger like pump water over an open flame. "We should have helped you. I didn't realize how much you were sacrificing."

"Doesn't matter now. It's over. I made my choices, and I'm proud of who I am. Pa didn't quit on us. Maybe it's time to think about why you believe he did."

"I guess we'll never know." Seth was touching on something Russ didn't want to recognize, and he backed away, physically and emotionally. Hitching his boot on the shovel, he switched conversational tracks. "There's someone in town buying up land from the ranchers."

Seth accepted the abrupt change of subject without flicking an eyelash. "That fellow with the mining company, Jason Mitchell? I know all about him. He made an offer on my land. Turned him down."

"Nah. Not Jason. Someone else. He may be sniffing around the Shawnee land, and he may have a woman working with him. Whatever is happening, something doesn't feel right."

"You know, now that you mention it…" Seth tugged on his ear. "My neighbor just sold. Took a real hit on the value. The land flooded. The dam just north of the railroad bridge gave out. Sheriff Getman says it collapsed under the rain, but I've seen worse weather, and we never had any problem before. Might be worth looking into."

"You think someone deliberately flooded the land?"

"Don't know. The sheriff isn't the most competent

fellow. If someone wanted to fool him, it probably wouldn't take much."

A chill swept over Russ. "If someone is causing trouble, I'll find him."

"I know you will." Seth adjusted his hat. "That's how I know we're different from Pa. I stuck it out and built the ranch again. You fight injustice."

"What about Adam?"

"I don't know. Maybe if he ever came home long enough, I'd find out what kind of man he's become. Until that day, I just don't know."

"I'll think about what you said."

"Good," Seth said as he hitched the horses' reins to the post. "Hate to think I'm wasting my breath."

Russ watched his brother's progress down the boardwalk, his thoughts spinning. He'd never known Seth to offer his thoughts unless prodded, and he didn't know if he liked this new side of his brother. Russ had made his peace with the past. There was no use dredging up old memories.

He'd just had a run of bad breaks with women, that was all. Maybe he'd even take Seth's advice and have dinner at the boardinghouse. He'd show Seth he wasn't afraid of getting to know a woman. Russ snorted. The idea was ridiculous.

He'd go there sometime next week if he wasn't too busy with work. There were the deeds from the land sale and property line dispute to settle. Might have to be the week after next.

Seth would be eating his words one day soon. But not this week. This week Russ was too busy.

Chapter Ten

A week following her dramatic arrival in Cowboy Creek, Anna paused while cleaning a guest room in The Lariat, pressed a hand to the small of her back and stretched her spine. She'd slept for eight hours the night before and felt no more rested than if she'd slept two.

True to his word, Russ had put in a reference for her with the management, and she'd been given the job of housemaid at The Lariat. The work was busy but not stressful, which was both good and bad. While she hadn't experienced a relapse of her illness, she was still battling fatigue, and the monotonous tasks gave her too much time to think.

She had a tiny room all to herself on the third floor, and the lead housekeeper had let her store her seeds in the cool, dry cellar of the hotel. All in all, she had nothing to complain about. She'd gotten exactly what she wanted. She had a job, she had a roof over her head, and she didn't have to worry about where her next meal was coming from. Her lingering lethargy was a bother, but she seemed to catch a second wind as the day wore on, which made working feasible.

Since her conversation with Sadie, time nipped at her heels. She'd been beside herself the first few days after Sadie discovered her secret, but true to her word, Sadie had kept quiet. So far.

Which meant there was no time for rest. Anna dutifully brewed the tea Dr. Mason had prescribed each evening, with vague plans of visiting the doctor again once her supply ran out.

These days she mostly worked and slept. Though unaccustomed to being alone, she was learning to tolerate the solitude. Most days she'd close her eyes for a few minutes only to discover she'd slept for hours.

A gentle knock sounded on the door frame. Expecting another assignment from the hotel manager, she plastered a smile on her face and turned.

Her heart tripped a beat before she wrestled control of her emotions when she saw who was standing in the doorway of the hotel room she was cleaning. "Russ! I wasn't expecting you."

"I came to check on your employment. Ready to quit yet? My offer still stands. You can stay at the hotel or room at the boardinghouse for free."

"Go away," she ordered gently, a smile softening her words. "You're going to get me sacked."

"Don't worry, I know the boss."

"You'd better be telling the truth, because this job has been a godsend." Stifling a yawn, she reached for another fresh pillowcase. "I'm doing fine. I'm feeling well. I'm eating enough food to feed a ranch hand. You don't need to check up on me every day anymore. While I appreciate your concern, you needn't worry about me. Surely your work keeps you occupied?"

Only yesterday she'd overheard someone in the lobby

give a glowing report on a land sale Russ had brokered. She'd yet to meet anyone who didn't admire his work ethic. His daily visits were a bright spot in her day, but she had to break the habit. She couldn't come to depend on him.

"I wasn't checking up on you." Russ intercepted her grasp and took the next pillow to help her change the linens. "I'm here on Leah's orders. I'm supposed to remind you that we've been invited to the Gardners' for dinner this evening."

"I'd forgotten all about that."

"You've been working hard. You deserve a night out. Besides, Leah will be disappointed if you cancel."

Anna tugged her lower lip between her teeth. As long as she kept her distance, he should be protected from the scandal if someone discovered the truth. "I don't want to disappoint Leah but…"

"If you're worried that people will think you're spoken for, Daniel, Will and I can discreetly spread the word that you're open to courting." He expertly shook the pillow into the fresh case and fluffed the feathers before replacing it on the bed. "If you've changed your mind, that is."

A violent shudder racked her body. "I don't want another husband."

Russ grew sober. "You must have loved your husband very much. I didn't mean to sully his memory by suggesting you replace him."

"It's not that." Anna's head throbbed, and she turned away to reach for a coverlet. Telling the truth about her marriage was far too humiliating. "You wouldn't understand."

"Try me sometime, Anna. You might be surprised."

One of them was going to be surprised, that was for certain. Philadelphia was miles away, but not far enough. She couldn't hide forever. The truth was bound to catch up with her. The unsolved murder of a prominent man was front-page news.

"If you ever change your mind about remarrying," Russ said, "promise you'll tell me. I'll steer you away from the scoundrels."

She looked up at Russ. "That's precisely what Mrs. Foster said."

"See? You're in safe hands."

"I won't change my mind." Unaccountably weary, she perched on the edge of a chair. "I shouldn't take advantage of your friends' hospitality."

"For the last time, we're not embarking on some great deceit. They're interested in getting to know you. Just you. This is a small town, and you're new. They're being nice. They'd do the same for any newcomer."

"Then I'd be delighted." She stood and flicked the coverlet into place. "I'll be able to repay you for the ticket soon."

She sounded annoying to herself, Russ must be heartily sick of her constant excuses.

"We've gone over this," he said. "You don't have to repay me."

Why did he have to be so kind and accommodating? She hadn't wanted to like him. When she'd taken the letter from Susannah, she'd expected to find the selfish man she'd invented in her head. The man who'd callously tossed her sister aside and left her life in shambles. His insistent kindness only exacerbated her guilt, and she no longer trusted her instincts. She couldn't afford any more mistakes.

"I don't want to be in your debt," she said.

"All right. Pay your fare. But there's no hurry. Neither of us is going anywhere anytime soon."

She tipped back her head and studied the wrought iron chandelier. She hated disappointing him, but staying in Cowboy Creek was out of the question. Russ wasn't the man she remembered, and she wasn't the naive girl she'd been all those years ago.

Russ reached across the coverlet and ran his hand along the seam, smoothing the crease.

She rested her chin on her palm as she watched him. She couldn't imagine Edward performing such a mundane task. "You're awfully good at making beds."

"Four years in the army earned me a few skills."

"Did you see much fighting?"

"No. I was an aide to a general. I already had two years of law school before the war started. The general was convinced my skills were more suited to the boardroom than the battlefield."

"There's no shame in that."

"There isn't much glory, either." He folded a towel in thirds and draped the length over a bar beneath the water pitcher stand. "They don't give out medals for paperwork."

Edward hadn't served at all. His father had known a senator. Money had changed hands, deals had been made, and Edward had somehow escaped conscription. Her father-in-law always said that wars were started by rich men and fought by poor men.

Russ prepared to take his leave, but he paused in the doorway, his hand braced against the frame. "Remember, Anna, there's nothing wrong with accepting an invitation to dinner."

As she looked at him, posed that way, she couldn't help but notice how handsome he was. Not only that. Russ Halloway was a handsome man who'd made something of himself. There was no reason he couldn't find a bride on his own. Her curiosity got the better of her, and suddenly she had to know. "Why did you send for a bride in the first place?"

If Russ was surprised by her directness, he didn't show it. He merely shrugged. "Will Canfield is running for the Senate next term. Someone needs to take over as mayor."

"And the mayor needs to be a family man. Is that what you're saying? Someone with a wife and children running underfoot?"

"Married men are seen as more stable. Men with children are viewed as more responsible."

She bent down to pick up the soiled linens, but when she rose, the room swayed around her.

Russ was at her side in an instant, lowering her to the mattress. "Sit. You're pale as a corpse."

"That's not very flattering."

"You haven't recovered properly from the influenza. You're going to make yourself sick again."

Her stomach roiled and the throbbing in her head intensified. "I simply stood up too fast."

He perched on the edge of the bed beside her. "You know, we're both at loose ends."

She wasn't quite certain what he meant. "I suppose."

"You could do worse."

"I don't understand."

"You could do worse than me."

Her heartbeat kicked against her ribs. "What are you saying?"

"I'm saying there are worse fellows than me. I make a good living. You wouldn't want for anything."

The dizzy spell had addled her brain. "You're not making any sense."

"We're friends, aren't we? We've both had our share of heartbreaks. I'm not asking to take the place of your husband. Perhaps we could take care of each other."

"I can't," she said, her throat tight.

"At least tell me why Charlotte isn't looking out for you."

"She's busy with her own family. Besides, I can take care of myself."

"I know you can, but you don't have to."

He had atrocious timing. If he'd said those words two years ago, she'd have leaped at the chance, even after he'd jilted Charlotte. Except too much time had passed. She wasn't the same person.

She didn't want to talk anymore. "I have work to do." She certainly didn't want to be reminded about her unsuitability as a wife.

When she went to rise, he stilled her. "We're both adults," he said. "We're both far past the stage of youthful infatuation. There's no need for us to be anything more than friends."

She pressed her hand against her rebellious stomach. There was one sure way to dissuade him, and the time had come. "You want a family, right?"

"Yes. Marriage. Children. Everything. Surely you want the same?"

"I can't marry you, Russ," she said, feeling more tired than she ever recalled being. More defeated than she'd ever thought possible. "Because you want the one thing I can't offer."

"And what's that?"

"Children." Saying the words lifted a weight from her chest. "I can't have children. I'll never be able to give you what you want. I'll never be able to give you a family."

"I'm sorry." Was that compassion she saw in his hazel eyes? "I don't know what to say except that my offer still stands."

"What about children?"

"If you want children, we could always adopt."

He didn't want her, he wanted a wife. There was a difference. And he certainly didn't want a wife that jeopardized his political career.

Though she was sorely tempted, she didn't trust herself. She didn't trust her judgment. She'd made excuses for Edward's behavior before she'd married him. There'd been signs of his temperament, signs she'd chosen to avoid.

While she didn't believe Russ was a cruel man, he didn't love her either. She'd already been in one loveless marriage. She couldn't bear to be in another. Especially since she suspected she could very easily fall in love with Russ. At least with Edward, her initial goodwill for him had soon withered and died.

She wouldn't be getting over Russ that easily.

"Are you certain you won't reconsider?" Russ asked her.

His guilt over jilting Charlotte had obviously caught up to him, and he was trying to make amends. He needn't bother. If Charlotte wasn't good enough for him, Anna had no delusions about her limited charms.

"I'm happy being alone," Anna said. "You don't have to look out for me."

Perhaps he felt some sort of obligation for her, she thought. But obligation was a poor foundation for marriage.

"I'm not asking you to love me, Anna. We're both alone. There's no reason we can't be friends."

There were reasons, of course. But those reasons were too personal, too raw to share.

She rose to her feet. "I should be going. I have three more rooms to clean before lunch, and you shouldn't be seen here, even if you do know the owners."

He followed her, standing only inches away. "I'll walk you to the Gardners' this evening."

"I'd like that."

"There doesn't have to be any awkwardness. We'll pretend this never happened, all right? I shouldn't have pressed you."

"You're a good man, Russ," she said, looking up into his eyes, her voice no more than a whisper. "You're a good man, and you deserve everything you ever wanted in life."

"We both do." He walked to the door, where he turned and gave her a small smile. "Don't work too hard. I'll be by around seven."

"I'll be ready."

Keeping her head held high, she forced her legs to take measured steps to the next room. She stepped inside and closed the door, then leaned back against the wood paneling with a quiet sob.

The sweeping sadness sucked the breath from her lungs. She'd done the right thing.

She'd never have to worry about the truth of her first marriage ruining her happiness. She didn't have to worry about falling in love with someone who only thought of her as a friend. She didn't have to worry about being a disappointment to anyone but herself.

It was more important than ever that she earn enough money to move on. She couldn't stay. Not now. She couldn't stay knowing that she'd once had everything she'd ever wanted within her grasp, only to watch it be torn away.

Leah and Daniel's delightful eight-month-old, Evie, perched on Russ's lap. The beautiful cherub stuck a fist in her mouth and drooled. Russ grinned and bounced her on his knee. She squealed and cooed, delighted with the game.

Daniel stood near the fireplace, his elbow perched on the mantel. "I heard Jason Mitchell is buying up more ranches."

The owner of the Gardner Stockyards was slightly shorter than Russ and solidly built. He had brown hair highlighted from time spent in the sun and perceptive green eyes. He and Will were friends, and together with Noah Burgess, the three war buddies had founded the town. They'd thrived, and they'd invested their profits back into Cowboy Creek, building it from a cow town into a thriving community.

"It's not just Jason," Russ said. "I did some digging. According to the register of deeds, there's a man named Maroni who's buying up land, as well. Jason is apparently fit to be tied. For his mining business to succeed, he can't afford to purchase easements for roads and bridges."

"And Maroni is trying to buy up the land between his parcels?"

"Looks that way, but he hasn't been successful just yet."

"Have you met him?" Daniel asked. "This Maroni fellow?"

"Not yet. According to Simon, someone came around the office to see me, but I wasn't in. He's never come back. At first, I thought it might be him, but the clerk didn't have a description. A woman filed the deeds for him." Russ carefully considered his next words. "I thought Maroni was trying to defraud the ranchers, but now I see he's just trying to make more money off the coal mines. Either way, I think we should check into this Maroni fellow's background."

Daniel drummed his fingers on the mantel. "If he's trying to buy the land Jason wants, let the Mitchell Coal & Mining Company incur the expense. It's no sweat off your brow if the coal mine has to pay more."

"There's still a slim chance he's using unscrupulous methods to obtain the land cheaply. After the dam failed, James Solomon sold his land below market value. What if he was sabotaged?"

"Sabotaged?" Daniel straightened. "That's another matter. I didn't spend half of last year dispatching the Murdoch gang only to have the town overrun by another outlaw."

"Near as I can tell, the world has never run short of outlaws."

Daniel muttered his agreement. "How do we find out what happened?"

"I think we should have someone other than the sheriff look at the dam. The sabotage might be hard to spot. Is there anyone who was part of the original construction living around here?"

"Gideon and Pippa are in town. With his connection to the railroad, he should know someone. I'll ask him for an inspection."

"Good," Russ said emphatically. "And the sooner the better."

"From the tone of your voice, this sounds almost personal, if you don't mind my saying."

Russ had never told another living soul about what his father had done, not even Will. He trusted the founders of Cowboy Creek—they were good men—but what had happened to his family remained within the family.

"Nothing personal," Russ said. "Just business. You brought me here to take care of the interests of the townspeople, and that's what I'm doing."

From across the room, he caught Anna gazing at the baby he held. He read the expression in her eyes. She looked as though Evie was the most precious thing in the world. His chest tightened. She couldn't have children, yet he sensed she wanted them. There'd been sorrow in her eyes when she'd told him her story this morning. Sorrow and something more. Defeat.

He wanted to tell her that adoption was an excellent option. Just look at his brother. There were plenty of children in the world who needed good homes.

When she'd swayed on her feet in the hotel, his protectiveness toward her had taken hold, and the words had tumbled out. He didn't regret them. He only regretted the awkwardness he'd created between them.

Leah stood. "If you two insist on talking about business, I'm going to get Anna's opinion on a new recipe."

"We can speak about something else," Daniel said. "We didn't mean to exclude you ladies."

"You two obviously have a lot to talk about," Anna

said, though her gaze never met his as she spoke. "We ladies have plenty to keep us busy."

Leah gestured. "I can take Evie."

"That's all right," Daniel pecked her on the cheek. "We'll be fine with Evie."

Russ watched them exit, his heart heavy. Ever since he'd called for her this evening, he'd sensed a change in their relationship, a hesitation on Anna's part, a tension between them.

"Are you listening?" Daniel asked.

Russ started. "I'm sorry, I didn't hear what you said."

"You haven't been present all evening." Daniel glanced in the direction of the kitchen where the two women had gone, then back to Russ. "I know we haven't known each other long, but if you need to talk about something, I can assure you I'll keep your confidence."

Russ looked down at Evie and fluffed the hair on the top of the child's head. "You enjoy being a father, don't you?"

"More than anything." Daniel's grin stretched from ear to ear. "It's a kind of love I never understood before. A kind of love I never expected to feel."

Leah had been pregnant when the two married, but Daniel appeared to love the child as though she was his own. The baby was beautiful. A delightful sprite with wide, curious eyes.

"I asked Anna to marry me," Russ said.

"What did she say?"

"No."

"I see."

"No questions? No curiosity?"

"Would you rather I asked a lot of questions?"

"Not particularly."

"I didn't think so."

Noises sounded from the kitchen followed by a burst of feminine laughter.

"The women are getting along well," Russ said.

The Gardner house was simple and elegant, with personal touches that gave the home warmth. Exactly the sort of house he'd always wanted and much different from how he currently lived. His bachelor residence was a shambles. Some of the rooms were empty, and others were overflowing with papers. His mother had cleaned a few spaces and bought a few pieces of furniture and some rugs, but she'd quickly abandoned the effort when she'd seen the dining room he used as a study.

Watching Daniel and Leah together had him craving more than the arrangement he'd made with Susannah. The two were obviously in love, and for the first time since his engagement to Charlotte, he yearned for something more than simple affection and mutual respect. Watching the Gardners together, he didn't want to settle.

Anna was mourning the loss of her husband, and she didn't have room for him in her heart. Perhaps things had turned out for the best. He'd rather be alone than live in a cold, loveless marriage. The decision might cost him a chance at running for mayor, but he'd sort out the difficulties later. There was no reason a single man couldn't run for office. Times were changing, and it was up to Cowboy Creek to change along with them.

Daniel refilled his glass with water from a pitcher. "She's a recent widow, isn't she? Leah had been recently widowed when we met."

"Was it difficult, competing with a dead man?"

Daniel stared into his glass. "Their marriage wasn't

as happy as it could have been." He cleared his throat. "You know that Leah is the town midwife?"

"Yes."

"Occasionally Dr. Mason asks her opinion about a case when a pregnancy is involved."

Russ wasn't quite certain what this had to do with the conversation. "I'm not sure I follow."

"I don't know. Just a feeling I had. It's probably nothing."

Russ sensed there was much more to the story, but Leah appeared in the doorway then, with Anna close on her heels. Leah radiated joy, and though Anna was a beauty, fatigue clung to the corners of her mouth and lines showed around her eyes. Perhaps Leah could talk to her about slowing down instead of working. She should be resting instead of cleaning rooms at the hotel. Her illness was liable to return if she didn't give herself time to recover.

Nothing, though, detracted from her natural elegance. Anna had swept her wavy, golden-brown hair into a knot on top of her head. Tendrils framed her face and highlighted her brilliant green eyes. Once again he marveled at the changes to her appearance. She'd been a girl before, but now a woman stood in front of him.

He couldn't help but wonder about her late husband. He recalled Daniel telling him that Leah's first marriage had been unfortunate. For the first time, Russ thought perhaps he'd been reading Anna all wrong. Perhaps her marriage to her first husband hadn't been as happy as he'd thought.

Daniel cleared his throat, and Russ shot to his feet, his thoughts put on hold. It was time for the gentlemen to accompany the ladies to dinner.

Anna gave him a shy smile, and after passing the baby to their hostess, he took her hand, escorting her to her seat.

Dinner passed quickly. Daniel and Leah kept up a steady stream of light conversation, and for that Russ was grateful.

He couldn't help but note the difference between the Canfield and Gardner households. While they were both full of love and warmth, a pervading sense of chaos surrounded Tomasina, while nary a hair would dare go out of place in Leah's presence. Russ craved something in between. Order with chaos around the edges.

The baby had long since gone to bed when Leah carried in a tray of coffee. "There's dessert, too."

Daniel rubbed his stomach. "Nothing for me just yet."

Leah anchored the top of the coffeepot and poured a steaming waterfall of rich liquid into a delicate rose-patterned china cup. "How are you liking Cowboy Creek, Anna? I admit I was a little taken aback when I first arrived. I was expecting something less rustic. The addition of the dress shop and the opera house have already smoothed many of the rough edges." She indicated the chocolate cake. "Perhaps we'll be adding a bakery soon."

"Cowboy Creek is delightful. I'm going to miss the cakes Miss Frazier bakes."

Leah righted the coffeepot. "Are you planning on leaving?"

Anna's cup rattled in the saucer. "No. Yes. I mean, um, I don't know yet. Things are uncertain."

Russ's gaze sharpened. She hadn't spoken of leaving before. Why would she leave? Where would she go? Had his proposal instigated the idea?

"Speaking of Miss Frazier," Leah began, smoothing over the awkward pause, "I think Preston Wells has set his cap for her."

"He isn't the only one," Russ added. "She's quite the baker. Did she study the craft, or is she simply a natural talent?"

Leah scooped sugar into her cup. "I'm not certain, really. She's not as forthcoming as some of the other brides."

"I met Sadie," Anna said as she added a dollop of cream to her coffee. "She seemed quite friendly."

"I heard she's been seen out and about with that photographer, Walter," Leah said. "I haven't had a chance to meet the newest brides. I've been shirking my duties. Did you have a chance to get to know any of them on the train?"

"Not really, no. I wasn't feeling well, you see…" A wash of color dusted her cheeks. "I mostly kept to myself."

Anna was visibly uncomfortable with the turn of the conversation, and Russ ached for her. "Leah, have you met Molly? She seems nice enough. I think perhaps she was hoping Seth might come up to scratch before Marigold entered the picture."

"Molly is a doll," Leah offered with a bit more enthusiasm than the comment required. "I know she's going to find love and start a family soon enough. Buck Hanley was seen ordering flowers for her recently."

The three of them descended into awkward silence once more, and Russ wanted nothing more than to kick himself. Anna had been reluctant to attend the dinner, and they kept dropping minefields into the conversation.

Anna rested her cup and saucer on the table. "Do you garden, Leah?"

Russ almost heaved a sigh of relief at the change of conversation.

"I grow a small kitchen garden," Leah said. "Although I've been having trouble with my sage. There's some sort of rust on the leaves. Do you have any ideas?"

"I'd have to take a look. The problem could be any number of things. Sometimes it's overwatering, and sometimes it can be just the opposite, not enough water. There could be an infestation or a mold problem. I haven't had an opportunity to study the predominant scourges in Kansas."

"Well, it sounds as though I've asked the right person. I'd be grateful if you'd take a look and give me your advice."

For the first time that evening, Anna appeared at ease and enthusiastic. "I'd be happy to assist. There's no time like the present."

Why hadn't he thought to bring up gardening?

"The evening is quite pleasant," Leah replied. "I'm sure we'd all enjoy a turn in the garden after our coffee."

Anna lifted her cup and turned pale. The saucer rattled to the table, and she placed two fingers against her lips. Recalling the incident at the hotel, Russ grasped her chilled fingers.

"Are you all right?" he asked. "What's wrong?"

"I don't feel well. Perhaps some fresh air."

She stood and swayed. Her eyelids fluttered, and she collapsed in his arms.

Chapter Eleven

Anna woke in an unfamiliar room, a cold compress pressed over her eyes. She blinked rapidly and struggled to rise but was held back by a hand pressed gently against her shoulder.

"Don't get up just yet," Leah ordered quietly. "Rest a few more minutes."

Anna was exhausted and disoriented, unsure how much time had passed, though she recalled she was having dinner at the Gardner house. "What happened?"

Leah had a natural elegance and ease about her that Anna found calming. She glanced around the pristine room—the curtains were draped at perfect angles, and the gray flocked wallpaper was sophisticated without being overwhelming. Leah did everything to perfection, even decorating her lovely home. Compared to her, Anna felt dowdy and disheveled and disorganized.

"You fainted," Leah said easily, as though women fainting in her parlor was a common occurrence. "Russ caught you just in time and carried you here."

Anna felt heat infuse her cheeks. "That's impossible. I don't faint."

With efficient movements, Leah rinsed out the rag in the ewer set by the bed, then dabbed the cool cloth against Anna's brow. "Did Russ tell you that I serve as the town midwife?"

"He mentioned something."

Russ had mumbled the words without meeting her eyes. Anna hadn't given his reaction much thought. Men were often reluctant to speak about topics that centered around children and women's bodies.

"There's something else I need to tell you," Leah said.

Anna propped herself up on one elbow. "What is it?"

What could possibly be worse than fainting before a virtual stranger?

"You're pregnant."

"That's impossible." Anna collapsed against the pillows and threw her forearm over her eyes. "I'm barren."

"Who told you that nonsense?" Leah shook her head. "I can assure you they were quite mistaken."

"I visited specialists in Philadelphia."

"Anyone can call themselves a specialist." Leah huffed. "That doesn't mean they are. I encounter this sort of thing all the time. I once had to counsel a woman after a so-called specialist convinced her that drinking rum each evening would cure infertility. Rum! Can you imagine?"

Anna had been given the same advice, but she couldn't abide strong spirits. "Actually, I can imagine."

"You poor dear. I'm sorry you didn't encounter a doctor with more sense."

Anna took a moment to think. The nausea, the fatigue... All these recent symptoms might indicate a pregnancy, but they were also symptoms of the flu and effects of the stress she'd suffered. Could she actually be pregnant?

"But I was married for two years. I've never had a regular cycle. I can't get pregnant or I'd have had children by now."

"Not necessarily. The human body is a delicate balance." Leah asked a few more questions and patted her hand. "Judging by your symptoms and your answers, I'd say you're due in November."

"How can you be so certain?"

"Dr. Mason suspected as much, as well."

"Dr. Mason? But she didn't say anything."

"She asked me about a rather unusual case. No names were mentioned, of course, but I'm not a complete fool. When you visited her after the shoot-out, she suspected a pregnancy."

"But why didn't she say anything?" Anna replayed their encounter in her head. "She did mention the possibility, but I discounted her suggestion."

"Dr. Mason is an excellent physician, but she's sometimes baffled by deeper, conflicting emotions. She's very practical, you see. She didn't understand why you weren't acknowledging the pregnancy. I thought perhaps grief had colored your thinking. Mourning takes a great deal of energy, after all. Dr. Mason simply assumed that events would work themselves out. That your advancing pregnancy would eventually force you to confront the issue."

"She was right." Joy and confusion together in a confusing tangle of emotions. Anna was excited and terrified all at the same time. "What do I do now?"

There was a child to consider now. A new life inside her. She pressed her hand over her stomach, and a growing sense of wonder filled her heart.

Tears burned behind her eyes and she choked back a sob. Why now? Why after all this time, when she had no means to support a child, had God finally granted her the gift?

Anna blinked rapidly. "I don't know what to do."

Her future had changed in the blink of an eye. She wasn't just looking out for herself, she was solely responsible for the innocent life of a child. From this moment on, all her decisions hinged on what was best for the baby.

"You're recently widowed," Leah said.

"Yes, three months."

"I understand if you're overwhelmed, but I'm here to help. I don't know Russ well, but Daniel and Will trust him."

Anna didn't have to question Leah. She knew what the woman was leaving unspoken. It seemed everyone in town was playing matchmaker between her and Russ. Her throat tightened with emotion. "He asked me to marry him."

"What did you say?"

"I told him no. I told him that I couldn't have children." She brushed at the blanket Leah had draped over her. "He was being kind. We knew each other in Philadelphia."

"He's a good man. He wouldn't have offered otherwise." Leah plucked a handkerchief from her sleeve and extended her hand. "It's all right if you want to cry. Pregnancy has a way of muddling our emotions."

"I don't cry," Anna insisted, her voice trembling.

"And you don't faint either." Leah offered an indulgent smile. "I know it's a lot to think about, but you're not alone anymore. You have another life to consider."

A sense of wonder and hope filled her. The sentiment was quickly followed by a shaft of abject terror. Anna pressed her hand against her belly where her child was growing. She had no money to care for herself. How was she going to care for a child?

"Russ is extremely worried about you," Leah said. "I'd best assure him that you're all right. He's pacing divots in the carpets."

"Would you mind sending him in?"

"Are you certain? Take as much time alone as you need. You're welcome to stay here as long as you like. We've got plenty of space. You've had quite a shock, and I'm sure you have a lot to think about."

"Russ has been very kind to me. I don't want him to worry unduly."

"If you're not ready to talk about your condition, your secret is safe with me. I'll only assure him that you're not dying of some terrible disease."

"It's all right. I don't mind telling him myself."

"I think you're making the right choice." Leah stood and swept her skirts aside. "I'll be right back. Would you like me to bring you some dessert?"

"Not just yet."

Russ appeared a moment later, his hair disheveled as though he'd run his fingers through the strands dozens of times. His tie hung loosely from his collar, and he'd unbuttoned his vest.

"Are you all right?" He took the seat beside the bed. "You gave us all quite a fright. I wanted to send for Dr. Mason, but Leah said it wasn't necessary. Are you certain you don't want the doctor?" He stood again and jerked his thumb over one shoulder. "I can fetch her."

"I'm fine, Russ." She drew in a deep breath, knowing there would never be a better time than the present to share her secret. "Remember when I said that I couldn't have children?"

Russ frowned. "Yes."

"I was wrong. According to Leah, I'm expecting a baby."

She felt as though a tremendous weight had been lifted from her shoulders. Hiding her pregnancy from Russ served no purpose. He was her closest friend in town, and she needed all the help she could get.

Russ bolted from his chair. "A baby?"

"Yes. I'd been told by the specialists in Philadelphia that I couldn't have children. I guess they were wrong."

"Are you certain?"

"Yes. Leah is certain, and when I think of all the symptoms I've been having, everything makes sense. The fatigue, the illness, the cravings. Everything fits." She rested a hand on her stomach. "Leah thinks the baby should be born around November."

"That's a marvelous time to have a baby." He took the seat once more and folded his hands in his lap. "My offer still stands. I'll take good care of you."

All her doubts came rushing back. Deep in her heart, she'd known he'd renew his offer. He was a good man, and he wouldn't let her face this alone. But there were other considerations. "What about the baby? Can you love the baby?"

"Yes."

She hesitated. "I don't think you should make any hasty decisions."

Hiding her past was more important than ever. The life growing inside her deserved a future untainted by the sins of the father. Sadie had proven she could be trusted. This far west, there'd been nothing in the news-papers she'd seen, and she reasoned that as the story faded into the past, there were no doubt other scandals crowding the front pages back east. Perhaps with a new name, she'd be shielded from any rumors that might travel this way. Dare she hope?

At her momentary silence, Russ seemed to grow unsure. He leaned back, and his eyes seemed to darken. "You know, Anna, you don't have to settle," he said. "If it's not me, there are other men in town, good men. Any man would be blessed to have you as a wife."

"I fear you'd be the one who was settling."

What did she have to offer? Another man's child? He was far better off with someone else, but a selfish part of her wanted him all to herself.

"I don't want you to feel trapped." He stood and turned toward the window, appearing almost boyishly uncertain. She could picture him as a child, smooth-cheeked and whip-thin, his eyes still that enticing shade of hazel. After a moment, he turned back to her, and she saw the tentativeness in his eyes. "You've had quite a shock. But I think we'd suit. We get along well enough, don't we? And you used to like my jokes."

Her heart ached at his uncertainty. "I still like your jokes."

She should be the one trying to convince him, yet it was he in that role. She found it endearing. If she wasn't careful, she'd fall hopelessly in love with this man. She feared she was already balanced on the precipice. It was best, though, if she protected her heart.

"What do you want Anna?" he asked, a heartbreak-ing note of doubt in his voice. "What's best for you?"

"I don't care what's best for me anymore. I have a

child to think about. I have to do what's best for my baby. You understand that, don't you?"

He leaned closer, and she fought the urge to collapse in his arms. He was strong and powerful; he'd keep her and her child safe. She wanted to lift this incredible weight from her shoulders, if only for a moment.

"I think so." He took her hand, his thumbs turning comforting circles in her palm. "Tomasina was trying to tell me something at supper the other night. She kept saying that life was different for a woman. That your choices were harder. I think she suspected. About the baby."

Snippets of conversations came rushing back. "It seem everyone knew but me."

Perhaps Dr. Mason was right. Perhaps she'd been denying the truth to herself because she didn't want to face it. These past few months had been uncertain chaos. Her future had crumbled. But now…this was her chance to start over. This was her chance to erase the past.

Russ cupped her cheek. "Sometimes we're simply too close to the problem."

Her skin tingled beneath his hand, and her gaze dropped to his lips. Loving this man would be very dangerous, indeed. He could hurt her worse than Edward ever had. She'd walled herself off from her late husband and built a barrier around her heart.

Russ's kindness had the potential to wound her far more than Edward's cruelty. She couldn't bear being a disappointment to him. "I won't be able to work as much after I have the baby."

"You don't have to work at all. You never did. Let me take care of you. Let me take care of you and the baby."

She desperately wanted to say yes. She wanted to hand over her burdens for a short while. She wanted to share the weight of all her worries. She wanted to be free of this aching loneliness, if only for a short time. But if she said yes, she risked ruining everything Russ had worked for in Cowboy Creek. He wanted a career. What if he followed Will into the Senate? A sharp pain radiated through her chest. Philadelphia was too close to Washington, D.C. There were too many people who ran in the same social circles. She'd never be able to hide.

Then again, maybe he wouldn't even want her to accompany him to Washington. Perhaps he hadn't thought that far ahead. She glanced at him, and her heart sank. Of course he'd thought that far ahead. Much as her late husband had done, he was building a path, stone by stone, paver by paver. But that was a path she couldn't walk beside him. If he decided to go to Washington, could she stay behind in Cowboy Creek?

"I need to think," she said. "I want to do what's right for everyone, not just me and the baby."

"You don't need to make a decision right away, but you haven't been feeling well. The sooner you're able to rest, the better."

If it were only herself she had to think about, she'd refuse. But it wasn't just her own life she had to worry about now. She had another life to think about. A precious, innocent life. There was a chance her past might never catch up to her, and she had to take that chance. She had to take the risk for the sake of her child.

"Are you quite certain this is what you want?" she asked Russ, her eyes searching his. If he wavered, even for an instant, she'd have her answer.

"I'm marrying a friend," he said. "What else could I want?"

Love. Passion. Devotion.

All those things seemed like the foolish dreams of a naive girl. She had practical considerations now. She needed a safe place to raise her child. She needed a roof over their head and food in their bellies. Love and devotion were for romantic fools who hadn't yet learned the cruel ways of the world.

"If you're certain…"

"Yes," Russ said, his voice firm. "I'm certain."

"Then, yes," she said, her voice growing less tentative with each word. "I accept your proposal. I will marry you."

Before Russ could speak, she rushed to ask, "What do we do now? How does this all work?"

He reached out and patted her hand. "I can speak with the reverend first thing in the morning. Considering your condition, we should get married as soon as possible. You'll have to quit your work at the hotel immediately. I can't have you standing on your feet all day."

"But I have to give them notice. I can't simply walk away."

"I own a ten-percent share in the hotel. Which, technically, makes me your employer. As your employer, Mrs. Linford, I'm officially giving you the sack."

Events were moving too quickly, and her head was spinning.

Russ turned her hands over in his. "Would you like to meet my mother? Why don't you have supper with us tomorrow?"

"I would like that," she said, more to put him off than anything else. "How is your mother going to feel about another Darby sister?"

"She's going to be delighted."

Anna wasn't quite as certain, but she'd come too far to turn back now.

On impulse, she leaned forward and kissed him. It was a light kiss, a gentle brushing of her lips against his. He froze, and she knew he hadn't expected her to be so bold. She started to move back, but his hesitation only lasted an instant before he pulled her close. He wrapped his arms around her and cradled her against the solid muscles of his chest.

And then he was kissing her, too. His mouth felt sweetly familiar against hers, and kissing him was like falling into a wonderful dream. She buried her hands in the silky texture of his hair, reveling in the feel of him. She could have spent the rest of the evening kissing him and running her fingers through his coffee-colored hair.

Aware they were still guests of the Gardners, she broke the kiss first, though her hands lingered on his broad shoulders. "You could have anyone. Your choice of any girl you want. Why…?" She couldn't bring herself to say *why settle for me*.

"If I have my choice of any girl, then I choose you. You're my first, last and only choice."

He touched the side of her face and she pressed her cheek into his palm. For a moment, she almost believed him.

For just this moment, she'd pretend his words were true.

Russ stacked several books in a teetering pile and grasped a handful of papers.

His mother stood on a chair beside him and dusted a wall sconce. "Are you certain this is what you want? I don't know why you think you need to settle. You're a handsome, successful man. You can have your pick of women."

He was drawn back to the sweet, intimate kiss he'd shared with Anna, and a flare of heat coursed through his veins. She was his first, last and only choice, though he sensed she'd doubted his words. For the first time in his life, he felt as though he'd shatter if a woman walked away from him.

He didn't know why his feelings were this strong, this fierce, and he feared looking deeper into his reaction to her. He'd told himself the news that she was expecting a child was the reason for his intense feelings, but he'd known the instant she fainted in his arms that he didn't want to ever let go. He wanted to care for her and protect her in the hopes that someday she'd return even a portion of his affections.

"Let's face it, Mother, Adam is the handsome son," he replied.

"Your looks are compelling."

"That's very diplomatic of you." He turned in a half circle only to discover there was no place to set his paperwork. "But I'm not settling. You'll see when you meet her this evening."

"I realize she's expecting a baby, and I'm delighted for more grandchildren, but darling, you don't have to save everyone. What happened with your father wasn't your fault."

"You sound like Seth. He was lecturing me last week."

"You could do worse than listen to your brother. He's changed since he and Marigold married. I didn't realize how much your father's actions had affected you boys until recently."

Facing the wall, Russ froze. "If I had been further along in my law studies, he'd still be here. I never would have let him sign those papers."

A soft hand rested on his shoulder. "You don't know that. I don't believe your father made a mistake. I don't believe he borrowed money from that awful man. I don't believe he abandoned us."

"We have the paperwork." Russ turned and caught sight of the stubborn set of her chin. "I'm sorry. I shouldn't have brought it up."

His mother grasped a stack of books and slapped the edges together, straightening them into a rigid stack. "I don't mind speaking about what happened. Your father would never turn his back on his family. I knew him for twenty years. He wasn't that sort of man."

"Then what happened to him? He's not here."

"He's dead. I know it. He wouldn't sell the ranch, and they killed him because of it."

Russ loved his mother, but he didn't like the idea of her believing a lie. She'd never find peace if she was clinging to the past. "Ogden already owned the surrounding land. There was no reason for him to buy our ranch. There was no reason for him to kill anyone."

"Your father was a good man. He's gone. I know it in my heart. Just like I know that Adam is coming back someday."

"Then why haven't you moved on? You're still wearing a wedding ring."

She clutched her hand to her chest, protectively covering the ring in an unconscious gesture. "Move on to what? To whom? I already married the love of my life. I wear your father's wedding ring because I'll always be married to him." She glanced at her clenched hands and dropped her arms to her sides. "That's why I want more for you than a loveless marriage of convenience. Tell me this. Can you love her? Can she love you? You deserve those things. Marriage is tough enough when two people love each other."

He knew his own feelings. He could love her—he feared he was already falling in love with her. He merely wanted to give her time to adjust to all the changes. Maybe in a few years, she'd develop an affection for him.

"She's recently widowed. I can't ask her to love me this soon after losing her husband. Maybe in a few years."

"That's a very big risk you're taking, young man."

For the first time since last evening, doubts invaded his thoughts. His mother was mourning a man who'd been absent from their lives for nearly a decade. Was he selfish to even crave Anna's regard? He'd made his offer, and he wasn't going to retract it. He wanted a wife, a family. They got along well. Why ask for more?

His mother heaved a sigh. "If this is what you want, then I'll support you. After watching Marigold and Seth fall in love, I'm filled with romantic hope."

Russ pressed a kiss against the papery skin of her cheek. "Thank you."

"Why do you have all these books at home?" She balanced yet another teetering stack. "Don't you have an office for that?"

"I need more hours in the day. The business is growing fast."

"Then have Simon organize your paperwork."

"Simon will be back in school soon."

She haphazardly shoved a sheaf of papers together.

"Wait," Russ protested. "Those items don't belong together."

"Fine." She threw up her hands. "I was only trying to help."

"And I appreciate your assistance. It may not look like it, but I have a system."

"A very chaotic system." His mother rubbed her fingertips together. "I'll start dinner if you won't let me help with the paperwork. Just remember, you only have a few hours until your fiancée arrives. If you want to make a good impression, then I suggest you clean up. You'll scare her off if she thinks she's marrying an eccentric hoarder."

"I'm not a hoarder," Russ grumbled.

"On second thought, leave everything as it is. Perhaps she'll change her mind about you. Then you won't be attached forever to another Darby sister."

Russ grew serious. "I understand you have reservations, but I won't have you speaking about her that way. This is my decision, and that's final. If you can't respect that, then perhaps it's best you don't stay for dinner."

His mother's eyes widened, and he caught a hint of admiration in her stunned expression. "Well said, my boy. Well said." She grasped his hand and gave a comforting squeeze. "You have my apologies. But you can't blame me for being skeptical considering your last encounter with the Darby family."

"For the last time, Anna is nothing like her sister. You'll see for yourself when you meet her."

"We'll be dining on tins of peaches if I don't start cooking." She pointed to a spot in the corner. "Don't forget to dust the baseboards."

Baseboards? Since when did people dust baseboards?

Russ shrugged. He had other things to worry about, like figuring out where he was going to stash all these books and papers.

Exactly four hours following their minor tiff, Russ and his mother led Anna into the sparkling dining room. Mouthwatering aromas wafted from the kitchen, and his mother's best china decorated the table.

Anna paused on the threshold. "Are you expecting more people?"

"Just you, dear," his mother said from the doorway. "It's not every day one of my sons proposes. It's a special occasion."

Anna blushed. "Your son has been very kind to me since my arrival in Cowboy Creek, Mrs. Halloway."

"Call me Evelyn," she said. "I didn't get to spend much time with your family in Philadelphia."

"I'm afraid my father wasn't much for entertaining."

Evelyn pursed her lips. "How is your sister?"

Russ loudly cleared his throat. "Shouldn't you be checking on dinner?"

"I'm sorry, darling." Evelyn blinked. "I thought you were over the fact that she jilted you for another man, then expected you to take the blame for her actions. My mistake. You won't hear another word out of me."

"Take the blame?" Anna turned to Russ, clearly bewildered. "I thought you jilted Charlotte. She is rather a handful, after all."

"That's an understatement," his mother said beneath her breath.

Russ glared at his mother before taking Anna's hand. "You probably don't remember because you were very young. Your father wanted Charlotte to marry me, but she was in love with someone else. We thought we might blunt your father's wrath if I took the blame."

Anna appeared stunned. "I had no idea. I thought she eloped with her husband because she was heartbroken. That's what she told me." She sank onto a chair. "I believed her."

His mother had the grace to appear abashed. "I'm sorry, dear. I thought you knew."

Russ clenched his teeth and tilted his head. "Do I smell something burning, Mother?"

"Oh, yes, I'd best check on dinner."

As she disappeared into the kitchen, Russ knelt before Anna. "I'm sorry about my mother. She's very protective of my brothers and me, but she owes you an apology for speaking about your sister that way."

"Your mother doesn't owe me anything. I think there was a part of me that knew the truth all along. I admired Charlotte. I looked up to her. She was so beautiful, and everyone loved her. I wanted to be like her. I couldn't admit she had faults."

"It's natural you admired your sister. That's how it should be. Don't let this color your regard."

"She treated you poorly, yet you're defending her. Why?"

"She did the best she could. We're both older and wiser. I'm happy for your sister. I'm happy she found someone to love, someone who loved her back with equal fervor."

"Are you certain she's loved?"

"Aren't you?"

"I don't know," Anna said. "I haven't spoken with her since she eloped."

"Not once?"

"No. Father shunned her. Then, after he died, I don't know...everything happened so fast. I was married, and there wasn't time."

Charlotte had always been selfish and self-centered, thinking only of herself and her own needs. Apparently, nothing had changed. She had never reached out to her younger sister.

Yet Anna dearly loved her, and he had to respect that love. "Perhaps you should write to her."

"I wouldn't even know where to begin. I don't know where she lives."

"I can make some inquiries if you'd like. I still have mutual friends in Philadelphia."

"No!" Anna paled. "That won't be necessary. I can find her myself."

Nothing was going to plan. His mother had insulted Anna while inadvertently revealing the truth about Charlotte, and Anna was indicating that she didn't want his help finding her sister. Understandable, considering their past connection.

He stood and reached for her hand. "I want to show you something."

At the touch of her fingers on his palm, pleasure flared through him.

"What is it?"

"It's a surprise." He led her through the first floor of the house, pointing out the different rooms in an informal tour, waving at his mother as they passed through the kitchen and out the rear door. He pointed toward the side of the house. "I planted a rosebush."

"For me?" she asked, her voice filled with wonder.

"Yes. For you." Even before he'd proposed, a part of

him had been preparing, he realized now. He held up his thumb. "Even pricked my finger on a thorn."

"Thank you," she said. The beautiful green of her eyes shimmered with unshed tears, and his chest swelled. "That's the most wonderful thing anyone has ever done for me."

He'd plant a thousand rosebushes and suffer a thousand sharp thorns to see that look again. "You can plant whatever like. Especially pumpkins. I want plenty of pumpkins."

A single tear caught the last ray of light from the setting sun and sparkled a path down her cheek before catching on her chin. "I'm going to plant the most beautiful garden you've ever seen. I promise."

"Can you be happy here, Anna?" *Can you love me?* With the pad of his thumb, he wiped the moisture from her face.

"Yes." She pressed her hand over his, and warmth radiated between them. "What about you? Are you ready for an instant family?"

"Yes."

He leaned forward, aching to kiss her, but uncertain how to proceed.

The screen door banged open, and Anna turned toward the sound. His mother shielded her eyes with her hand. "There you are. Dinner is ready."

The moment broken, he pulled away. "We'll be right in," Russ called.

Anna offered him a shy smile. "I can't wait to plant more rosebushes."

"And I can't wait until my mother moves back with Seth."

Holding his forearm for balance, Anna rose on her

tiptoes and kissed his cheek. "Be nice. I want her to like me."

Tossing a last look over her shoulder, she skipped toward the house.

Russ's heart lightened. He must be doing something right. He hadn't seen her this happy since he'd known her in Philadelphia. He'd missed this side of her, and wanted to see more. Seeing her joyful smile was worth risking his heart.

She needed him, and for now, that was enough. Maybe later, she'd even come to want him, too.

Chapter Twelve

Filled with anticipation, Anna stepped into Dr. Mason's workroom. Marlys had arranged for her to meet Touches the Clouds that morning. Thankfully, Friday was her day off. Russ had insisted she quit immediately, but she'd ignored his order. She still didn't trust the future, and the more money she saved, the better off she'd be if something happened.

Dr. Mason showed her into the workroom. "Excellent timing. He's just arrived."

The doctor made the introductions, and Anna sat down across from Touches the Clouds. He was a small man, shorter than she was, with straight dark hair he kept in a long braid that dusted his belt. He wore faded denim pants and a threadbare chambray shirt topped with a beaded vest. When he shook her hand, his grip was light, and his fingers bent with rheumatism.

"The lady doctor says that you are interested in seeds," he said in a deep baritone, his diction precise. "I am pleased to meet a fellow student of the earth."

She blinked, covering her surprise. "Yes."

"You did not expect my excellent English. I was taught in a school back east."

Heat flushed her cheeks. "You're the first, um, Indian that I've ever met."

"I am the first Shawnee Indian that you have ever met," he corrected with a gentle smile. "Tribe is very important. I am called Touches the Clouds." He grinned. "My mother expected a taller son."

She liked him instantly. "It's a pleasure to meet you, Touches the Clouds."

"What questions do you have for me?"

"I'm interested in the indigenous plant life of the area. What seeds do you harvest each year? How do you store them?"

Touches the Clouds proved knowledgeable, and she soon lost track of time discussing various plants and seed types. Fearful she'd forget something, Anna hastily jotted down notes. Her pencil flew over the pages until her hand soon ached.

At least an hour had passed when the bell over the door chimed.

Dr. Mason peered into the room. "Russ Halloway is here."

"Russ?" Anna's hand fluttered to her collar. "I wasn't expecting him."

"He's here to speak with Touches the Clouds."

"Oh." Anna half stood. "How silly of me. I thought… Never mind."

"Don't get up on my account." Russ stepped into the room and tucked his hat under his arm before greeting the Shawnee. "Dr. Mason said you might have some information that could help me."

Anna sidled nearer the door. "I should be going. You two obviously have business."

"Stay," Russ said. "I was hoping you'd do me a favor. I need someone to take notes for me. The Shawnee have been having some trouble, and I'm investigating the matter. Simon says my handwriting is atrocious."

The idea of spending time with him left her feeling slightly breathless. "I'd be happy to help." She turned to a clean sheet of paper.

How silly of her, considering they'd be spending every day together once they were married. She'd best get control of her emotions, or she'd be hyperventilating like a schoolgirl.

Russ sat down and stretched out his legs. "I hear someone has been trying to buy your land."

"Trying to steal my land," Touches the Cloud answered, his tone flat. "He offered us a quarter of what the land was worth."

"Who?"

"A man named Maroni."

Anna glanced between the two men. She'd heard that name before, when Russ was speaking with Daniel.

"Let me guess," Russ said. "When you refused to sell, he tried to convince you that your land was worthless."

"He said the land would flood when the coal mining came. He lied. The land will not flood."

"Flood, you say? That's interesting. The dam broke over at James Solomon's place. He lost half his herd, and his feed crop rotted at the roots before the water receded. Sheriff Getman looked at the damage, and declared the breach an accident."

"That was no accident," Touches the Clouds said.

Russ sat up. His gaze intense, he leaned forward and planted his hands on his knees. "Are you certain?"

"There was no reason for the dam to break. There were no heavy rains. No beavers. Whatever happened was caused by man. Your sheriff did not inspect the dam properly."

"The sheriff isn't known for his thoroughness." Russ made a sound of frustration. "The damage was done weeks ago. Any evidence of foul play has long since washed away. In any case, I'll take a look for myself."

Anna glanced up and flexed the fingers of her writing hand. "What do you think happened?"

"I think someone is trying to buy land cheaply from the settlers, including the Shawnee, in order to charge Mitchell Coal & Mining Company a high price for the easements." He stood and leaned over her shoulder. "Can I borrow some paper?"

He touched her shoulder, and her pulse quickened. "Let me tear off a sheet."

She handed over the paper and pencil, and he sketched a map, then laid the paper on Dr. Mason's work table. "The Solomon property is here." He pointed. "And the Shawnee land is to the north. If Jason's coal mine sits in the middle, then these are the best places to build a road."

"Who owns that land?" Anna asked.

"My brother Seth, and he's not selling. Jason already knows that."

Understanding dawned on her. "Which means whoever tried to buy the Shawnee land wants to block the road."

"I've seen this scheme before," Russ said. "He'll

charge the mining company to use the easement, and make a tidy profit."

"Isn't Jason concerned?"

"He's not happy."

"Then we should speak with him. As soon as possible."

"My thoughts exactly. I don't care about his bottom line, but I do care about the people of this town. Whoever is buying that land is doing it on the sly and taking advantage of the ranchers. I should speak with Artie Henriksen. If the sale of his place hasn't been finalized, perhaps he can ask for more money."

Touches the Clouds pressed a hand against his chest. "Thank you. Your help is much appreciated by the Shawnee."

Russ extended his arm and the two briefly clasped hands. "If there's anything else I can do for you, let me know."

Touches the Clouds nodded and turned to Anna. "I look forward to your visit this afternoon."

"Visit?" Russ quirked an eyebrow.

"Touches the Clouds has invited me to tour the Shawnee land. I'm interested in their growing techniques and the seeds they've cultivated over the years. The land is owned by the tribe, and the seed collection is held communally. It's quite fascinating. I can't wait to see the varieties."

"I'll be happy to accompany you."

"That's not necessary. I'm sure I can find my way on my own." Although she had no idea how. She couldn't afford to borrow a wagon from the livery. She'd simply have to walk.

Touches the Clouds crossed his arms over his beaded

vest. "It is not safe for you to travel alone. It is best you bring your man."

"You can't argue with that." Russ puffed his chest. "You'd best bring your man."

The Shawnee stood and touched his forehead. "I will see you this afternoon. I will introduce you to my children, and we will share the evening meal."

"You don't have to do that…"

Her words fell on empty space. Touches the Clouds stepped out the door with his long, purposeful strides.

Russ chuckled. "It's best not to argue with him."

"Despite what he said, you don't have to feel obligated to accompany me."

"You'd be doing me a favor. I was hoping to speak with some of the other members of the tribe. There's a chance someone knows more about the man who was trying to buy the land. There's even a chance someone might have seen what happened to the dam."

"All right," she conceded. "As long as you have other business. I don't want to trouble you."

"It's no trouble, Anna. No trouble at all."

That breathless feeling took hold of her once more. He was so handsome and kind. She felt as though she was climbing too high, as though she was being granted more than her fair share of happiness. She felt as though she was living on borrowed time.

It had been so long since she'd been comforted by someone, she gave herself over to the feeling. Unable to resist, she wrapped her arms around his waist and nestled against his chest.

This time he didn't hesitate. He held her close, resting his chin on the top of her head. "Everything is going to be all right, Anna. You don't believe me, I know. But you'll see. We're going to just fine."

"Yes."

She desperately wanted to believe him, but she was afraid, too. Afraid of showing too much joy. Afraid of having her happiness snatched away. Everything seemed too good to be true, and she couldn't shake a sense of foreboding.

Nothing good ever lasted.

Russ took Anna's hand and assisted her into the wagon before taking the seat beside her.

He patted the basket he'd placed between them. "It's a long drive. I brought a snack."

"You didn't have to do that for me."

"I didn't." He chuckled. "I never travel without food. I eat every two hours, or I get cranky. You should know this about me."

"You do not."

"Every three hours, perhaps." He glanced at his companion. Her elegant features were flushed a becoming shade of pink. In the short time she'd been living in Cowboy Creek, her cheeks had filled out, and her eyes had brightened. "Cowboy Creek agrees with you."

"I've been sampling all of Deborah's desserts."

"I don't mean to gossip, but I've heard Preston Wells, the telegraph operator, is pining over Miss Frazier. I'm surprised she hasn't accepted a proposal yet. She arrived in town wearing a wedding dress, after all."

"She did not! You're teasing me."

"She absolutely did. You can ask anyone. Surprising then, that she hasn't been seen courting anyone since her arrival."

"Perhaps she's shy."

"Perhaps," he said.

They spent the next few miles talking amiably about the various people Anna had met since her arrival in town. Russ pointed out the notable landmarks along the way and spoke about his law practice. He even asked her opinion on a case. Something Edward had never done.

He indicated the horizon. "See that bend in the road? There's a lovely little pond just beyond the curve. It's the perfect place to stop."

Though she hadn't thought she was hungry, her stomach rumbled, and she didn't protest the delay.

Russ had thought of everything. He tamped down the grass and spread a plaid blanket over the surface. Next, he retrieved the picnic basket and two mason jars of lemonade.

He flipped open the basket and studied the contents. "Let's see what Mrs. Foster has packed for us. There's sure to be enough for a small army."

"Mrs. Foster? And here I thought you were toiling over a hot stove all morning."

He took her good-natured teasing in stride. "She mentioned that she'd spoken with the housekeeper at The Lariat. You haven't quit your job yet."

Anna plucked at a blade of grass, her gaze averted. "There's no reason I can't work until we marry. I have nothing else to do, after all."

"Would you consider working at the law office? Simon is swamped. The office is becoming disorganized."

She lifted her head. "Are you certain?"

"Sure. Why do you ask?"

"I assisted my husband once or twice, but he didn't like me being around the office. He said it didn't look professional, having his wife hanging about. I think I embarrassed him."

"You'd never be an embarrassment."

"Isn't there someone from town you can hire?"

"I'd rather have you," Russ said. "Simon isn't nearly as pretty."

She tossed the feathered head of a dandelion at him. "I'm going to tell Simon you said that."

"He'll only agree."

The breeze ruffled the prairie grasses and sifted through her hair. All the work that had always seemed pressing faded into the background. Russ spent so much time in the office, his head bent over a stack of paperwork, that sitting in the sun, enjoying a jar of lemonade, was pure luxury.

Anna stared into the distance, a hint of sadness in her expressive features.

"You're looking melancholy again," Russ said. "What are you thinking?"

"I was thinking that it's been a long time since I've looked forward to the future." She touched her stomach. "It's been a long time since I've felt this hopeful."

"I promise I'll do my best for you and the baby."

"I know you will."

Stretched on his side, Russ leaned his weight on his elbow and crossed his ankles. "It must have been very difficult for you, losing your husband at such a young age. You couldn't have been married very long."

She never spoke of her late husband, and when she did, her words left Russ feeling uneasy.

"Two years. After my father died, I felt adrift. I'd never had much of a plan for the future." She popped the head off another dandelion. "Charlotte wanted the fairy tale, the happily ever after. I was content with less."

She spoke as though she was picking her way through a field of nettles, trying to navigate carefully. That same sense of unease nagged him, drawing him back to his work with soldiers after the war. Some of them were beaten down and quiet, turning inward. Others were angry, and they lashed out. Their loved ones often had the same way of speaking around the wounded soldiers, as though afraid they might trip a live wire at any moment.

"I'm glad you're not like Charlotte," he said.

"Why?"

"Because Charlotte wasn't nearly as adventurous as you are. She'd have stayed in Philadelphia and found someone else to take care of her." An ant scuttled over his outstretched hand. "I don't mean to speak ill of your sister, but I'm happy you came to Cowboy Creek. I'm happy you took hold of your life and came west. I'm glad we were able to meet again."

"I never thought of it that way." She sat up a little straighter, as though surprised. "I thought everyone would think I was running."

"What does it matter what others think? Susannah stayed behind. Charlotte eloped. Only you took the initiative. That's a brave thing."

"I suppose."

He brought the conversation back to the topic he wanted to discuss, with another question. "Was your late husband in the war?"

She tore off a piece of bread and added a slice of cheese. "No." She laughed, a hollow, humorless sound that gave him chills. "His father was wealthy. Edward had an issue with his foot or something. You know how it was."

"I do."

People with enough money bought their way out of the war, leaving the fighting to the farm boys and the immigrants. They left the war to people who couldn't afford to bribe doctors and congressmen for waivers. He'd never had much respect for those folks.

"We should go." She tossed the bread aside and rose on her knees to gather the mason jars. "I don't want to be late."

"There's no rush." He rested his hand over her trembling fingers. "We can stay awhile and talk."

A lock of her hair fell loose, covering her eyes. "But I'm already keeping you from your work." She went to work packing the picnic basket.

He didn't mind the delay, but she'd obviously made up her mind. They gathered the rest of the food and Anna folded the blanket into a neat square. He assisted her into the wagon once more, carefully watching for signs of fatigue. Perhaps he should speak with Leah about how best to care for her in the coming months.

As he drove the wagon under a sunny sky, he saw clouds gathered along the horizon. In minutes, they passed a brick marker that noted the edge of the Shawnee land, and they rode for a while before seeing signs of dwellings. The Shawnee land rolled into the distance, beyond the creeks, reaching to the railroad tracks. The tribe had planted trees and cultivated crops, built houses and barns alongside more traditional dwellings. The settlement was a curious mixture of the old and the new, of the traditional and the modern.

Russ guided the wagon around the last bend. Touches

the Clouds had wanted to show Anna the communal barn where they stored the seeds each year, which wasn't far from the main lodge.

A familiar, saddled horse was tied to the hitching post outside the large communal building that served as the lodge. He recognized it as Jason Mitchell's.

"I was hoping to speak with Jason," Russ said. "I didn't expect to see him this soon."

"He's here?"

"That's his horse. I suppose I shouldn't be surprised he's visiting the Shawnee."

"Will he pressure them to sell?"

"Jason isn't like that. Still, it doesn't hurt to speak to the man. He might have some insight."

A flash of movement in the distance caught Russ's attention. "Did you see that?"

Anna followed his gaze. "I didn't see anything."

"I thought I saw a horse and rider." -

"Surely that's not unusual. We're very near the Shawnee settlement."

"Yes."

Yet something nagged at him. The Shawnee had a certain way of sitting in the saddle—tall and proud, their movements perfectly aligned with the horse. The man he'd seen had been wearing a hat as he hunched over the pommel of the saddle. Russ shook off the uncomfortable feeling. Probably it was nothing. A visitor or one of the younger men of the tribe.

Since the encounter on the road with the outlaws, he was reading something sinister into even the most mundane events.

He slowed the horses and steered toward a shady patch beneath a brace of poplar trees.

Jason Mitchell ducked through the doorway of the lodge and shielded his face from the afternoon sun streaming through the growing cloud bank. He caught sight of them and recognition spread across his face in a welcoming smile.

"Mr. Halloway," Jason called. "I didn't expect to see you here. And who's your lovely companion?"

Russ glanced between the pair. Jason was young, in his early thirties and a handsome, successful bachelor. The owner of the coal mine cast Anna an admiring glance, and Russ's stomach dropped. Was he selfish? Was he keeping her from the chance at finding love again? She'd agreed to marry him, yet he couldn't even talk her into lingering over a picnic on a beautiful day. He didn't know what to think anymore.

"This is Mrs. Anna Linford. My fiancée," he added without an ounce of regret. "Anna, this is Jason Mitchell of the Mitchell Coal & Mining Company."

"I believe I've heard your name around town," Anna replied.

"I see my reputation precedes me." Jason hooked his thumbs in his vest pockets and grinned. He caught the sharp glint in Russ's eye, and his smile faded a notch. "Pleasure to meet you, Mrs. Linford. Congratulations on your engagement."

"Thank you," Anna said, inclining her head.

Russ only trusted Jason to a point, so he asked sharply, "Bought any more land?"

"Not today, I'm afraid."

Anna's gaze flicked over Jason without any hint of interest, and the tension eased from Russ.

He'd taken Susannah's defection without an argument, and he'd even accepted Charlotte's change of heart with little more than an annoyance. But he'd fight for Anna, and it was best the rest of the single men in Cowboy Creek understood that—sooner rather than later.

Jason was tall and dark and strikingly handsome—and appeared to be well aware of his own countenance. His smile was charming and his demeanor sure. He was a man accustomed to having women fall at his feet, but Anna wasn't just any woman. The heart of a man mattered far more to her than the superficial trappings.

"You must call me Jason," he said, offering a wink that was probably meant to be endearing.

"Call me Mrs. Linford." Anna found the gesture annoying, and winked broadly in return, hoping he'd recognize the silliness of the gesture. "I don't want to be forward."

"You're from back east, I presume." Jason removed a silver case from his breast pocket and extracted a slender cheroot. "I detect a Pennsylvania accent in your speech."

Before Anna could reply, Russ crossed his arms over his chest and spoke up. "What's your business here, Jason?"

"What do you suppose?" He tapped the end of the cheroot against the case. "I wanted to see if the Shawnee were interested in selling their land. Much as you'd expect, the answer was no."

"You'll respect their decision?"

Jason's eyes widened. "That's an odd thing to say. Have I ever given you a reason to doubt my sincerity?"

Something very akin to anger flared between the two men. Anna glanced between them. They both had their hands on their hips, their chests puffed. Even with Russ sitting up on the wagon, the men reminded her of two bantam chickens pecking around each other in the barnyard.

"Not yet," Russ said, an edge of threat in his voice.

He climbed from the wagon and reached up for her. She expected him to take her hand, but he caught her around the waist, gently lowering her to the ground. When she would have stepped away, he kept his arm circling her waist.

Gracious, if she didn't know any better, she'd think he was acting like a jealous man.

Touches the Clouds appeared in the doorway then and splayed his arms in an encompassing gesture. "Welcome."

Anna stepped from Russ's proprietary hold and took his hand in greeting. "Thank you so much for inviting me."

Jason tipped his hat to the Shawnee. "It's been a pleasure doing business with you, sir."

"The pleasure is mine," Touches the Clouds said, then he motioned for Anna. "I will give you a tour of our seed collection."

She turned toward Russ, and he waved her on. "Jason and I have some business together. I'll catch up with you."

The owner of the mine raised his eyebrows but didn't dispute the claim.

Touches the Clouds motioned her forward. "Follow me."

The two of them made their way across the clearing to the enclosed barn. Painted red, the structure was built in the shape of an octagon with a domed roof that peaked in the center. Enormous double doors opened beneath a dormer hayloft.

He tugged open the doors and ushered her inside. "We farm as a community. There are twenty families who share in the harvest."

"You combine all your resources?"

"It is our tradition. We work and live together as a community, as did my father and his father before him."

The air inside the barn was heavy with the scent of hay and feed. Light shimmered through the vented opening at the peak of the roof. Grain bins containing seeds lined the walls, and an enormous table, almost like an altar, featured a carved wooden box.

"What's that?"

Touches the Clouds flipped back the lid and retrieved a leather pouch. "This is called the medicine bag. The bag contains the most holy of relics among the tribes of the plains. Though few men may hold the medicine bag, its power is sacred to the whole tribe. It is opened only on sacred occasions."

His tone indicated his reverence for the item, and she was fascinated by the tradition. "What holy relics does this medicine bag contain?"

"Each object has a spiritual meaning to the keeper. There can be animal skins or ceremonial pipes. Seeds or arrowheads. Some items are too sacred to name."

He replaced the medicine bag with equal reverence. She sensed he was honoring her by merely showing her the item, and she was awed by his consideration.

For the next twenty minutes, they toured the supply of seeds. Some of the varieties had been provided by the government's bureau of land administration, while others had been passed down through generations.

There was even a drought-resistant strain of maize the Shawnee had developed through the years. She desperately wanted a sample, but asking felt far too presumptuous. Speaking with someone who understood her passion for collecting and saving the different varieties of vegetable seeds warmed her soul.

"We have several fields planted," Touches the Clouds said. "We keep some of the seeds back from planting in case we lose the crops. The weather is uncertain. There are droughts and rains. Sometimes fire."

Touches the Clouds lifted a leather pouch from around his neck and knelt before the wooden bin containing the maize seeds. He scooped three large handfuls into the pouch and tightened a leather strap around the top. When he finished, he handed her the satchel. "This is for you."

"I can't. They're far too precious to your tribe."

He jostled the bag. "They are a gift."

She sensed refusing him would be an insult. Unsure how to respond to such a precious gift, she hugged the satchel to her chest. "Thank you. I'm honored."

She slipped the leather straps around her neck as Touches the Clouds had done.

He smiled, and his eyes crinkled around the edges.

"May I see the crops?" Anna asked.

If she was going to grow the maize, she wanted to see how a healthy plant should look.

"Certainly."

Touches the Clouds strode ahead of her, and she struggled to keep up with his brisk pace. He pushed open the door and exited without looking behind him. Anna turned and tugged closed the heavy doors. A flash of movement just inside caught her attention, and she paused.

She glanced over her shoulder and discovered Touches the Clouds had moved well ahead of her. She shrugged and finished closing the door. The barn was communal, after all.

Ten minutes later, sweat trickled from her brow and dampened her bodice. Though considerably older than her, Touches the Clouds had an endless supply of energy. She skipped to keep up as he strode down the neat lines of corn. He stopped, and she nearly collided with him.

He knelt and speared the dirt with his fingers. "We dig each hole and add a dead fish to nourish the roots."

The plants were young but healthy, and she marveled at the different varieties. The sun was barely starting to sink in the sky, and sweat trickled down her back. Her feet ached, and she was incredibly grateful that Russ had packed a picnic meal.

The heat was making her a little woozy, but she didn't want to halt the inspection lest Touches the Clouds think her rude. When his path led them back toward the seed barn once more, she slowed her steps and clutched the stitch in her side. The afternoon sun was sapping her strength.

They'd nearly reached the barn when the scent of burning hay teased her nostrils.

Touches the Clouds stopped and cocked his head. He searched the horizon and pointed. "There's smoke coming out of the barn."

He broke into a run. She secured her hat with one hand and caught her skirts with the other, rushing behind him.

Upon reaching the barn, he yanked open the door, and a wave of smoke poured from the opening.

Staggering back a step, he flung his arm over his eyes. His heel caught on the uneven ground, and he fell, his knee bent awkwardly. He attempted to rise but fell back once more.

Anna fished a handkerchief from her sleeve and covered her nose and mouth. She knelt beside Touches the Clouds and rested her hand on his shoulder. "Are you all right?"

His face rigid in pain, he merely held his knee with both hands.

Anna searched the clearing for any sign of Russ or Mr. Mitchell, but they were nowhere to be found.

"We need to move away," she said, hooking her arm beneath his shoulder. He was slight, but she struggled beneath his weight. "This way."

Together they staggered toward the lodge. When they reached the steps, he lowered himself onto the bottom riser.

The smoke poured thickly from the partially open door, and the fire crackled. *The medicine bag.* Fearing Touches the Clouds might try to stop her, she sprang to her feet and dashed toward the barn. She tugged the doors open wider and peered inside. The worst of the flames were at the far end of the barn. She had plenty of time to retrieve the sacred bag.

Taking a deep breath, she covered her nose with her handkerchief and scooted toward the raised table. Her eyes watered and she groped along the top until her fingers caught on the rough, carved surface of the box. Even in those few moments, the smoke had thickened.

Barely able to see, she grasped the medicine bag and

held tight. Pivoting on her heel, she started toward the exit once more. Smoke clouded the cavernous space and tears streamed down her face. Struggling for air, she made halting, awkward progress toward the door.

The space had gone black, and her lungs burned. Reaching out her hand, she encountered a solid wall.

Her heart hammered against her ribs. She'd lost her way in the dense smoke. The exit must only be five or ten feet away, but which direction? Sweat beaded her forehead, and the growing heat made her dizzy.

The fire crackled and popped, growing stronger by the moment.

She collapsed to her knees and felt along the floor. A sliver of light caught her attention, and she crawled toward the exit.

Her lungs screamed, and her legs would barely cooperate. She clutched the medicine bag and crawled toward the elusive light in the distance.

Chapter Thirteen

Jason and Russ stood at the bottom of the creek bed. They'd walked behind the main lodge to survey the valley Jason had purchased for his coal mining company.

"He's trying to buy up the land for the roads," Jason said bitterly after Russ explained what he'd learned. "I can't believe I was so blind."

"I probably wouldn't have found out either, except Simon discovered the deeds."

"Who is it?"

"Don't know. It's not public knowledge until the deeds are filed with the county. There's a man named Maroni flashing a lot of money in town. I'd check him out first."

Jason spun away. "Do you smell something?"

Russ tilted back his head. "That's smoke."

"There was nothing cooking when I was inside," Jason said, a note of panic in his voice. "We'd best check."

Moving quickly, the two men climbed the steep embankment. Jason shielded his eyes from the sun and searched the horizon.

"There!" He pointed. "It's the barn."

Russ caught sight of the flames licking the side of the barn, and his chest seized. They crossed the distance to the main lodge and discovered Touches the Clouds limping toward the burning barn.

He pointed. "She's inside."

Neither man had to ask who.

Jason started toward the building, and Russ caught the man's arm. "I'll go first. If I'm not out in ten minutes, it's your turn."

The other man reluctantly stilled. "She doesn't have ten minutes."

Russ offered a wry grin. "There's no use three of us dying today."

"I'll see to Touches the Clouds." Jason gave his shoulder a quick clasp. "God be with you."

Russ's heart skipped an uneven beat before a strange sense of calm descended over him. He shrugged out of his jacket and wrapped the fabric around his nose and mouth. Pausing outside the door, he gazed inside. Thick, black smoke poured from the barn doors and heat shimmered from the building. Opening the second door would feed the flames, growing the fire, but he needed the larger target for an exit.

He crouched to avoid the worst of the smoke as he entered. He shouted Anna's name, inhaling smoke and coughing.

Instantly blinded, he dropped to the ground where there was at least some relief. His hands probed the ground ahead of him and bumped against warm flesh.

"Anna!"

"Russ, I can't find the way out."

She coughed weakly.

His heart soared, and he slid his fingers down her arm till he clutched her hand. "Stay low, and I'll lead you out."

Heat singed his cheeks and he feared the roof collapsing. Lungs burning, he crawled toward the exiting plume of smoke. Once they'd cleared the door, he stood and scooped Anna into his arms. Fearful of the heat and flames from the burning building, he carried her a safe distance away before collapsing onto the hard-packed dirt.

Jason was at his side in an instant, a tin cup of water in his outstretched hand. Russ accepted the offering and pressed the cup against Anna's lips. Her eyes fluttered open.

"Drink," he ordered gruffly.

She took a long swallow before gasping and coughing.

Knowing she was alive sent a wave of emotion shuddering through her chest. He clasped her tightly in his arms, his eyes and throat burning, then rocked her back and forth.

"Why did you go into a burning building?"

She struggled away from him, revealing a leather satchel clutched in her hands. "The medicine bag. Touches the Clouds said the bag was sacred."

A bell clanged incessantly, sending his head throbbing. Soon dozens of Shawnee were jogging toward the building. A fire brigade formed and bucket after bucket of water tossed on the inferno.

Russ appreciated their tenacity though the effort was useless. Flames devoured the dry wood, and the barn collapsed inward, shooting plumes of smoke into the sky. Beams crackled and popped, exploding into showers of sparks.

Anna gasped and sat up. "There might have been someone else inside. I thought I saw someone in there earlier." Her eyes red, she blinked rapidly.

Gooseflesh raised on his arms. "How well did you see the person?"

"Not well. Just a flash of movement."

"As though he didn't want to be seen," Russ said more to himself than Anna.

She held her hands against her lips. "I hope he got out in time."

"I'm sure he did," Russ replied with certainty. The rider he'd seen earlier and the person Anna had seen were too much of a coincidence on top of the sudden fire. "Are you all right?"

"I'm fine." She swiped at her forehead, leaving a trail of soot. "The Shawnee seeds were in there. They've lost everything."

"But it's spring. Surely everything has been planted."

"They always keep a supply of seeds in case something goes wrong with the harvest. If there's a drought or a flood before the plants bear fruit, they'll lose everything. One of the varieties of corn is specific to the Shawnee." She gasped and clutched the satchel hanging around her neck. "Touches the Clouds gave me some. It's not much, but it can be used to rebuild a crop if the worst happens."

Russ gently rubbed the soot from her forehead. "No seed or medicine bag is worth risking your life. Promise me you'll never again run into a burning building."

She appeared suddenly shy. "I didn't expect the flames or the smoke to spread so quickly."

"Fire is like that."

"I'm fine. Go and help."

"Promise me you'll stay here. Don't try to rescue anything or anyone."

"I promise."

Leaving Anna, he joined the fire brigade, which was concentrating on containing the flames from the collapsed building. Jason joined a large group of men digging a fire trench between the barn and the main lodge in case a grass fire spread.

After another hour, their labors proved fruitful. The fire still burned, though not quite as strong, and they'd significantly reduced the risk of spreading.

The men gradually backed away, weary and resigned to the destruction. Despite her brush with the flames, Anna circulated among the thirsty men with a pail and scoops of water.

Russ watched her carefully, noting the signs of exhaustion, and elbowed Jason. "I'd best see to Mrs. Linford."

Jason mopped his forehead with his blackened handkerchief. "You're a fortunate man."

"More than you know."

He'd known the instant he'd discovered Anna was inside the burning building that he needed her. He'd do more than fight for her love. He'd die for her. She may not love him now, but maybe in a few years, she'd grow to love him. Until that time—if that time ever came—he'd care for her and the baby as best he could. He'd ease the burden from her shoulders and maybe even catch a glimpse of the carefree young girl he'd known before. Either way, he was doing the right thing by marrying her.

Her shoulders drooping, Anna had taken a seat on a low bench. He walked over to her and gestured beside her. "Is this seat taken?"

"I was saving it for you." She smiled at him but it was a fleeting glimmer. "If only we could have done more."

He sat next to her and wrapped his arm around her shoulders. "We'll help them rebuild. This fall, we can even help them gather more seeds. We can't change the past, but we can help build a better future."

She collapsed against his side, and he savored the feel of her. She trusted him, and he'd do everything in his power to assure her that trust was not squandered.

Touches the Clouds limped toward them, his shoulders stooped, the lines in his face deep. "This is a sad day."

"I've got something for you." Anna twisted and reached for the medicine bag, and presented Touches the Clouds with the bundle. "This is for you."

His hands trembling, the older man reached for the medicine bag. "Thank you," he said simply.

"You're welcome," she replied.

Jason trudged wearily toward them. Perspiration drenched his shirt, and he collapsed beside the bench. "This town is never short on excitement." He grinned, a handsome, engaging smile that probably made the girls swoon. "Or is it you, Mrs. Linford? Are you the source of the excitement? I seem to recall that you were involved in a shoot-out not more than a week ago."

Her cheeks flamed. "I was simply in the wrong place at the wrong time."

Russ glared at the man and stood. "We should be returning."

Anna stood, as well. "I'm so sorry about your barn, Touches the Clouds." She retrieved a pouch from around her neck. "At least we were able to save these. All is not lost."

She extended her arms, but Touches the Clouds put his hands over hers, dwarfing the small pouch. "You keep them safe."

Seeds. No doubt. She nodded, and her throat worked.

Russ placed a hand on the small of her back. "You're dead on your feet. You need rest."

Touches the Clouds gave a shallow bow and moved back toward his people, resting from fighting the fire. Jason shrugged into his coat.

"Do you need a ride back to town?" Jason asked.

"No," Russ replied, his tone clipped. "I'll see her back to town safely."

"Good." Jason whistled a merry tune. "Because I only brought one horse."

His hands in his pockets, he strode toward the hitching post.

Anna rolled her eyes. "He's quite the charmer, isn't he?"

"He thinks a lot of himself. I suppose he has a right. He's quite successful. He'd be a good husband for any woman."

"I'm not so sure." She tucked her hand into the crook of his elbow. "I prefer a humbler man."

"I can't think of anyone humbler than me."

"Really?" She laughed. "How humble are you?"

"I'm so impressively humble, I rarely even mention all my dazzling successes."

She paused, and he halted beside her. "Is something wrong?"

"I don't want you to regret your decision."

"You don't have to settle for me either, you know."

Her smile was tinged with sadness. "We don't think a great deal of ourselves, do we?"

"I think a great deal of you. And I'm going to spend the rest of our lives trying to make you see in yourself what I see in you."

"You'll be sorely disappointed."

He faced her and caught her hands, pressing them against his chest. "What did he do to you?"

She glanced away. "Who?"

"Your husband. Anna, I'm not a fool. I knew you before you married him, and I know you now. Something happened to that beautiful hoyden I knew back in Philadelphia. *Someone* happened to her."

Her chin trembled, and she refused to meet his gaze. "He's gone now. It doesn't matter."

"It matters."

"Why? You said it yourself, we can't change the past. We can only make a better future."

"Did you love him?"

"I could have loved him, if he'd let me."

A wealth of meaning infused her words. She'd told him all he needed to know. For now. She was not austere by nature. He simply had to find the key to set her free once more, to regain the vivacious nature she'd had before.

"All right." He had all the information he needed, for the time being. He'd known the instant he'd seen her on the road from Morgan's Creek that something had gone terribly wrong in her life. Now he knew what. "Then I guess we'll just settle for each other."

"It's agreed." Her relief at closing the subject was obvious. "I can't think of anyone else I'd rather settle for."

It wasn't much, but it was a start. He'd find a way to bring the light back to her eyes, even if it took the rest of their lives.

* * *

Anna paced the small church vestibule, the skirts of her borrowed dress fluttering behind her. A soft knock startled her from her troubled thoughts.

She answered the door to Seth's wife. Marigold was tall and slender with red-gold hair she'd rolled into an elegant chignon. Her cornflower blue dress brought out the delicate flecks of gold in her hazel eyes and highlighted the luster of her porcelain skin.

"Seth sent me to check on you," she said, her voice gentle. "Can I get you anything?"

"Nothing. I'm fine. How long before the ceremony?"

Marigold checked the watch pinned to her fitted bodice. "Ten more minutes."

"Thank you. For everything." Anna brushed her hands over her silk skirts. "For finding me something to wear. The railroad still hasn't located my trunk."

The dress was a delicate ivory confection of silk and lace with a pin-tucked bodice and full, billowing skirts. She'd forgone a veil and decorated her hair with a posy of flowers instead. Having been married before, the less formal arrangement suited her.

"If they don't find your trunk real soon," Marigold said, "have Russ talk to them. He'll make them reimburse you for the loss."

"I will. Where did you find something this lovely on such short notice?"

Marigold tweaked Anna's capped, flutter sleeve. "You can thank Hannah Johnson, the local dressmaker. She's married to James, who works at the stockyards. He takes the boys fishing sometimes. I'm babbling now. Hannah has been working on a collection of wedding gowns. She had several dresses in various stages of completion for just such an occasion. Given the town's growing population, her forethought was inspired."

Anna turned toward the looking glass and ran her hand along the modest, draped neckline. "Her work is exquisite."

"We're extremely fortunate to have such an accomplished dressmaker in town. I've only been living here a couple of months myself, mind you. But I've come to love Cowboy Creek."

"Did you come as a bride?"

"The schoolteacher. I never thought I'd find a place where I belonged until I met Seth. I can't imagine living anywhere else now."

The door creaked, and a tiny face framed by red-gold curls, the exact shade of Marigold's hair, appeared in the narrow opening. "Can I see the bride, Aunt Mari?"

"Of course you may," Anna spoke first. "What's your name?"

The door opened wider, revealing a young girl about the age of seven.

"My name is Violet," the girl answered shyly. She was petite and delicate with her aunt's hazel eyes and gentle speech. She wore a crisp white dress with a wide, pink sash tied around her waist and matching pink ribbons woven through her hair. "I'm wearing a new dress."

"It's lovely."

"Uncle Seth helped me pick this out. Daddy never bought me new dresses. I like this one the best of any dress I ever owned. Aunt Mari says I can wear it every Sunday for church."

Anna's heart melted. She recalled having the same feelings herself as a young girl.

Marigold draped her arm around the girl's shoulders with a grateful smile. "Violet has only just come to live with us. She's a little overwhelmed with her new brothers."

"I like Tate the best," Violet offered.

"He's the closest to her age," Marigold said. "I suppose that helps."

Anna knelt before the girl. "It's very nice to meet you, Violet."

The girl's expressive eyes blinked. "Before I came to live with Aunt Mari, I was with my daddy. I like living with Aunt Mari better. She took care of Momma and me before Momma died."

Marigold blushed. "My brother-in-law traveled a great deal when she was younger, and I'm afraid Violet didn't get to know him very well. He and Violet traveled together for a brief time after my sister died. But now Violet has come to live with us forever. My brother-in-law passed away recently."

Anna caught Violet's hands in her own. "My mother died when I was your age. My sister took care of me. We're both very blessed, aren't we, that we had someone to take care of us?"

"I love Aunt Mari. Is your sister coming to the wedding?"

"No." Anna sniffled quietly. "I'm afraid we don't keep in touch."

"Do you miss her? I miss my momma sometimes."

"I miss her a great deal, but I'm very fortunate. Since moving to Cowboy Creek, I've made new friends."

Violet glanced between the two women. "If you're marrying my uncle Russ, does that make you my aunt?"

"Yes." Anna's throat worked. "I'm delighted I'll be part of your family now."

Violet stuck out her lower lip. "You won't be delighted when you find the frog Harper has in his pocket. He said he's going to set it free in the church during the ceremony. The kissing part."

Marigold gasped. "He did not!"

Violet gave a solemn frown. "He might have changed his mind, but I don't think so."

"If you'll excuse me." Marigold pursed her mouth. "I'd best go check on the boys."

Anna stifled a grin. "That's quite all right. Violet and I will be okay together, won't we?"

"Yes, Aunt Anna."

Muttering to herself, Marigold briskly exited the room. "I'm going to tan that boy's hide if I find a frog in his pocket."

Violet and Anna erupted into peals of giggles. After a moment, Violet sobered. "I hope I didn't get Harper in very much trouble."

"I think you saved Harper from getting in a lot of trouble later, by getting him in a very little amount of trouble now."

The girl considered the declaration for a moment before nodding. "Yes. I think he would have been in much more trouble if he'd set loose a frog during the ceremony. During the kissing part."

Anna blushed and patted the fluff of red-gold curls. She was quite looking forward to the kissing part. Her pulse quickened, and her mouth went dry. Having kissed Russ once, she discovered that she quite liked the experience. She hoped he did, too. He seemed to anyway.

Violet threaded her hands behind her back and

rocked on the balls of her feet. Anna's heart went out to her. She recognized the hesitant uncertainty in the young girl's expressive eyes. She'd been much the same herself, all those years ago.

"Violet, I have a very special favor to ask you."

"What?"

"Do you know what a flower girl does during a wedding?"

"She walks ahead of the bride and scatters petals."

"That's right. Would you like to be my flower girl?"

"Yes!" Violet exclaimed. An instant later, her face fell. "But I don't have any flowers or a basket."

Anna considered the possibilities and snapped her fingers. "I know just the thing. Wait here."

She stepped outside and turned the corner, running headlong into a solid wall of male chest.

Russ grasped her upper arms and steadied her. "Are you all right?"

"Yes," she replied with a breathy laugh. "You?"

"Never better."

She could have stepped back and put some space between them. She didn't. She looked up at him. He'd trimmed his goatee and slicked back his hair. The delightful aroma of bay rum teased her senses.

A red rose peeked out from his lapel. She adjusted the stem and smoothed his lapel. "Where did you find the flower?"

"Shh." He held his index finger to his lips. "There's a lovely flowering rosebush just outside the back door."

"Do you think you could gather some more? I want Violet to be my flower girl."

"That's a marvelous idea."

"I think I saw a basket in the vestibule. Do you think

Reverend Taggart would mind if I borrowed it for a spell?"

"I'll give the church a generous donation. That should smooth any rough edges."

"Are you always going to be this kind to me?"

His expression sobered. "Always. You don't believe me, I know, but someday you will."

"Are you certain you haven't changed your mind?" she whispered, afraid of saying the words and afraid of leaving them unsaid. After today, there was no going back.

"Are you certain that you haven't changed your mind?" he asked.

"No turning the tables. I asked you first." A million doubts suddenly filled her heart. Would she ever be truly free of the past? "What if...what if something happened and you couldn't be mayor? What if you lost the election?"

He lifted one shoulder in a careless shrug. "I decided to run for mayor because the idea suited me at the time. There's nothing set in stone. There's nothing that can't be changed. If you'd rather I didn't, say the word."

"You'd do that? You'd step out of the race for me?"

"In an instant."

Like the petals of a flower unfurling in the morning sun, she felt as though her heart was opening. The scandal was a thousand miles away. Living in Philadelphia had given her a false sense of the scope. She'd existed in a tight-knit circle of petty, scheming people, and they'd colored her thinking. No one here cared what happened in Philadelphia. Sadie had kept the secret, and there was no reason to think the story was even interesting in Philadelphia anymore. By now, something else had stolen the headlines.

She was no longer newsworthy. She was no longer important.

Marigold careened around the corner of the church and gasped. "What are you two doing? You're not supposed to see each other before the wedding. Get back in the church, Russell Halloway." She flapped her hands. "Shoo!"

Ignoring his sister-in-law, Russ leaned down and kissed Anna's cheek. "I'll see you at the altar."

Anna's heart slammed against her ribs and breathing grew shallow. "I'll be the one in ivory."

Marigold dabbed at her eyes. "Stop it, you two. Weddings always make me cry." She hooked her arm through Anna's and led her away. "Come along. There'll be time enough for kissing after the wedding. You'll have the rest of your lives together."

Marigold released her once they entered the vestibule once more.

Anna paused. If she looked over her shoulder, and Russ was there, then she'd know he cared. With her heart pounding, she slowly turned her head.

He was there.

"Go," he ordered gently. "I don't want Marigold to tell me to shoo again. I feel like a schoolboy."

Pressure built behind her eyes and her throat grew tight. He cared.

This was actually happening. She was marrying Russell Halloway. She was going to have a baby. This time she was going to be happy.

Russ stood at the altar, his hands quaking. A joy unlike anything he'd ever known filled his heart. He felt as though everything in his life—all the pain, all the sorrow, all the joy—had led him to this moment.

He glanced at his mother, and she offered an encouraging smile. There was only his mother, Seth, Marigold and the children in attendance, and that's all he wanted. Anna had requested a small gathering, and he'd been happy to oblige.

This moment was for the two of them, and he only wanted the people dearest to his heart in attendance. The occasion felt more intimate, more solemn that way.

The double doors at the back of the church swung open. Marigold scooted through and slid down the aisle, taking her seat next to Seth.

Violet appeared next. She held her basket in both hands, concentrating on her task. As she started down the aisle, she dropped the first petal with delicate precision.

Then Anna appeared, and suddenly he felt as though he could conquer mountains. She was stunning. He'd seen her moments before, and yet he felt as though he was seeing her for the first time. He hadn't realized how soul-weary he'd become until she'd transfixed him. She'd stolen into his heart like the first breath of spring, giving him new life. He felt regenerated and invincible.

She approached, and he held out his hand, clasping her warm fingers. They stood side by side, and she leaned close, whispering near his ear. "Is this for real?"

He felt as he had the day of the fire, as though a soul-deep peace had washed over him, giving him a clear vision of the future. "I cannot imagine passing through this life without you at my side."

What had she said before? *I could have loved him if he'd let me.*

Russ would have no trouble letting her love him. No trouble at all.

Chapter Fourteen

Russ had arranged a cozy, private room in the restaurant at The Lariat for the tiny wedding party. The three boys, Harper, Tate and the youngest, Little John, huddled over a game of marbles in the corner. Much to Marigold's relief, Harper had only been teasing Violet when he'd claimed there was a frog in his pocket.

Violet took a seat next to her aunt Marigold, the flower basket still clutched in her hands. Anna hadn't had the heart to take the basket from her, and the reverend had cheerfully declined any compensation.

With everyone seated and the conversation lively, Anna caught Russ's attention and gave him a shy smile. She couldn't imagine a more perfect day. Even her stomach had cooperated. She hadn't felt a bit queasy all day.

Her new mother-in-law, Evelyn, turned to Marigold. "How are the plans progressing for the new library?"

"I'm starting to regret my impetuous behavior," Marigold said. "Everything is costing more than I expected. The books cost more. The furniture costs more. I don't know how we're going to pay for everything.

I can't ask the town founders for any more money. I sincerely hope Tomasina's fund-raiser is successful."

Russ leaned nearer to Anna and spoke low. "As a local teacher, Marigold has been helping transform Will's previous home into a library. Will sold the house to Daniel at a shocking discount, and Daniel donated the property to the town."

"So essentially they split the cost of donating the building?"

"Apparently."

Marigold heaved a sigh. "I was hoping to have the library open this summer, but we'll be fortunate if it's ready by Christmas if we can't raise enough money."

Seth wrapped an arm around her shoulder. "Everything will work out, darling, you'll see."

"I'd feel better if I could assist Tomasina on the committee. There's simply no time with Violet and the boys and school."

"I can help," Anna said. "I assisted with several community projects in Philadelphia."

Marigold's eyes lit up before her expression fell. "I can't ask you to do that. It's too much work. Too much of an imposition."

"I think it's an ideal way to meet people around town." She turned toward Russ. "Unless you have an objection?"

"I'm only worried about your health. A fund-raiser is a lot of work."

"I'd rather keep busy."

Evelyn planted her chin in her hand. "I'll help, too. I've been getting bored."

She'd moved back to Seth and Marigold's house in anticipation of the wedding.

"Then it's settled," Anna said.

Marigold brightened. "Tomasina has boundless energy, and we've already arranged for the food, but we're having trouble coming up with a theme for the event."

Evelyn tilted her head. "I'm worried that people have grown weary with the usual celebrations. We've already had two dances, a wild west show and a charity dinner in the past year. Do you think attendance will suffer?"

"Then we should think of something unique," Anna said. "Something unusual that will stir interest."

"Perhaps a charity bake sale," Marigold said.

Evelyn rolled her eyes. "Deborah would win all the prizes."

"True," Anna agreed. "There'd be no competing against Deborah."

Seth leaned back in his chair. "How about current events for inspiration? What's happening in the world today?"

Russ stood. "I'll get a newspaper from the front desk."

Anna's pulse quickened as it always did when the newspaper was mentioned, and she held her breath. He spread the pages over the table. Everyone leaned in. She quickly scanned the headlines and sat back in her chair, her pulse slowing. No news from Philadelphia.

She nearly laughed at her foolish worry. She felt as though she'd passed over a threshold. Worrying was an annoying old habit she'd have to work on breaking. As long as she kept moving forward, she could finally forget about the past.

Russ read aloud. "On May 10, 1869, the ceremony featuring a golden spike officially marked the meeting of the Central Pacific and the Union Pacific railroads, joining the east and west coasts by railroad for the first time in United States history."

"That's it." Anna snapped her fingers. "We'll have a transcontinental charity dinner celebrating the event."

"Seems fitting since the railroad is what put this town on the map," Russ said.

"At least the deal was finished before the Murdoch Gang started causing trouble." Seth groaned.

"We'll have everyone purchase a ticket for the event," Anna said. "Is anyone an artist?"

"I can draw," Marigold said.

"We can have each ticket represent a city along the path. Everyone can have their ticket punched when they enter the event."

Russ leaned closer and adjusted one of the flowers in her hair. "I'm afraid a rose has come loose."

"I should go fix that."

She stood, and he caught her hand. "Don't be long. I've ordered a very special dessert to celebrate."

A happy smile on her face, she slid shut the pocket doors to their private room and crossed the lobby. A skeletal-thin man in a black suit and dark hat sat on a bench. He lifted his head, and the brim revealed his eyes.

"Detective Latemar," Anna gasped. "What are you doing here?"

"You remember me." He unfurled from his seat, rising to his full, dizzying height. "You're looking well, Mrs. Linford."

He had a long, smooth face with graying hair, and his suit hung off his slender frame.

She touched her skirts. "What are you doing here?"

He glanced over his shoulder toward the clerk at the desk. "Perhaps we should speak in private?"

"Yes. Of course."

Her heart hammering, Anna ushered the detective into a small parlor off the main lobby and closed the double doors behind her.

Detective Latemar leaned one hip against an ornate buffet and studied the polished tips of his boots. "Finding you wasn't easy, Mrs. Linford."

"I'm under no obligation to you," she said, her voice firm. She wouldn't let him intimidate her. "I was cleared of any wrongdoing. I was under no obligation to inform you of my whereabouts."

"Professional courtesy then? Aren't you the least bit curious about who killed your husband?"

Her pulse jerked. "Then you've made an arrest?"

"Not yet, no. But I will."

"Then I'll read about it in the newspapers. He's gone. Finding the killer won't change anything."

"Aren't you afraid? What if your husband wasn't the only target?"

"No." He was toying with her. He'd done the same in Philadelphia, only times had changed. *She* had changed. "My husband was the one with the enemies."

"True, true. I've learned a lot about your husband over the past few months."

"I'm very busy, Detective Latemar. If you have nothing to add, I'll be going."

He casually slid before the door, blocking her exit. "My mother passed away two weeks ago."

"I'm very sorry for your loss, but that has nothing to do with me."

"She lived in Wichita. I came home for the funeral.

I knew you borrowed a train ticket, but I lost the trail. I saw your name in the papers. An encounter with out-laws. Did a little checking in Wichita. Found your name and your transfer."

"Here I am, Detective Latemar." She splayed her hands. "If you don't have any new information, I'll be going."

"I said I hadn't made an arrest." He grasped his lapels and leaned against the closed doors. "I didn't say anything about new information."

She wasn't falling for his bait. "Goodbye, Detective Latemar."

"Nice dress you're wearing. Special occasion?"

"I was married this morning. If you don't mind, I have guests waiting."

There was no use hiding. He'd find out the truth sooner or later.

"I'm happy for you. I truly am. I discovered quite a bit about your husband. Don't think I'd have liked him if we'd met. Some people get what's coming to them. But you, you I like, Mrs…"

"Halloway."

"You I like, Mrs. Halloway. I'm not here to hurt you, but I think you might have some information that could be useful to me. Since I was only three hours away, I figured I'd visit you in person and search your memory."

"I've told you everything I know."

"Did your husband ever mention a man named Fair-fax?"

"No."

"He was having an affair with his wife."

The sting barely registered. "My husband had many affairs. I chose not to keep track of them."

"Did Mrs. Fairfax ever contact you?"

"Never." Voices sounded in the lobby. "I can't stay long. I'll be missed."

He moved away from the door. "Yes. Your wedding day."

She paused beside him. "I don't want my husband to know about this."

"I'm in town for a few days. If something comes to mind, I'll be staying at The Cattleman."

"I want to help you. Truly. But I don't know anything."

"You don't have to be afraid of me, Mrs. Halloway. I'm here to help you."

She threw back her shoulders. "My husband wants to run for mayor of this town. How well do you think he'll be received if the local newspaper discovers that his new wife was once a suspect in her late husband's murder?"

"Politics is a tricky bedfellow."

"Then you understand."

"The best way to clear your name is by catching the true killer."

"That's your job, isn't it? You've questioned me. You've splashed my name across the front pages of the Philadelphia newspaper. Your investigation drove me from town. If I knew who killed my husband, you'd be the first person I'd tell."

He retrieved a letter from his pocket. "Do you recognize this handwriting?"

She tossed a cursory glance in the direction of the handwriting. "That's Edward's."

"He sent this letter to Mrs. Fairfax. He was severing his relationship with her."

"What does that have to do with me?"

"A woman scorned. The classic motives are always the most universal."

"I don't recognize the name. I don't remember ever meeting the woman. Where is she now?"

"That's the thing. She's disappeared, Mrs. Halloway. You see, your husband's letter wasn't very gentle. He'd decided to focus his attention on his wife. On you."

"He was lying. He was like any other man trying to escape a difficult situation. He was lying to get himself out of a tight corner."

"According to her friends in Philadelphia, Mrs. Fairfax was acting rather agitated in the weeks before she vanished." He pinned her with his direct gaze. "If she's still after revenge, she may come for you."

"Why? She has no reason to come after me. Especially if she killed Edward."

"I learned a long time ago that logic never applies to the human heart, Mrs. Halloway. Tell your husband what happened in Philadelphia. Soon."

Her ears buzzed, and her vision blurred. "No. He doesn't deserve this. He doesn't deserve any of this."

"You misunderstand me. I don't believe you're deliberately concealing something. I think you may have a vital piece of information, and you don't realize the importance. It could be anything. A name your late husband mentioned in passing, perhaps. An item in his possession that seemed out of place. You assisted him at his law practice. Perhaps you overheard something. Something that didn't seem important at the time."

"I saved nothing of Edward's. Nothing. His family wasn't very welcoming of me after you named me as a suspect. The debtors took everything of value after he died. I donated his clothing and personal items to charity. I gave him a Christian burial, and I left God to pass judgment. I can't help you, and you'll only harm me if you stay. You said you liked me, so go. That's the best thing you can do for me."

"Think about what I've said, Mrs. Halloway."

"Anyone who knew Edward knew that I meant nothing to him. There's no reason for anyone to harm me. I have to go now. I have guests."

"Then let me be the first to offer you my congratulations."

"Thank you, Detective Latemar." She touched her stomach. She had the future of her family to consider. She had to be strong. For Russ. For her child. "I know you're driven. I know you won't stop until you solve the case, but if you approach me again, I'll have you arrested for harassment. Do you understand?"

"Yes."

"Good."

She stepped from the room and pivoted on her heel. The detective remained standing just beyond the threshold. She slid the doors closed and turned her back on him.

She wasn't afraid of him any longer. She even trusted that he'd find the killer. She didn't care either way. What was done was done. He was her past.

Russ was her future.

The afternoon of the fund-raiser, Russ felt as though he no longer recognized his normally calm, cool and collected wife. She spun around the house, a whirling dervish of chaotic energy.

She thrust a basket into his hands. "Can you load this in the wagon?"

"Yes. Is there anything else you'd like loaded?"

"All the boxes on the porch."

"Done."

She paused, slightly breathless, a sheen of sweat on her forehead. "Already?"

"Yes." He placed his free hand on her shoulder. "Relax. Everything is going to go splendidly. The weather is perfect. The planning committee has done an impeccable job. The fund-raiser is going to be a raging success."

"Do you really think so?"

"I know so. Now relax and enjoy the party. We'd best go, or we'll be late."

"Late?" she exclaimed. "What time is it?"

"Time to leave." He took her hand and led her gently but urgently toward the door. "You're going to give yourself an apoplexy."

She took a deep, gusty breath. "This is the first time I'm going to meet many of your friends and business associates. I want everything to be perfect."

"And everything *will* be perfect. Don't worry."

Though he worried about her health, he enjoyed seeing the fire of excitement in her brilliant green eyes. The first hesitant steps of their marriage were progressing quite nicely, though he always sensed she was holding something back from him, keeping something just out of his reach.

He did his best to erase whatever sad memories she had of her first husband. He encouraged her hobbies and sought her opinions—even her passion for seeds and gardening was contagious. He'd come to appreciate the miracle of growth from the tiny seedlings.

Though he'd always admired her looks, something about her had changed. "You look more beautiful every day."

She blushed becomingly. "I already had to let out the waist of this dress."

He pressed his hand against her stomach, marveling at the even greater miracle of life. "When will you feel the baby move?"

"Leah said between four and five months." She pressed a quick kiss to his cheek. "We'd best be going."

He brushed the spot with his fingers. She was growing bolder each day, and he liked the change.

She stepped onto the porch and spun around. "The wagon is gone!"

"I delivered everything earlier. Half the town is already crowded outside the new library. There's no room for another wagon. We can walk the distance if you're up to it." He dangled the basket on one arm and held out the other to Anna.

She hooked her arm through his. "I'd enjoy a walk."

They made their way toward the town. Before they'd reached Eden Street, they were already rubbing elbows with jostling crowds of people.

Beside him, Anna's grin was wide and infectious. "The whole town has turned out!"

"Yes," he agreed. A gentleman and his wife approached them, two young girls in tow. The man caught his eye in recognition. Russ drew Anna aside, and the man and his family joined them. "Anna, I'd like you to meet Noah and Grace Burgess and their daughters, Abigail and Jane."

Noah Burgess wasn't overly tall, but he was solidly built with wavy blond hair that seemed a little long and piercing blue eyes. Scars from a burn he'd gotten in the war covered part of his face, disappearing beneath his shirt. His wife was petite and delicate with wavy dark brown hair and red highlights that caught the afternoon sun and golden-brown eyes. The girls were seven-year-old twin replicas of their mother.

After the round of introductions was made, Russ added, "Along with Will and Daniel, Noah is one of the town founders."

Noah brushed off the title with a self-effacing gesture of his hand. "Pleasure to meet you, Mrs. Halloway. Thanks for all your hard work on the fund-raiser. I keep up with the town council, and they're quite impressed with you."

Anna drew up taller. "Thank you. It's been a pleasure."

The two families separated, and Russ used his superior height to navigate them through the throng. By the time they reached the library, an enormous crowd had formed on the front lawn. From the makeshift stage, Reverend Taggart gave a blessing, and Tomasina opened the festivities with a rousing speech that had everyone in peals of laughter.

The redhead stepped aside, and a group of Shawnee and Seneca Indians in full tribal costume appeared. Each of the groups performed a ceremonial dance to the delight of the crowd.

Russ directed Anna's attention to a group of people beside the stage. "Looks like Minnie and Millie have found love."

The two girls were talking and giggling with two men. Three children sat on the grass at their feet.

"Who are they?"

"The dark-haired man holding the banjo is Freddie Simms, and that's his brother, Billy. Billy is a widower who owns a ranch on the outside of town. Those are his kids, Dwight, Frank and Jenny."

Judging from the smitten looks passing between the brothers and the cousins, there'd be two more marriages before long.

Anna giggled herself. "I can't believe those two are going to marry brothers. Could anything be more perfect?"

"I hope the Simms brothers are prepared," he said. "Come along, we'd best deliver this basket to the barbeque." They passed a gentleman with a striking brunette clinging to his arm. "That's Buck Hanley and Molly Delaney. Buck was the sheriff in town before he left the job to open his own business. Molly had her eye on Seth before Marigold."

"I thought Sadie had her eye on Seth."

"Everyone loved Seth."

She tugged on his sleeve. "Not everyone."

His heart did a little flip. "Speaking of Sadie, there she is now."

The buxom lady strode toward them on the arm of a fellow holding a camera box hitched over his shoulder.

"Anna, have you met Walter Kerr? He's the town photographer." As Russ introduced them, he felt Anna stiffen beside him. "Is there something wrong?" But she merely shook her head.

Walter adjusted the enormous camera box on his

shoulder. "If you like, I can take your picture. A belated wedding photo."

Sensing something amiss with Anna, Russ said, "Maybe later."

When the couple dissolved into the crowd, Russ turned to Anna. "Is everything all right?"

Anna squeezed his arm to her chest. "Everything is fine. Let's watch the canoe races after we drop off the basket."

The rest of the day passed in a flurry of activity. Russ worried about Anna, but she appeared to be energized rather than fatigued by all the activity. There was a strength contest where men took turns pounding spikes into a mock railroad tie, and crossing signs directed the crowds. Different stations had been set up, and Anna had her ticket punched at the 'Omaha' stop before moving to the next town on the transcontinental railroad line.

As the sun set low on the horizon, the stage was taken by the band, including banjo player, Freddie Simms. When the band struck up a slow tune, Russ took Anna's hand. "May I have this dance?"

"Yes," she replied, her voice slightly breathless.

He spun her gently to the dance floor. "I like the new dress."

She'd donned a peach calico dress with lace at the sleeves and collar. "Hannah Johnson is the seamstress. She's quite good."

He pressed her closer, his hand around her back, his other hand clasping hers. With her close like this, the scent of the rosewater rinse she used on her hair teased his senses. This morning, she'd brushed it out before the stove, and the sight had caught him unaware. He'd lingered in the doorway, longing to feel the silky tresses beneath his fingers. He'd scooted into the shadows before she'd caught him staring.

She hadn't married her late husband because she loved him. He hadn't been kind to her, that much Russ knew.

She stumbled, and he righted their steps.

"I'm sorry," she said. "I never had much of a chance to dance."

"Not even when you were married?"

"Especially when I was married," she said, her tone filled with bitterness.

Another thought occurred to him, and he halted on the dance floor. "Did he hit you?"

"No." She glanced around. "Keep dancing. People are watching us."

A weight dropped inside him, a spiraling downward sensation. The tight knot in his chest eased somewhat. Unbearably relieved, he forced his feet into the familiar pattern, concentrating on the feel of polished cotton beneath his fingertips. He needed to know what happened with her husband if he was ever going to break the barriers standing between them. He knew that with a sudden clarity.

"I'm sorry," he said. "I had to know."

"Why? What does it matter now?"

Russ guided them toward a quiet part of the dance floor. "I always feel as though you're hiding something. As though you're keeping a part of yourself hidden from me."

"You know everything to know about me. I'm from Philadelphia. I have a sister. I'm a widow. I'm going to have a baby."

"We're going to have a baby. We're a family now."

She smiled. "Thank you. Thank you for saying that."

"Why are you always surprised when I'm kind? I'd never hurt you or the baby. You know that, don't you?"

Straining away, she glanced over her shoulder. "I know."

"Then what happened to you? You're not the girl I knew." Something twisted in his chest. "I thought I could be patient. I thought I could wait months and even years for a glimpse of that girl, but I was wrong. There's a part of you that's closed off to me, and I want to know why. Is it because of what happened with me and Charlotte?"

"No," she replied, her voice thick. "It's not that."

"Then what?"

"I'm trying to do everything right. Tell me what I'm doing wrong, and I'll fix it. I promise."

The desperation in her voice shattered something inside him. "You don't have to fix anything. Not for me."

They'd made their way to the side of the dance floor, and she broke away from him, pacing the darkness between the stage and the side of the new library. "Are you disappointed?" she asked.

"In what?"

"In me."

"How can you even ask that?"

"I thought we were having a nice time." She pressed a fist against her mouth. "Why do you want to know about him? I don't want him to be a part of our lives."

"He is part of our lives, as long as you let him be. I know he's here, between us. You tiptoe around me like you're afraid of me, and I've done nothing. I've done nothing to make you feel that way."

"I'm not afraid of you," she said, her voice no more than a whisper.

"But you don't trust me."

She rubbed her palms together. "Have you changed your mind?"

He scratched his head and turned in a frustrated circle. "About what?"

"About me."

"No." He caught her shoulders. "Of course not. Where did you get that idea?"

"The way you were talking just now. I'm trying, really I am. I shouldn't have worked on the fund-raiser. I didn't realize how much time it would it take. I'm not as tired anymore either. You'll see everything will be different." Tears shimmered in her eyes, and her voice sounded tight when she added, "It's not you. I promise."

"Then what can I do differently?" He was desperate to reach her.

"Nothing." She covered her face with a sob. "I'm sorry."

He took her in his arms and hugged her against his chest. "Shh. I'm sorry. I don't know what's wrong with me. Forget I said anything."

Her fingers trembled in his. "Can we dance some more?"

"Absolutely." He cradled her face in his hands and wiped away her tears with the pads of his thumbs. "Just please don't cry."

"I'm sorry."

"Why do we keep saying that to each other? What are we sorry for?" He tucked two fingers beneath her chin and met her watery gaze. "Nothing you could ever tell me would change the way I feel about you."

She turned her face up toward his, an invitation if ever he'd seen one. Russ surrendered to the temptation. Lowering his head, he kissed her softly.

The music swirled around them, and they drifted to the dance floor once more. Dancers crowded nearer, and his thoughts swirled. He wondered about the man she'd married, the man who'd scared her off men, and a white-hot rage filled his soul.

He'd thought she might grow to feel something for him, but he was only driving her away. He was falling hopelessly in love with Anna. He was falling in love with her, and his love was driving her further away.

A feeling of emptiness and yearning gaped in his chest. He had the uneasy sensation she'd just told him goodbye.

Anna tugged her wrapper around her shoulders and slipped onto the porch. She closed the screen door behind her, making sure the hinges didn't squeak.

Moonlight glinted off the dew-covered grass, illuminating the path. Her bare feet padded over the soft grass. She knelt before the rosebush and plucked the single bloom from the leafy bush. Returning inside, she carefully trod up the stairs and tiptoed past Russ's room and into her own.

She feared she was falling in love with him, and she feared what that meant. She recalled their kiss that afternoon, and the way he looked down at her right before he captured her lips. That was how she wanted to remember him. Gazing at her as if she was the only bloom in a barren desert.

She'd picked the rose to remember the day. Now she

tucked the flower between the pages of a thick book and pressed the cover shut.

He deserved the truth. He was right, they couldn't go on living with walls between them. He deserved more than she could give him. She'd hurt him this evening. It devastated her to think she could hurt such a kind and loving man. Of all the regrets she had in her life, hurting Russ stood above the rest.

She'd tell him. She'd tell him and face the future without the past haunting her. If he was ashamed of her, then so be it. If he never wanted to see her again...

At that thought, she felt as though her soul was being ripped from her body. Pressing her hand against her stomach, she choked back a sob. When he returned from work tomorrow, she'd tell him the truth.

No matter the consequences.

Chapter Fifteen

Russ propped open the door of his office to take advantage of the temperate spring weather and resumed his place behind the desk. In his effort to clean up his house for Anna, he'd brought all his papers from home. They remained in a haphazard stack near the door. He had vague plans of organizing them later, when business slowed, though he doubted he'd ever see that day.

A tall, gaunt figure darkened the doorway, and he glanced up. "May I help you?"

"I was hoping you might," the man said.

Russ motioned him toward a chair set before his desk. "Have a seat. Can I get you something? A cup of coffee?"

"No, thank you." The man folded his tall frame onto the seat. "I was hoping to speak with you about your wife's late husband."

In the outer room, Simon glanced up from his paperwork. He looked between the two men and cleared his throat. "I have some business at the register of deeds. Best get it done before they close for lunch."

He stood and donned his coat, silently closing the door behind him.

Russ folded his hands over his stomach and leaned back. "I'm afraid I can't offer you any help, Mr..." He let his voice trail off.

"Detective Latemar."

Though surprised by the title, Russ kept his expression neutral. "I never met my wife's late husband."

"Has she told you anything about him?"

Russ's scalp prickled. "I don't have time to play games, Detective Latemar. Say what you have to say and leave. As you can see, I have stacks of work."

"Your wife wasn't concerned about finding her late husband's murderer, but I was."

"He was murdered?"

"You look surprised, Mr. Halloway."

Russ suppressed a muttered oath. "If you have nothing else to say, good day to you, sir."

"Mr. Linford was killed in a very public, very shocking fashion. A woman was observed fleeing the scene." The detective rose from his chair. "You can imagine the list of suspects."

Russ was a lawyer. He knew full well what the detective was insinuating. In a crime of passion, the police always looked toward the spouse.

"You don't believe for an instant she killed her husband," Russ said. It was a statement, not a question.

"Not after I met her. But I'm a detective, Mr. Halloway. I have to follow the rules. Most people think of the spouse first."

Russ didn't know the details, but he knew something had gone very wrong in Anna's life. Regret squeezed his chest. He hadn't realized her husband had been murdered. No wonder she'd been skittish and afraid. He certainly didn't believe she'd had anything to do with his murder, but the tale was salacious. People talked. People speculated. And Anna had no doubt been at the center of that gossip.

He wanted to rush home and gather Anna in his arms, but he held himself in check. The detective was here for a reason. He had to figure out why.

Before he could question his visitor, the man spoke. "I had a few suspects. There were several mistresses." He flipped back his coat, revealing his gun holster, and put a hand on his hip. "But I couldn't prove anything. My prime suspect had disappeared, you see."

Mistresses. Plural. Everything fell into place. Anna's marriage had been miserable. She'd suffered, and instead of giving her time to heal, he'd pushed her—into marriage, into talking about the past. A past she probably wanted to keep buried.

"Then find your suspect," Russ said, refusing to show the detective his riotous emotions.

"She's dead." Detective Latemar studied the spines of the books perched on Russ's barrister shelf. "Killed herself. Found out this morning. Thought Mrs. Halloway should know."

"Then why tell me?"

"Because I can't prove anything. The woman took her secrets to the grave. I'll never be able to prove it, but for me, this case is solved."

Russ stood. "Then go back to Philadelphia and close the case."

"I can't. I don't have proof. It will always be out there—the suspicion about your wife. Thought you should know. Rumor around town has it that you're running for mayor."

Russ leaned back in his chair and clutched his head in his hands. He felt as though a fog had lifted and everything was suddenly crystal clear. Anna had only married him when she'd discovered she was pregnant, when she was alone and desperate. She'd kept him at arm's length because she hadn't wanted to hurt him. She was keeping her distance, just in case.

She'd been trying to protect him the whole time.

The detective cleared his throat. "You all right, Mr. Halloway?"

He looked up. "Why are you here? Why are you telling me all this?"

Detective Latemar adjusted his gun belt, then leaned forward and braced his hands on Russ's desk. "I like what I've heard about you around town. I wasn't going to speak with you originally. Your wife asked me not to. But I like Mrs. Halloway, too. She didn't deserve that fool. I think I made the right choice in coming here. I think maybe she deserves you."

"I don't deserve her."

He'd made so many mistakes along the way. Why hadn't he been more patient? Would she ever forgive him? Could she ever love him?

"Yep." Detective Latemar grinned. "I did the right thing coming here." He turned and walked to the door, then paused as he grasped the door handle "Tell Mrs. Halloway the case is closed. Tell her that I'm sorry I couldn't do more. Tell her..." The detective hung his head. "Tell her I'm sorry I failed her. I wanted to clear her name, but I'll never have the proof."

He turned his head, and their gazes met. An understanding passed between the two men.

"I'll take care of her," Russ said.

"I know you will." With that, the detective left.

Russ stared at the door for a long moment before swiveling in his seat. He thumbed through the stack of papers. He'd nearly reached the bottom when he found the item he'd been seeking.

He spread the newspaper across the desk—the *Philadelphia Morning Post* his friend had sent some months ago—and searched the headlines. When nothing relevant appeared, he thumbed through the pages to the obituaries, but there was no Linford listed. He'd nearly given up when a headline caught his attention: Case of Murdered Lawyer Remains Unsolved.

He skimmed the article before sitting back in his chair once more. Rubbing his nose with his thumb and forefinger, he read the article again.

Digging through his desk drawer, he retrieved a tin of matches and set the corner of the newspaper on fire. He dropped the flaming bundle into the metal wastepaper can and watched it burn.

Simon strode through the door and skidded to a halt at the sight of the fire. "What's that?"

"The past," Russ said quietly. "The past."

Anna answered the knock on the door and discovered a train porter wearing a sharp green uniform and matching cap. "Mrs. Linford?"

She exhaled her frightened breath. For a moment, she feared Detective Latemar had returned.

"It's Mrs. Halloway now."

"I have a trunk for you, ma'am. I tried to deliver it to the hotel, but they said you were staying here."

Anna glanced behind him and noticed her trunk for the first time. "Finally! I was starting to think I was never going to see it again."

"Sorry about that, ma'am. Someone forgot to take your trunk off the train in Cowboy Creek. This thing has been to California and back."

Anna shook her head. "It's quite a sobering thought to realize one's trunk is more well-traveled than one's self."

"Where would you like it?"

"In the parlor, please."

The young man hoisted the trunk onto his shoulders and delivered it to the parlor. Once she sorted through the contents, she'd have Russ take the trunk upstairs.

After showing the young porter out, Anna knelt, unlocked the mechanism and flipped open the lid. The familiar scent of a lavender sachet wafted from the layers of tissue and clothing. How odd, living in this great house when all her possessions fit in such a small space.

She sifted through the layers of clothing and petticoats, relieved to discover her looking-glass hadn't broken. The hairbrush and looking-glass were the only items she had beyond a pair of earbobs from her mother.

Several favorite books lined the bottom of the trunk, and she placed them on the shelves beside Russ's law books. She retrieved her copy of Andrew Jackson Downing's *A Treatise on the Theory and Practice of Landscape Gardening* and hugged the book to her chest. Having familiar, beloved objects around the house made her feel more at home, as though she belonged.

She sat back on her heels. She'd always been a bit of

an outsider, but Russ was doing his very best to ensure she felt as though she belonged, and she appreciated his effort. She wasn't here only to cook and clean. He wanted a true companion. The experience was heady and frightening at the same time.

Distracted, she set the treatise aside to read later. There were several more burlap sacks of seeds in the bottom of the trunk. She'd packed the less precious varieties here, and carried the others in her satchel. She'd brought far more seeds than she could ever use. With that in mind, she began separating each of the sacks into two piles. She'd give the extra seeds to Touches the Clouds. There might be some varieties he found interesting.

Another bundle, deeper in the trunk, had been knotted with twine, and she struggled to unravel the tight bow tied around the top. As she grasped the bundle, her fingers closed around a sheet of paper. She sat back on her heels and lifted the sack to the light. How on earth had paper gotten into her seed collection?

Curious now, she wrestled the knot loose and dumped the contents over the table. A letter fluttered down with the seeds, and the pungent odor of cheap perfume sent her stomach curling.

She gingerly pinched the envelope between her fingers. Large, florid writing scrawled over the front. The letter was addressed to Edward. A neat slit across the top indicated he'd read the letter. Hesitating, she tugged her lower lip between her teeth. Reading the missive felt like an intrusion.

Then again, why had the letter been placed in the bag with the seeds? Edward must have placed it there knowing she would find it.

She tugged the letter free and quickly scanned the contents, before returning to the top of the letter and reading more slowly.

"Oh, Edward."

The nauseating scent of the perfumed envelope turned her stomach as she read the looped handwriting. He'd treated the woman badly. More even than a romantic relationship, Edward had taken money from her with promises of investing the funds for a profitable return. He'd promised her an income secret from her husband. Judging by the contents of the letter, Edward had the taken the money for his personal use. The lady also claimed that she knew several other women who had suffered at Edward's hand.

She threatened to kill him in a specific manner. She threatened to shoot him.

The letter was signed, *O. Fairfax*.

Her heartbeat picked up rhythm, and she dropped the letter as though she'd been burned, then backed away from the offending object.

Was she reading the letter of a killer?

Lines from the last newspaper story she'd read circled in her head. Edward's many affairs had exclusively involved married women. At the time, she'd assumed he sought them out as a matter of convenience. But what if something more sinister was at hand? If he stole a lady's money, she could hardly petition her husband for assistance.

"Edward, you idiot," she muttered into the empty room.

His tastes had always run toward the expensive. The finest horses, the most expensive clothing, membership to the best clubs. He'd needed all that, he'd said, to support his career as a successful barrister, as well as his political dreams. Had he ever been a successful barrister? She'd always taken his word. She'd discovered early on that he wasn't as successful as he'd led her to believe, but she'd assumed his exaggeration was limited.

Her stomach dropped. She remembered how he devoured the money left to her on her father's death. No doubt he'd convinced his colleagues that her inheritance funded his lush lifestyle. When he'd run out of that money, he'd gone back to his old ways. He'd stolen it.

The crime was perfect. Or almost. Someone had obviously exacted revenge.

It seemed Edward must have suspected something might happen to him, and he'd placed the letter in the one place he was certain it would be discovered. In that way, he'd led her to his killer. He'd given her what she needed to clear her name. Tears burned her eyes. Perhaps he had cared for her. Just a little. Though he'd mocked her hobby, he'd at least understood the importance the seeds held for her. He'd known she'd find the proof there.

A carriage sounded in the drive and heart pumped faster. She set the letter on the buffet and straightened her spine.

Russ appeared in the doorway, and her heart did a little flip. He'd loosened his tie and unbuttoned the top button of his shirt.

She jumped to her feet and brushed at her skirts. "I'm sorry. Dinner isn't ready. I wasn't expecting you this early." She grasped a handful of clothing and stuffed the assortment into the trunk. "This was just delivered."

"I was starting to worry they'd lost it for good."

"According to the porter, this trunk has been all the way to California and back."

"Hmm," Russ said, tugging his tie even looser. "How was your day?"

She stuffed the rest of her belongings haphazardly into the trunk and slammed shut the lid. "I'll check on dinner."

"What are we having?"

"Stew." She smoothed her hair and brushed past him. "I'll see to it."

He caught her arm. "There's no rush."

"Can I fix you something to drink?"

"Nothing. I'm fine." He tugged her gently. "Sit down. Tell me about your day. I'm sorry I rushed you at the dance. I was an idiot. I'm sorry. Take all the time you need to trust me."

"I do trust you." She was putting off the inevitable. She took a seat and stared at her clasped hands. "I found a letter."

"A letter?"

"Yes. From one of my husband's mistresses." The rest of the story poured out of her. The shame. The embarrassment. Edward's treatment of her. "I thought it was me. I thought I wasn't good enough, and that's why he cheated. I thought if we had children, he'd love me. Nothing worked. Nothing ever worked."

He knelt before her and took her hands. "He's the past, Anna. I'm your future."

"There's more."

He pressed two fingers against her lips. "I know, and it's all right."

"You know?"

"The detective came to visit me today. He thinks he

found your husband's murderer. Only she killed herself."

"What?" Her thoughts whipped around her head. Why was he here if he knew already? "He promised me that he wouldn't speak with you."

"He was trying to help."

Feeling numb, Anna stood and reached for the letter. "I think I have proof, but I don't know if it's enough. That's why Detective Latemar was here. He thought Edward might have left a clue, and he did." A sob clutched her throat. "I should have told you sooner. I should have never married you. When we kissed the other night, I knew I had to tell you the truth. I won't fight an annulment." The sob broke free, and tears spilled down her cheeks as she made her way out of the room.

Russ blocked her rushed exit. "Don't you see, Anna? I don't care. I love you."

"How? Why? I'll ruin your career."

"I don't want a career. I want a life. With you. If you won't think about me, at least think about the baby."

"I am thinking about you." Tears streaming down her face, she pressed her fist against her mouth. "But don't you see? I'll always be tainted."

"Not to me."

Revealing the truth left her feeling as though she'd dropped the lead weight she'd been carrying since Edward's murder. The burden had lifted. She felt as though she could breathe again. She loved him. She'd always loved him. She'd been jealous of Charlotte because she wanted him all her to herself.

She'd written to Charlotte, and if her sister didn't answer, she wasn't pursuing the matter. From now on, she was concentrating on the people in her life who valued her.

She grasped the letter. "Sadie said you brother is a detective. Can you ask him? Can you ask him if the letter is enough to clear my name? I think Edward left it for me. In case something happened."

"I don't care about the letter. I don't care about proof. I only care about you."

She could hardly believe she was hearing those words. Words she'd only hoped he'd utter one day. She felt a smile budding through her tears, but before she could let it blossom, a sharp, stinging pain pierced her side. She lurched forward to clutch his sleeve as it gripped her in a vise. "Oh, no."

His face pale, he caught her in his arms. "What's wrong?"

"It's the baby," she moaned, the pain sharpening. "Fetch Leah."

She'd known her happiness was too good to be true. Sobbing, she collapsed in Russ's arms. The edges of her vision blurred. "I love you."

"Don't try to speak." He took the stairs two at a time, hastening to lay her on the bed. "Everything is going to be fine."

"What's going to happen?" she begged.

"I don't know. But whatever happens, we'll face it together. The two of us. Don't give up on me, Mrs. Halloway."

She touched his cheek. "You never gave up on me, did you? Even though I pushed away the whole time."

"I never gave up on us, and neither can you."

She'd hoped for Russ, for a baby, for a happy life.

Pain radiated through her side, and she grimaced. She'd hoped for too much.

"I won't," she said. "I promise."

Leah appeared, and Russ sprang to his feet. It felt like she'd been with Anna forever. "What's happened? How is she? Is she all right?"

"She's fine."

His legs gave way and Daniel caught his arm, lowering him to a chair. "Easy there, old boy."

Russ grasped his head in his hands and choked back a sob. "You're sure? She's all right?"

"She's fit and healthy and ready for visitors." Leah smiled. "The baby is fine, too."

He'd been too afraid to hope, too afraid to wish. "Are you certain?"

"Yes. These things happen sometimes."

"It's my fault. She was upset. She had a secret and—"

"She told me all about it. Don't worry. None of this is your fault. Bad timing is all."

"Can I see her?"

"Of course."

Russ ran up the stairs but paused in the hallway and brushed his hair into place before pushing open the door.

Anna reclined in bed, her hair spread across the pillow. She smiled and held out her hand, tears streaming down her face. "The baby is fine. It was just a scare."

Russ sat on the bed and gathered her in his arms. "I was a fool. I—"

She gently placed two fingers over his lips. "No, let me." Her eyes twinkled with tears. "I love you, Russ Halloway. I think I always have."

"And I love you."

"You don't have to say that." She threaded her hands through his hair. "Would you still be saying that if I'd lost the baby?"

"If you'd lost the baby, I'd be assuring you that we'd have more children. I'd assure you that we'd have our own children, and when we stopped having our own children, we'd adopt ten more."

"You know, I'm going to hold you to that promise," Anna said.

"Which one?" Russ asked, his heart full to bursting.

"Having another child. Your child."

"This is my child," he replied, pressing his hand over the growing life inside her. "Our child. Our family. Just what we've both always wanted."

"I love you, Russ Halloway. I thought it was too good to be true. I didn't think I deserved happiness."

He kissed her with a love and passion neither had ever known, kissing all the traces of tears from her cheeks, absorbing them as though he could take her pain.

"You deserve everything," he said. "I love you, Anna. Now and forever."

"Forever," she whispered.

* * * * *

Dear Reader,

I was fascinated to learn that a vault on the Norwegian island of Spitsbergen contains almost a million packets of seeds, each variety an important food crop. The Global Seed Vault is an international initiative that provides protection for these valuable commodities against the challenges of natural and man-made disasters.

When Anna was collecting seeds in 1869, there were at least 285 varieties of cucumbers for her to plant. If she were gardening now, she'd have limited varieties from which to choose. While savings seeds from year to year was common, Anna was ahead of her time in post-Civil War America in cataloging the heirloom seeds for future generations. Seeking historical varieties of seeds has become a hobby for many people in recent years.

While gathering and growing different varieties of seeds is a fun and important way to remember our history, cultivating these seeds can also protect against blights. The Great Famine in Ireland was caused, in part, by heavy reliance on only one or two high-yielding types of potatoes. Cultivating genetic variety is often used as a protection against losing an entire crop to a disease.

The next time you're at the grocery store, think about all the different varieties of fruits of vegetables!

I hope you enjoyed Anna and Russ's story. Don't forget to read book one of the series by Cheryl St. John, *The Rancher Inherits a Family*, and book three by Karen Kirst, *Romancing the Runaway Bride*.

I love connecting with readers and would enjoy hearing your thoughts on this story. If you're interested in learning more about this book or others I've written in the Prairie

Courtships series, visit my website at SherriShackelford. com or reach me at sherrishackelford@gmail.com, on Facebook at Facebook/SherriShackelfordAuthor, on Twitter @smshackelford, or with regular old snail mail: PO Box 116, Elkhorn, NE 68022.

Thanks for reading!
Sherri Shackelford

We hope you enjoyed this story from
Love Inspired® Historical.

Love Inspired® Historical is coming to
an end but be sure to discover more
inspirational stories to warm your heart
from **Love Inspired®** and
Love Inspired® Suspense!

Love Inspired stories show that
faith, forgiveness and hope have the power
to lift spirits and change lives—always.

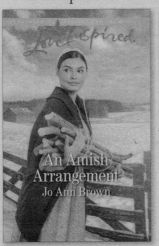
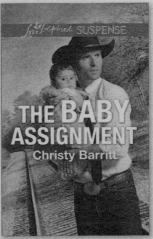

Look for six new romances every month
from **Love Inspired®** and
Love Inspired® Suspense!

www.Harlequin.com

LIHST0318

COMING NEXT MONTH FROM
Love Inspired® Historical

Available June 5, 2018

ROMANCING THE RUNAWAY BRIDE

Return to Cowboy Creek • by Karen Kirst

After years of searching, Pinkerton agent Adam Halloway is
finally on the trail of the man who destroyed his family. Then
tracking the scoundrel throws him in the path of sweet, lovely
Deborah Frazier. Can he trust in love—and in Deborah—when
he realizes she's hiding a secret?

A COWBOY OF CONVENIENCE

by Stacy Henrie

Newly widowed Vienna Howe knows nothing about running
a ranch, yet now that she's inherited one, she's determined to
make it a home for herself and her daughter. Ranch foreman
West McCall wants to help—can his plan for a marriage of
convenience lead to something more?

ORPHAN TRAIN SWEETHEART

by Mollie Campbell

Orphan train placing agent Simon McKay needs Cecilia Holbrook's
help when his partner suddenly quits. The schoolteacher
agrees to help him ensure all the orphans have been safely
placed with families in town...but keeping her heart safe from
Simon won't be so easy.

HANDPICKED FAMILY

by Shannon Farrington

The Civil War is over but the rebuilding in the south has just
begun. Newspaperman Peter Carpenter arrives seeking stories
to tell...and the widow and child his soldier brother left behind.
After pretty Trudy Martin steps in to assist, Peter's search for
family takes a turn no one expected.

---

*After years of searching, Pinkerton investigator
Adam Halloway is finally on the trail of the man
who destroyed his family. The clues lead him to
Cowboy Creek and a mysterious mail-order bride
named Deborah. She's clearly hiding a secret—could it
be a connection to his longtime enemy?*

Read on for a sneak preview of
ROMANCING THE RUNAWAY BRIDE
by **Karen Kirst**
the exciting conclusion of the series,
RETURN TO COWBOY CREEK.

"You're new. A man as picture-perfect as you wouldn't
have gone unnoticed." The second the words were out,
she blushed. "I shouldn't have said that."

Adam couldn't help but be charmed. "I'm Adam
Draper." The false surname left his lips smoothly.
Working for the Pinkerton National Detective Agency,
he'd assumed dozens of personas. This time, he wasn't
doing it for the Pinkertons. He was here for personal
reasons.

She offered a bright smile. "I'm Deborah, a boarder
here."

Her name is Deborah. With a D. The scrap of a note
he'd discovered, the very note that had led him to Kansas,
had been written by someone whose signature began with
D.

He ended the handshake more abruptly than he'd intended. "Do you have a last name, Deborah?"

Her smile faltered. "Frazier."

"Pleased to make your acquaintance, Miss Frazier. Or is it Mrs.?"

She blanched. "I'm not married."

Why would an innocuous question net that reaction?

A breeze, scented with blossoms, wafted through the open windows on their right. In her pretty pastel dress, Deborah Frazier was like a nostalgic summer dream. Adam's thoughts started to drift from his task.

He couldn't recall the last time he'd met a woman who made him think about moonlit strolls and picnics by the water. At eighteen, he'd escaped his family's Missouri ranch—and the devastation wrought by Zane Ogden—to join the Union army. There'd been no chance to think about romance during those long, cruel years. And once he'd hung up his uniform, he'd accepted an offer to join Allan Pinkerton's detective agency. Rooting out criminals and dispensing justice had consumed him, mind, body and soul. He couldn't rest until he put the man who'd destroyed his family behind bars.

That meant no distractions.

Don't miss
ROMANCING THE RUNAWAY BRIDE by Karen Kirst,
available June 2018 wherever
Love Inspired® Historical books and ebooks are sold.

www.LoveInspired.com